**A
PUBLIC
SPACE
No. 29**

D1497602

In these times of fragments and
fragmented times, what are the shapes
of our comfort. Built and imagined. What
gives boundaries and connection, healing
and shelter, familiar pathways and
points of rebellion.
—Brigid Hughes

Knox Martin

TABLE OF CONTENTS

A PUBLIC SPACE
(ISSN 1558-965X;
ISBN 9781733973069)
IS PUBLISHED BY A
PUBLIC SPACE LITERARY
PROJECTS, INC. PO BOX
B, NEW YORK, NY 10159.
PRINTED IN THE UNITED
STATES BY SHERIDAN INC.
ISSUE 29, 2020. ©2020 A
PUBLIC SPACE LITERARY
PROJECTS, INC.
POSTMASTER PLEASE
SEND CHANGES OF
ADDRESS TO A PUBLIC
SPACE, PO BOX B, NEW
YORK, NY 10159.

**A PUBLIC SPACE
IS SUPPORTED
IN PART BY**

**A PUBLIC SPACE IS A
PROUD MEMBER OF**
The Community of
Literary Magazines and
Presses

[clmp]

No. 29   A PUBLIC SPACE

FOUNDING BENEFACTOR
Deborah Pease
(1943-2014)

BOARD OF DIRECTORS
Charles Buice
Elizabeth Gaffney
Kristen Mitchell
Katherine Bell
Yiyun Li
Robert Sullivan
Brigid Hughes

ADVISORY BOARD
Robert Casper
Fiona McCrae
James Meader
Josh Rolnick

EDITOR
Brigid Hughes

MANAGING EDITOR
Megan Cummins

ASSOCIATE EDITORS
Sarah
Blakley-Cartwright
Sidik Fofana
Laura Preston

POETRY EDITOR
Brett Fletcher Lauer

EDITORIAL FELLOW
Taylor Michael

COVER DESIGN
Deb Wood

COPY EDITORS
Anne McPeak
Noreen McAuliffe

CONTRIBUTING EDITORS
Yiyun Li
Annie Coggan
Martha Cooley
Edwin Frank
Mark Hage
John Haskell
Fiona Maazel
Ayana Mathis
Robert Sullivan
Antoine Wilson

INTERNATIONAL CONTRIBUTING EDITORS
A. N. Devers
(England)
Dorthe Nors
(Denmark)
Natasha Randall
(England)
Motoyuki Shibata
(Japan)

EDITOR AT LARGE
Elizabeth Gaffney

SUBSCRIPTIONS
Postpaid subscription
for 3 issues: $36 in
the United States;
$54 in Canada;
$66 internationally.
Subscribe at
www.apublicspace.org
or send a check to the
address below.

CONTACT
For general queries,
please email
general@apublicspace.org
or call (718) 858-8067.
A Public Space
is located at
PO Box B
New York, NY 10159

INTERNS
Elisha Aflalo, Claire
Margot Dauge-Roth,
Maria Santa Poggi

READERS
Madeline Crawford,
Hannah Nash

Knox Martin

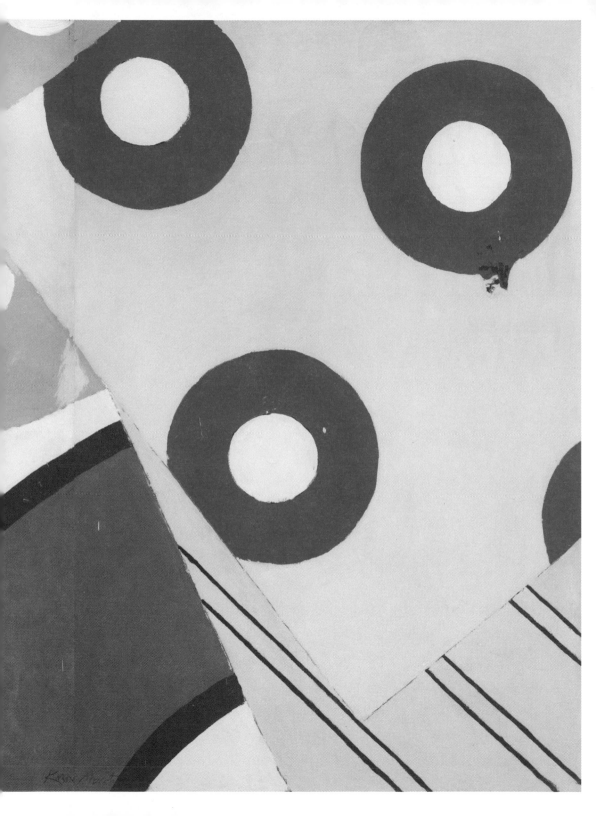

THE DELIVERY
JHUMPA LAHIRI

———

1. A package comes while the signora is on vacation, sent from overseas.

   But there's a fee to pay on delivery, so the postman leaves a message with the doorman.

   It says the package is being held at the post office. When I stop in one day to water the plants, I set the slip of paper aside. It looks like a postcard. I put it on the bookcase along with the bills and other things that look important.

The signora is spending time in the countryside, staying with friends. She'll be back at the end of the month, when the weather turns cooler.

Instead she calls after a week and says she's already returned to the city.

She tells me she was walking across the lawn in the dark when she fell into a hole and sprained her ankle. She thinks it was probably the den of some sort of animal.

Fortunately, the evening after her accident, there was a doctor among the dinner guests. He told her she needed to be in the city for a scan and to begin physiotherapy.

She couldn't drive, so the son of the family that was hosting her drove her car home, then went straight back to the countryside on the train.

"To be honest, it's a blessing," the signora says as I help unpack her suitcase. "I slept horribly up there, I kept having nightmares. I'd get up every night at three o'clock and stay awake."

I don't think she's pleased to be back. She seems disappointed to be stuck on the couch all the time. She can't manage the steps that lead to her bed in the loft space where she likes to sleep—a little den of her own—surrounded by her costume jewelry: colored beads that hang thickly on the wall, fat shiny bangles organized on a shelf.

The signora is an architect. She isn't that old even though the skin above her cheekbones is creased like dried figs. She's an active woman who tends to work from home and travels frequently. She usually asks me to come by a few times a week to do the laundry and tidy up.

She's been to my country a number of times, so now and again we have a conversation. She travels there in the winter, to a town along the coast I've never seen.

She goes to visit temples and cleanse her system of toxins. She follows strange diets. For example, she has to drink a lot of lemon juice.

When she comes back her skin is tanned and she's thinner, more energetic. She tells me that she loves the textiles and the colors of the buildings and the way the women move their bodies. She shows me pictures on her cell phone of the ruddy dirt roads, the white sandy beaches.

The signora lives alone. Once she lived in a different apartment with her husband and two children.

The son is studying to become an engineer and the daughter moved away to be close to her boyfriend. They both live overseas, in different countries.

The father of her children, a journalist who talks on television sometimes, married a woman three years older than their daughter.

That's what she tells me.

The signora can't go out now, she needs to rest her ankle, so I come by every morning with groceries and stay all day.

The signora always likes to accomplish things, so now that she's recovering with a bandaged ankle, she'd like to tackle a few projects around the house. I don't mind helping.

For instance, she asks me to empty out some of her closets and throw their contents onto the bed, the sofas, and the floor. I've inherited some of her clothing as a result.

At first I hesitated, given that her skirts and dresses all end at the knee and I'm used to longer garments.

But she insisted. She said, "Enough with covering yourself from top to bottom. It's so hot, you've got great legs, you'll feel much better in these."

One day she asks me to hand her all the mail I'd set aside and she discovers the notice about the package at the post office.

"Who knows what it is. Probably a book. Or maybe one of the kids sent me something. Stop by the post office and pick it up for me."

And she signs the card, authorizing me to go in her place.

II.   It's so hot, I don't feel up to crossing the bridge on foot at this hour. The sun's beating down. I take the bus instead.

But the bus gets on my nerves. It rattles like a drill that's about to split the sidewalk in two.

Sitting down is no better. The seats are uncomfortable, and they're so high that my feet barely touch the floor.

Standing in that unfriendly crowd, I never feel at ease.

On the other hand, I like the polka-dot skirt handed down from the signora, with two deep pockets and soft pleats. The material is dark blue and the small dots are white. I haven't worn something like this since I was a schoolgirl.

The post office is crowded. I take a number and wait.

The wooden seats are attached to a bar that's anchored to the marble floor.

I look at the windows and the red numbers on the screen that change now and then. When they change there's a buzzing sound, and the current number flashes.

The employees, all of them women, sit behind the windows and chat with one another.

The rest of us sit like the members of a small audience watching a performance. On the upper level there's even a sort of balcony. It's curved and made of glass.

All told, things could be worse. It's a chaotic place but at least it's cool.

A man next to me is reading the newspaper. And out of the corner of my eye, on the front page, I see a photograph. I learn, from the headline, that it was taken in a village close to my city, where it rains a great deal in summer.

Here, on the other hand, all summer, it hasn't rained. People say that they're going to close the water that flows out of the drinking fountains day and night.

The photograph shows a row of bodies. All of them are children.

They were crossing a river at the border when they drowned.

In the photograph, two mothers cover the bodies with an enormous tarp as if to keep them warm as they sleep.

The children lie facing the sky. But then I notice that one of them, a very small child, has turned his head to the left, eyes closed as if he's just dozed off.

I wait for about half an hour before my number appears on the screen.

I walk up to the window but I still need to wait, because the girl in front of me, who appeared to be finished, lingers, talking to the woman behind the window.

She's got a few more questions. Her dress is transparent, it exposes her black bra and nearly the full length of her legs.

Her shoulders are bare and she wears flat sandals.

One of the thin straps of her dress has fallen but she doesn't seem to care. She never bothers to adjust it.

She's still talking with the woman behind the window. They have so much to say to each other, it's as if they're friends.

The employee was smiling while she was speaking to the girl but the smile disappears when it's my turn at the window.

I pull out the card signed by the signora, and my identity card.

But the employee says, briskly, "We're not holding this anymore. The package has been sent back."

Then she makes me see, with the edge of her fingernail, the part where it says that the package was only going to be held for seven business days once the notice was left.

"Where was it sent back to?"

"I wouldn't know."

"Who sent it?"

"I have no idea."

"And now what?"

"Now I help the next person in line. Goodbye."

I feel terrible and I hope the signora won't be too angry.

There's finally a bit of breeze outside so I decide to walk back.

It's lovely to feel the skirt billowing around me like a cloud as I cross the bridge.

I stop on the bridge for a moment to look at the river that always flows more quickly than I think.

The river is green, as are all the plants and the giant leaves of the plane trees lining the banks.

On the wall, just by my elbow, I notice a mass of ants. They're scattered but clustered. They're transporting a dead fly much larger and heavier than they are. Their determination always moves me.

And as usual I notice a young couple slowly kissing, without a care, ensconced in their own world. He's standing. She's seated calmly, daringly, on the parapet.

A light push, perhaps even a gust of wind, would be enough to send her backward over the edge.

After crossing the bridge, I walk beneath a derelict archway sprouting weeds.

I proceed past a series of shops that all sell bicycles.

Suddenly I feel the urge to ride one, to go back to the river and pedal along the path.

I can't remember the last time I rode a bicycle. Do I still know how? I learned when I was a girl, my brother had taught me. We'd go exploring wide, dusty dirt roads together. I still remember the feeling of the air rushing into my face.

Instead I keep walking toward the signora's house, in the cool green shade, along a quiet street with only a few cars on it.

I think, What a pity about the package. I should have gone right away to pick it up.

I'm caught up in various thoughts when I hear a *motorino* behind me.

It's quite close and seems to slow down when a voice calls out, "Go wash those dirty legs."

I turn my head and for a second I see them. They wear helmets and sunglasses with thin frames. Then I feel a tremendous pain in my shoulder and also in my foot and see the sky overhead.

III.   The boy and his friend decide to go back to the same beach as last time. Maybe those same girls will be hanging out at the bar. The boy had liked the one with the blue nail polish and the tattoos running down her arm. They'd talked for a few minutes. Maybe he'll bump into her again.

To get out of the city they take a road with walls on both sides. It's like a long thin ribbon. They climb uphill and coast down. Then they ride through the countryside. It's pretty, with the sea spreading out to the left. Now the ground is so flat that they can see a lot of sky, with big white clouds that sit low over the landscape.

The highway is smooth and dark. The asphalt looks brand new, it's as if they are the first people to ever travel on it. At one point they pass by a city perched high on a hill and the boy remembers something his grandfather once told him when he was a kid: that a long time ago the sea came right up to that city, before this road existed. It's past four when they get to the beach. It's still hot and everything looks parched. People say it hasn't rained for over a hundred days. The parking lot is full of dust and they can hear all the insects teeming in the brush. While his friend parks his *motorino*, the boy sees a guy pushing a wheelchair. Another guy is sitting in it, maybe it's his brother. They kind of look alike but the legs of the one in the wheelchair are deformed. They're too short and they taper off at the ends.

The boy takes off his shoes, all he wants is to get into the water, but his friend bumps into someone he knows so they stop at the bar and have a coffee. While they're talking the boy feels something bothering his feet and when he looks at them, he sees that they're covered with ants crawling quickly, without any purpose. His friend wants to eat something but the boy isn't hungry. He waits while the friend eats a sandwich and asks for a glass of water. He looks down at his plate as he eats. Then the boy leaves his friend on the sand. Even though the air is oppressive the friend says he feels cold and lies facedown in the sun.

The water is full of people, kids, women talking to one another. Along the shore a father calls: Fede, Federico, Fe-de-ri! His cries go unheard.

More of those low clouds surround the boy, it's like they're sitting on top of the dunes. The water is a little muddy but it's refreshing, it's just that he feels tense the whole time. He floats and looks at all the people in the water and at the separate beaches along the sand. Looking at the sky, so blue and clear overhead, calms him more than the crowded water.

He swims for a while, then gets out and takes a walk. He sees the guys zigzagging between groups of sunbathers. They're selling hats, towels, and cotton skirts. They come up to one beach chair after another, approaching reclining women who are half-asleep, who are a bit annoyed by them, also a bit curious. One of the men has a row of purses hanging from his forearm, as if they were a row of empty hangers hooked over a bar in a closet. When the boy comes closer, he spies an arm covered with tattoos. It's her, she's with the same friend.

The boy lingers and watches the guy crouch over their beach blanket, talking up the stuff he's selling, draping the merchandise over their legs in a cocky way. He's selling scarves in a bunch of different colors, at least a dozen. They look so soft, one can almost see through them.

The girls chat with him. They're impressed, undecided. They're tempted.

The guy looks like the others who have moved into the boy's part of the city. Once it was a quiet neighborhood between the train tracks and an aqueduct built by an emperor. The foreigners have their own little grocery stores. They put signs in their windows that the boy's family can't read. They pray barefoot in squalid buildings. Their kids play soccer on the other side of the aqueduct, on a dry patch of ground. The boy's parents complain that there are too many of them. They say that soon enough they'll be outnumbered. Meanwhile the bar his friend's parents own isn't making enough money because, he says, people from that part of the world don't crowd the counter in the mornings or after lunch to drink coffee.

The guy selling scarves bothers the boy. He thinks, He's been hanging around these girls too long. He can't understand why they don't just tell him to get lost.

The boy wants to say something but he knows he shouldn't draw attention to himself right now. The girls are smiling and laughing, they're pulling money out of their wallets, they're buying this and that. What's your name? the one with the tattoos asks him. She hasn't glanced once in the boy's direction.

The boy starts sweating so much he gets back into the water. He stays in until the sun starts to set and the bodies of everyone on the beach start to turn that same glowing gold. He dives down a few times to try to touch the bottom. There's not much to see. Just a few drab-looking fish wandering around looking lost. A few twisted-up branches.

Nothing shiny like the pistol his friend tossed from his *motorino* into the river.

He'd fired twice and she'd fallen to the ground. She was short and had a long dark braid with a thick red elastic wrapped around the bottom. A skirt with dots.

The boy said, Fuck, you really shot her.

But his friend didn't reply, he just sped up.

The boy hollered, "You said you weren't going to aim at anyone!"

He added, "She was just a girl."

His friend waited to toss the gun before saying, "It's only to scare them, it's not like she'll die from it."

But now the boy is scared. He doesn't feel the adrenaline of those nights they get drunk and take markers to write messages on the walls or on the backs of street signs.

As the sun keeps sinking into the sea, the lifeguard working on the neighboring beach starts closing up the umbrellas. They're all red, just like the elastic at the bottom of the young woman's braid. And once they're closed up and bound tight, they remind the boy of her long braid, too. But the skirt, while she was walking, was light and flowing around her dark legs.

The boy swims a little more but he's getting cold, and he doesn't like being the only person left in the water other than a guy taking a long swim far out behind him. The boy wonders if someone saw him and his friend on the street that sells bicycles. Maybe someone remembers that he was the one who yelled out those words at her.

He comes out of the water. He doesn't have a towel, and by now the guys who sell them have left. The boy feels tired but he's not happy like the others walking, baked from the sun, toward the parking lot to go home. As he waits to dry off the waves hiss in his ears like snakes.

He finds his friend, who tells him that he took a nap and that it's time to go. The friend complains that his shoulders got too much sun. As they ride back to the city, the boy notices that the back of his friend's neck got a little burned, too. There's a mix of white clouds and dark ones. All of them are huge and low, like smoke billowing up from a fire under the horizon. The cold air strikes the boy's face the whole time. When they notice a cop car gaining speed the friend slows down a little and the boy quickly looks back.

No one stops them. They're after someone else up ahead.

The sky is pale above them, a thin crescent moon visible all day.

IV.   At the hospital they tell me they'd fired from about ten meters away and that I'd fainted. A man passing by on his bicycle had called for an ambulance.

They're taking care of me in the emergency room. In the end they don't need to admit me. They've found the pellets, they explain that they were fired thanks to bursts of compressed air. They send me home with two big x-rays that show the scattered pellets. They look like a series of lights in a town seen from a hilltop at night, or the little dots on the signora's skirt.

I need to recover now, just like the signora. I can't work for her until I'm better.

She tells me to take all the time I need. To be honest, I'm glad I don't have to spend time in her house, where I would keep thinking about the afternoon I went to the post office to pick up the package that hadn't been delivered and that had already been sent back.

One of my cousins is helping her out while I work for another cousin who has a store that sells bottles of beer, cereal, cases of water, and toilet paper until two in the morning.

I run the cash register. As long as I sit still, I can manage.

My cousin tells me I was lucky, that wounds like mine will eventually heal. He knows someone who was beaten up waiting at a bus stop and lost his eye.

He discourages me from filing a report. In his opinion it's better not to get mixed up with the police.

They were young, that's all I took in. Maybe they were friends who had nothing better to do, like the teenagers who turn up around eleven at night to buy beer and smoke in front of the convenience store.

These kids don't bother me. They chat late into the night, in the dark, seated on the steps outside the store or leaning against a parked car.

They're like cats or insects that only come out at night, that meet up and colonize the edges of the streets. They prowl in the dark, fueled by lust.

I hear their voices but I can barely follow what they say, all the words blend together. Their premature, awkward desire for one another floats up, unleashed, along with occasional laughter. It sails, weightless, as high as the stars.

When I was their age I did more or less the same, I'd stop with my friends after school on a certain street where students tended to gather.

We'd flaunt ourselves to the world and have something to eat. I remember one boy, skinny, who was already going to college. He'd single me out with his eyes. He'd bought me something to drink once.

But I left that world behind. Wanting more out of life, I came here willingly.

Now and then I take in a specific face: full pale lips, shiny skin, a glance lit up from a heavy shaft of light streaming down from a lamppost. At this lonely hour this ancient city belongs only to them.

I notice a few kids among them with different features, with darker complexions, growing up here. They're bound together by a strange harmony, by nocturnal complicity, by their identical gestures.

I like seeing them scattered but clustered and hearing them talking quietly, sometimes laughing. They're unaware that I'm soothed by their presence, even though, now and then, it's as if one of those pellets is lodged in my heart, and I nearly die from envy.

THE ALICE TULLY SHOW
COLM TÓIBÍN

Alone in America,
I tiptoe on the blurred line between the First and Second Amendments
And am even vaguer on the difference between
Father John Murphy and Father Michael Murphy.
And only Maureen Murphy can tell Standish James O'Grady from Standish
     Hayes O'Grady.
And who can distinguish the Alice Tully who paid for this hall from Alice Tully
     the bag lady
Who was popular with the workmen as Lincoln Center was being built?

Alone in New York,
I am unsure if either of the Alice Tullys is related in any way to Jimmy Tully,
Whose enthusiasm for the gerrymander knew no bounds.

The 9 has disappeared. We make do with the 1, those of us going uptown after
     the concert.

There was a time when I had reason to cross the Verrazzano Bridge.
But that is no more.

In the old dead cities, they wrote the music that starts off low,
Wisps of sound, something curled now sharp and piercing.
I can tell the difference between the first and second violin
And between the shiny shoes of the cellist and the outpouring of grief from
     the viola.

It is all quartet today. No piano.

Alice, both of you, do you hear what I hear?

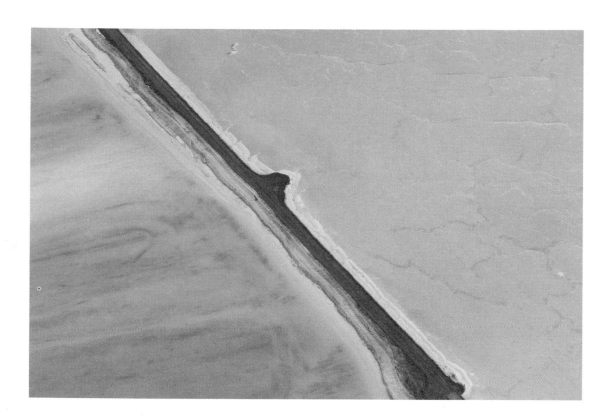

Neal Rantoul

TWO WOMEN
CLAIRE MESSUD

When my father was first dying—that's to say, in the time we thought he would die but he did not; the time when he made a belated and miraculous recovery and was returned to us, like a character in a fairy tale, for two years, three months, and five days—my aunt, his younger sister, tried to insist upon a visit from the priest. My mother, although diminished (as yet undiagnosed, she was already undermined by the

Lewy body dementia that would fell her), resisted valiantly, because my father (at that time off with the fairies, as the expression has it; apt, for the fairy-tale-like nature of that time) could not; and the priest was kept at bay.

But two years later, when he was actually dying, fully and utterly presently himself, my father—my obdurate and fierce father, whose will we feared and admired in equal measure—could not resist his sister in her zeal. Which is how he came, in the nursing home, reluctantly to take Communion from Father Bob, the once-a-week visiting Indian pastor in a baby-blue open-collared short-sleeved summer shirt, who, with short, plump fingers, unwrapped the host from a rolled hankie in his breast pocket like a wee snack saved from lunch.

"Isn't there someone," my father asked me pleadingly, "who could do this in French?"

Alas, I shook my head, I did not think so.

Being a man of his word, having promised his sister, my father opened his mouth for the host with all the enthusiasm he might have shown for a cyanide tablet. It was, of course, in addition to a display of religiosity from one who abhorred falsity and religion both, the first moment in which he had performatively to acknowledge that he accepted his imminent death. There were many reasons to balk at the preposterous scene of which he was unwillingly a part, carefully shaved and combed though his skin was a blotched mess, his Brooks Brothers button down tidily ironed, his torso pinned awkwardly in his wheelchair, in the antiseptic white-tiled room overlooking verdant gardens in Rye Brook, New York, where the nursing aides, all as Catholic as my aunt, were visibly relieved to see my father saved from damnation at the last. One woman in fuchsia scrubs, standing out in the hallway, clasped her hands and gave thanks to God. The morning of this encounter was almost the last time my father forced himself from bed, his pain by then too great. A few days later he would be transferred to hospital, and thence to the strange, liminal calm of hospice, to be granted the benison of morphine, and soon thereafter, of eternal rest.

But he accepted all this—the muttered prayers of Pastor Bob, who drew the sign of the cross upon my father's inviolable forehead, and the aides' hallelujahs—only when my mother was not in the room. Even half-witted—by then she'd lost many of her wits, though she'd struggled so valiantly and for so long not to let it show that I feel a traitor even now to acknowledge it—she would not have permitted my aunt's meddlesome Catholic hand. After the fact, she fumed; and remembered that betrayal longer than, by then, most things.

They had vowed when they married to keep religion out of it: she was a mild Anglican, and he a lapsed Catholic, child of passionately devout parents. (My French grandparents, their unconventional union blessed by papal dispensation, slept all their married lives beneath a crucifix draped with a rosary from the Vatican.) For each of my parents, the other's religion carried swathes of meaning—or, in the case of my mother's for my father, of meaninglessness. My father had rebelled against the swaddling quotidian faith in which he had been raised, but considered my mother's watery Christianity to be no faith at all. My mother, meanwhile, raised petit bourgeois and socially aspirant in midcentury Toronto, fully of her place and time, considered Catholicism sentimental and vulgar—by which she meant working class. We had at home a framed professional portrait of my French grandparents, black and white, both in profile: "It's very Latin," my mother would whisper, with evident distaste. "Very Catholic." She would have turned it to face the wall if she could.

This meant, in practice, that the pact against religion had been against Catholicism, first and foremost. I don't know whether my father knew, when he and my mother married, how the edict might shape their lives and ours. I don't know whether he ever wanted, before his deathbed, to return to the church of his childhood; but in that moment it was to his childhood that he returned: he longed for the prayers in French because only in French did they have meaning for him; it was only to his French self that they could speak.

His sister, my aunt, our Tante Denise, never left the church. She, like her parents, slept beneath her crucifix, and indeed ultimately died beneath it, watched over by nuns paid to pray at her bedside, rather than by us, her faithless North American nieces. Years before, contemplating retirement, she wondered often aloud whether to join a convent; in fact, when she stopped working, she gave herself—her time, her love, what little money she had—to the church, and more specifically to a particular priest, the fantastically named Père Casanova, with whom she more or less fell in love. Always meticulous, she undertook for years, pro bono, the accounts for his parish; but more indulgently, she fed him—gorged him, even, upon luxuries: filet mignon, truffles, expensive cognac—and lavished him with gifts; an expensive Aubusson carpet was, we came to know, among her donations. She blushed and grew giddy when he waved his carved ivory cane or swirled his embroidered raiment in her direction and praised her piety, or when, in mufti, he stopped by her apartment for an aperitif or two. She spoke so earnestly of leaving her property and worldly goods to the church that we assumed she'd written it into her will.

This was late in life, of course, when my sister and I had spouses and children of our own. We made fun of my aunt behind her back for being so perfectly like an aging spinster from a Trollope novel—by we I mean my mother, of course, and my sister and I. Our father remained silent, his face darkening when we joked about his sister: her lifelong defender as well as ours, he was, in such moments, rudely torn. With distance, I have to acknowledge that he was thus torn throughout his life, possibly almost all the time. After they'd all died—first our father; then, two years later, within months, my mother and my aunt—my sister observed that it was as if he'd been married to both of them, as if he'd shuttled all his life between two competing women. Needless to say—and it was never said—they hated each other.

As the story went, my mother met my father on a bus in the rain at Oxford, where they both attended summer school in 1955. Their first date was a picnic with an intimidatingly sophisticated American woman also in my mother's program named Gloria Steinem, and a Texan chap she brought along. My Canadian mother, tall and slender, resembled Ingrid Bergman; my father, who then had (albeit briefly) a full head of hair, was Latinly handsome. Both were shy. Their romance blossomed not only in Oxford but over the subsequent months in Paris, my mother's European foray prolonged on my father's account. By letter, she threw over her Canadian boyfriend—a young solicitor of the society to which she had been elevated, in adolescence, by her family's improved fortunes; my sister and I knew his name because our Canadian grandmother, when cross with our father, would mutter darkly that Margaret should have married Armstrong instead—and did not return home until she and my father were engaged.

Margaret's parents were far from entranced by the match: for starters, François-Michel was French, not to mention Catholic—in their small world the French were reputedly philanderers. He was only a student (and would remain one for some years), his prospects unclear. Apparently his parents—then en route to Buenos Aires, a city the very existence of which may have seemed doubtful to the Canadians—had no money.

Margaret's parents, amusingly surnamed Riches, had only lately risen from scrimping modesty to modest grandeur (my grandfather, a patent attorney, wrote the insulin patent for Banting and Best): a mink, a sheared beaver, and a belated diamond engagement ring for Marjorie; a Jaguar and a convertible both, for Harold; a lakeside summer cottage for all three to enjoy, though they remained in their same little house in their then-dowdy neighborhood in Toronto's West End: their expansion had its limits. My Canadian grandparents promptly wrote a letter to their future in-laws inquiring about their son's future plans, about how he proposed to keep their only daughter in the style to which she was accustomed. I've seen the letter; they actually used that phrase.

My parents were in touch only by correspondence for over a year, until my father arrived in Toronto a few days before their wedding, in late July 1957. Algeria, the land of his forebears going back over a century and the complicated home of his later childhood, was at that time in violent turmoil; his parents, recently resettled in Argentina, could not afford the journey to Canada. They sent instead my father's younger sister, Denise, my only aunt, to represent the family.

In the photos, she smiles gamely. She'd had a horrendous crossing from Paris by plane, with severe turbulence and a long layover in Gander (this, her first air travel, instilled in her a permanent aerophobia); and once she'd arrived, with only minimal English, she had to put on a dumb show of eager jollity. Still plump then—her obsessive thinness came later, a lifelong near-anorexia made possible by chain smoking—she was pale and rather horsey-looking, but you can see the courage and willing with which she stands alongside her brother, among these strapping, alien Canadians: my grandfather Harold, who died before I was born, looks like a bona fide giant. And yet it's strange, surely, that in so many photos my father is flanked on one side by my tall mother—in her pristine cream peau de soie faux-Dior dress that accentuates her fine waist, her elegant calf, her swanlike neck—and on the other by my plain and solid aunt (whose physique I unfortunately inherited), in floral chintz.

From the beginning, my father had two women to take care of: in his old-school, patriarchal worldview, that was how he understood it. At the time of their wedding, he and my mother surely didn't know that my aunt would never marry; they did not anticipate her imminent nervous breakdown, nor her subsequent lifelong fragility—she was never not on lithium after that; even when, toward the end, she drank so heavily that she'd collapse naked in her own vomit in the front hall of her apartment, even then she was on lithium—nor her inability to be alone. Although even as a child, nicknamed Poupette, little doll, she'd been timorous and highly strung, asthmatic and sickly, and had been billeted for months to an aged relative in the Algerian countryside because she was so traumatized by the bombardments in Algiers. And she was, except as a young girl, plain, and as I say, at that point in her young womanhood, plump, with thick ankles—the sort of thing that my grandfather surely pointed out to her (he told me, when I was a teenager, that I'd be good-looking were my legs not so heavy and wondered whether there existed an operation whereby my ankles might be slimmed). She would have been clear in her own mind that she wasn't readily marriageable.

Immediately after my parents' wedding, they boarded a ship for Le Havre. I can only imagine their bafflement: having known each other intensely for just a few months, they then hadn't seen each other for many more; had met again in the flurry of festivity and wedding preparation; had married; and were suddenly cast into greatest intimacy, in a tiny cabin on a rolling ship upon the high seas. My aunt doesn't feature in the shipboard photographs; I assume she had a return ticket by airplane, though there's nobody left to confirm this. I think of my prudish mother, my extremely private father, embarked not only upon a newly sexual life in their tiny cabin, but sharing seasickness, too—vomit? Diarrhea?—at a stage of uncertainty when they may still have eyed one another warily, thinking, "You don't look quite as I remembered. Your left eye is smaller. Your skin is a bit bumpy. Your laugh sounds strange." And at the same time: "Here we are, joined for life, till death do us part." Of these early months, my mother confessed that she'd have turned tail and fled for home were it not for her mother's voice in her ear muttering "I told you so." Though it might, of course, have been the best move for all concerned.

    Their first months together were spent in a small town in northern France, where my father completed his military service, and my mother—her French still a work in progress—spent such lonely days that she welcomed the pair of black-clad Mormon missionaries when they rang the bell and chatted with them for an hour. They then moved for a time to my grandparents' apartment in Paris, where my father had a job—though they would soon decamp again, for Boston, where he enrolled in graduate school at Harvard, in Middle Eastern studies.

The salient fact about their Paris sojourn is that they shared the small flat with my aunt. She'd been living in Paris for some months by then. There, working in an office, she fell in love with her married boss. This love, like all the romantic loves in her life that we know about—including her passion for the Père Casanova— proved unrequited. Denise spiraled into depression. It was 1958, and as she told it, the hostility toward her *pied-noir* background was everywhere palpable, sometimes even malicious. The Algerian War raged. The famous Pontecorvo film *The Battle of Algiers* describes events of 1956–57, culminating in the arrest of the FLN leaders in September of '57; the following months saw the rise of the OAS, a right-wing colonial terrorist organization fighting against the FLN with the support of certain military factions. The attempted coup in Algeria on May 13, 1958, led to the collapse of the Fourth Republic in France—Algeria's troubles brought France to the brink of civil war—and precipitated the return of an aging Charles de Gaulle to the French presidency. A new constitution was drafted; the Fifth Republic was launched. But the Algerian War would not end for another four bitter years.

A lyrical or mythic narrative of what resulted, for lonely young Denise, might glancingly propose that the violence and distress of the nation—France's inability to maintain power over its colony, Algeria, while at the same time being unable to liberate it—manifested as a crisis in my aunt's psyche, she a young woman who could neither be free from her abandoned homeland (whence her parents also had departed, of course, first for Morocco and then Argentina) nor at home in metropolitan France. Whether her collapse was precipitated by unattainable love of a man; a family; or a country, her Algeria; or whether by the political unrest around her, and the ways in which she saw herself as implicated in that unrest, as a young *pied-noir* woman in Paris passionately committed to a French Algeria, surrounded by peers who largely felt otherwise and considered her, a colonial in the metropole, an interloper—it's impossible now to know, and was perhaps impossible to know even then. She fell, through no fault of her own, on the wrong side of history. She fell through the cracks of history, perhaps. And she fell alone, while around her, for better or worse, her family was coupled: woebegone, she slid between her parents (their union legendarily happy), and mine (theirs not).

Which is to say: when my aunt's breakdown began, on the cusp of twenty-five (she was four months older than my mother; in 2010, she would die just two months after her), she was alone in Paris: her parents on another continent, in another hemisphere; her brother and his new wife some distance away. But then they moved into the flat on the avenue Franco-Russe along with her: Denise, François-Michel, and Margaret. My still newlywed parents—less than a year married; I think: they hardly knew each other! They tried to make room for themselves—my mother tried to make room for herself, I should say—among my grandparents' furniture and the matter of Denise's troubled life. Denise quit her job; she stayed in, sitting, when not sleeping, on the sofa; she wept; she smoked; she did not eat the meals that my mother prepared (because my mother understood preparing meals to be her wifely role); she shed the extra weight that had so discomfited her; she stared into space; she wept some more.

This too, I try to imagine, from my mother's point of view, or even from my father's. Many years later, my mother would say to my sister and me, apropos apparently of nothing, "Always remember that when you marry someone, you marry their family, too." Those months in that small flat: a month is comprised of weeks, a week of days, a day of many hours, each hour of many minutes. My father out between breakfast and supper; my mother and my aunt at home, together, bridging the language gap as best they could, harboring and hiding their mutual dislike. My aunt histrionic; my mother cool to the point of unresponsiveness; my father, in the evenings, the go-between, himself tempestuous and hardly intuitive, nightly mixing cocktails, his sole domestic talent, in an effort to keep the peace.

Eventually my aunt was dispatched to Buenos Aires, to the care of her parents. There she spent an exhilarating decade, made great friends, became fluent in Spanish, and again fell fruitlessly, impossibly, in love, once more with a married man, always with lithium as her guardrail. She never again left her parents: they traveled the world as a trio, and when the old couple retired to Toulon, she went with them and found employment nearby. They signed their letters "Pamande"—Papa, Maman, Denise.

These two women, Denise and Margaret, so profoundly different, were yet not wholly unalike. Each lived by a set of unspoken rules, complex webs of necessity inferred by my sister and me, internalized and absorbed without explanation. Figuring out the world, in childhood—figuring out how to be a girl, how to be a person—meant learning these women's signals and, in time, attempting to parse their meaning. (Our father loomed large in our lives, but, during those years, in the way of a Greek god: he was rather frightening, and usually not at home. Many fathers then weren't: a business suit, a sort of passport, liberated them to travel.) We were issued occasional Delphic pronouncements—such as our mother's about marrying families; or another of her infamous comments, about my aunt: "Getting the idea she was a good person is the worst thing that ever happened to her." Sometimes, we encountered instead inexplicable actions, as when my aunt, the night after my wedding, in a crowded hotel elevator in London, attempted to press into my hand a wad of French francs—a gift? Why, in that moment? Why at all, when she and my grandfather had already presented us with an expensive set of luggage? When I declined to accept it, she flew into a rage, the quelling of which required our best diplomatic efforts—not only mine and my husband's but also those of my sister and my father and my grandfather too. My mother, needless to say, did not get involved, and later simply rolled her eyes. After threatening to return to her room, Tante Denise was eventually persuaded to join us for supper, and in the photos at the Greek restaurant she smiles as if nothing had happened. Years later she said, out of the blue, "If I'd known you were going to keep your name, I would never have come to your wedding."

The rules that shaped my aunt's world were those of devout Catholicism above all; but also those of petit-bourgeois *pied-noir* society in the first half of the twentieth century, influenced too by the rigid French naval order of my grandfather's profession. Denise was profoundly devout; she collected religious artifacts, rosaries and holy water, and believed in signs and wonders. She kept secrets only, as she saw it, to make others' lives better: she hid the worst, which is why, in the end, we heard about her terminal diagnosis only from her doctor—she never mentioned it. We were always told that her terrible (solo) car accident occurred because she fell asleep at the wheel; though the timing suggests, in retrospect, greater volition. Still, she maintained a sunny face for as long as she possibly could. She had a terrible temper—what could she say? God had given it to her—but she was loyal. Deference to the patriarch, and to all elders, was absolute. The role of women in her world was clear, and fixed: we were on earth to marry and bear children. My aunt, a spinster with a successful career—a lawyer, which was the profession that my mother longed to practice, Denise worked also as an accountant—was referred to by her parents as "*pauvre* Denise"—in part because of the breakdown, the lifelong lithium, but chiefly because she'd failed to fulfill her role. They were sad that she was childless; sadder still that she remained unmarried. Theirs was not a secret pity, but overt, accepted. It was understood that in her single, childless state, Denise would stay close to home: caring for aging parents had been, for centuries, the lot of unmarried daughters. They had resigned themselves to this as far back as Buenos Aires— Pamande!—and took care of her at least as much as she did them.

After my grandmother died, my aunt guarded my grandfather like a wolf: when, at a restaurant with a close friend, he tripped and fell while my aunt was parking the car, she banished that friend from their lives. Ensuring his welfare and longevity became her focus, and she did her job well: at ninety-four, my grandfather died in his sleep, after a short illness, with all his wits—and his family—about him. After which, my aunt turned her attention to her older brother: thereafter, she rang François-Michel daily. They discussed the weather, their ordinary activities, her parish, her neighbors. She did not complain, not to him, not ever, no matter how desperate she felt. Theirs was "*la famille du sourire*" and her job was to bring him happiness. From across the Atlantic, Denise would care for him, in spite of my mother (who clearly didn't know properly how to do so). She would do so in a spirit of religious and relentless self-abnegation and self-sacrifice.

Meanwhile, her own existence grew ever more monastic and spartan: having saved very little, she embraced poverty almost like a child playing at being poor. She accepted gifts from my parents—from my father, really—as her birthright: an emerald ring, an amber necklace, a Burberry raincoat, her apartment—but for herself, she ate little, bought nothing, wore clothes and shoes until they fell apart, dried her husk of a body with rough and threadbare ancient towels. She did keep up always her Clarins foundation, her expensive lipstick—a deep dried-blood color, from Yves Saint Laurent: my mother loathed it, called it ghoulish—and her weekly *mise en plis*; these appearances were a matter of Catholic dignity, of French patriotism almost, a sunk cost. Beyond that, with the exception of cigarettes, she could forego almost anything. She could, and she would, want less, use less, need less, demand less than anyone else: in this, at least, in being last, she would be first.

Even as she whittled down ever farther her person and her material desires, she grew desperately needy and enraged. She became a hurricane of fury. This was when and why she took to drink, the drink that would ultimately, along with the cigarettes, kill her; but which proved the only means by which she could allow herself unfettered. She drank Johnnie Walker when my parents bought it for her, but otherwise Label 5, a lowly brand of scotch sold in chunky embossed bottles, some of which she saved to refrigerate tap water—not for herself, who preferred all drinks tepid, but for her visitors.

Drunk, Denise became greedy, garrulous, avid. When we were away, she kept count of how long since we'd visited, and a few drinks in would throw out the exact tally in astringent reproach. She quarreled with lifelong friends, taking issue with their inconstancy, their insufficient attention. When we were there, she'd force our arms around her neck, pull us close, plant loud, soggy kisses on our cheeks, rumbling in our ears in her raspy Louis Armstrong fag-end of a voice, in a fug of tobacco smoke—French Marignys had, with time, turned to Marlboro reds. Scrawny in age, and haggard, she developed particular tics when drunk, a way of tucking her hands into her waistband and rocking back and forth in unseemly pelvic thrusts; a way of thoughtlessly licking her forefinger, then pawing with the saliva at a raw, red patch on her face; a way of grinding her loose lips, ruminating almost, so that you couldn't ignore the prominent teeth behind them. Her pale-blue eyes, always watery behind their thick glasses, grew filmy and red-rimmed—and frightened, and sad.

Repelled by her, we were also guilty, even loving, in our repulsion: Tante Denise became a doppelgänger, a part of me that I feared, abhorred, accepted, and defended in equal measure. God forbid we should end up like Tante Denise— *pauvre* Denise. She was our Christian test, or one of them—mad, pathetic, noble, generous, oppressive, funny, deluded, brave, so lonely, and trying, always trying, until she couldn't try anymore. In her ignominious last years, of her naked drunken self, I was reminded always of Jane Bowles's character Mrs. Copperfield, who wants to drink gin until she can roll around on the floor like a baby. Being a woman was too difficult; in the end, maybe all along, Denise wanted only to renounce.

My mother's set of life rules, on the other hand, was that of a Protestant Anglophile with social aspirations in the Toronto of her youth. Effortless superiority and keen wit were de rigueur: you were supposed to be beautiful (or not, if you weren't) without making a fuss about it; wear practical, sturdy shoes; get straight As without being seen to work; you were to be always polite and, when necessary or even amusing, cutting in your politesse. Gentle and considerate, even passive by nature, Margaret had nevertheless developed the sharp tongue her adolescent milieu (a private girls' school) had required, and often spoke like a character out of Anthony Powell or Muriel Spark. Of a college friend of mine, she memorably said, after the girl's one visit, "I've never met such a nonentity. I kept forgetting she was in the car." Insecurity could make her mean; matters superficial got under her skin: she envied her friends their mink coats, their Caribbean vacations, their husbands' deaths. She enlisted us, her daughters, as her defenders in arguments with our father and raised us to understand that her life had been ruined by marriage to a man who didn't support her liberation or believe in her capabilities. "Never, never be financially dependent on a man," she would hiss, or, because she felt our father dismissed her intellect, "Never, ever marry anyone who isn't as smart as you are." "I've wasted my life on his dirty socks," she said. "Don't ever get stuck like me."

But the messages confused, because she never left him—she never so much as went overnight to a friend's house or a motel. She railed against François-Michel, but when we criticized our father, she'd defend him; when we told her our secrets, she'd pass them on to him. We came to know that her allegiances were more complicated than she wanted to let on. Moreover, for someone who bitterly described being a wife and mother as "the waste of a life," she mastered the housewife's tasks with stellar preeminence: a magnificent cook, she prepared three-course meals even on weeknights (my favorite dessert was zabaglione, an egg yolk and marsala confection whipped over heat into a fiery, airy froth: it took twenty minutes over the stove top at the last minute, but she'd make it sometimes just for the four of us, for fun); she kept house impeccably; everything was ironed, from shirts and dresses to sheets and pillowcases, nightgowns, underpants, my father's linen handkerchiefs. She could remove any spot from any fabric, darn socks, invisibly repair moth holes. She saved leftovers in tiny dishes in the fridge, and old twist ties, and washed out plastic bags and hung them up to dry.

She taught us that good stewardship was a moral strength; so too was thrift. This was not incommensurate with her sense of superiority and her sharp judgments of others—for a child of the Depression, greater continence was an expression of superiority, indeed. She came from, aspired to, a Canadian society of hardy, broad-shouldered women, capable and resilient. She eschewed makeup and fine clothes: when my father bought her beautiful things, she stuffed them, tags on, in the back of her closet. She used Eucerin as her face cream, and in my entire life, possessed one ancient blue eye shadow; her waxy lipsticks came from the drugstore. She never paid more than thirty dollars for a haircut and seemed almost to take pride in having great bone structure (Ingrid Bergman!) but looking shabby—the perfect counterpoint to Tante Denise, who, although homely, always made the most of herself. (My sister and I thought of it—think of it still—as Protestant versus Catholic and Canadian versus French.) She knitted elaborate sweaters; she created and tended beautiful gardens; she trained beloved dogs, and walked them miles, and played ball with them, and talked to them: she adored dogs. She read thousands of books, developed unexpected areas of erudition (e.g., nineteenth-century female travelers in Asia and Africa; histories of fonts and presses; all facts about the Bloomsbury group). And she wrote letters, amazing letters, many of which I am fortunate still to possess.

Both women formed me, even as they shaped my father's life. Albeit differently, they taught my sister and me that we should ask for, and expect, less, even as they encouraged us to strive for more, lessons that seem quaintly old-fashioned now. In the parking lot of the nursing home where Father Bob delivered the last rites to my father, my mother, mildly demented, remarked, with sadness in her voice, but also with considerable calm, "There's still so much of life to get through, once you realize that your dreams won't come true." She'd never taken up much space, but in those last years she took up less and less, ever polite, obliterated but gracious to her ten-month-bedridden end. Tante Denise, meanwhile, erased herself little by little in a different, uglier way, with the help of Label 5. She called the Atlantic "that accursed ocean," but managed nevertheless to cross it to be with her brother when he was dying. She largely ignored her sister-in-law at that point and picked fights instead with my sister. Once François-Michel was gone, Denise saw no reason to hold on, and her alcoholic suicide began in earnest.

My father had, all his life, two women to take care of (four, if you count my sister and me). He was devoted to his sister, and he adored his wife; though they irked him, each in her way. He, who had no time for gossip, said nothing behind their backs; in fact, I never heard him criticize my aunt at all; though he and my mother rowed a great deal over the years.

Denise knew what she was supposed to be (married, a mother, sweet, submissive), approved wholeheartedly, even judgmentally, of those traditional ideals, but couldn't for the life of her fulfill them. We've often wondered whether her unrequited heterosexual loves were for show, and whether, in our era, or without the pressures of her Catholic faith, her intimate life might have unfolded differently. Margaret, in contrast, despised what she was supposed to be (married, a mother, sweet, submissive) and yet was most successfully all of these things. What she wanted instead, she was too submissive to attain. From the two of them I learned that to hope for happiness, or peace, even, I should strive to be everything, but also that I was probably doomed: there's still so much of life to get through when you realize that your dreams won't come true.

Painfully, both my mother's and my aunt's identities involved profound self-loathing: they believed, as so many women have been brought up to believe, that they were inadequate as they were. I have struggled, with uncertain success, to divest myself of that legacy. Yet much that I internalized from these two women I still uphold: the joy and dignity of small pleasures, the gift of requiring less in order to find contentment, the Christian ethics that teach us to put others before ourselves, to be humble, to be kind. Curiosity, openness, fearlessness, generosity of spirit, above all, love—these things I also learned from them. To live with an open heart and an open mind, and to live with kindness—truisms, perhaps, but not less admirable goals for that. If there's an afterlife, I don't believe access to it lies in the hands of Father Bob, with his hankie-wrapped host; nor do I believe there's particular merit in my mother's urge to banish potentially assuaging rituals of faith. If I'd only found the priest between Stamford and White Plains who could deliver the last rites in French, my father might have been consoled. Even without believing, he might have been consoled.

Here's how I like to remember them, my aunt and my mother. When I was small, perhaps six or so, I knocked over my water glass on the table in the Vietnamese restaurant in Le Pradet, near my grandparents' home in the south of France. My father, who couldn't tolerate mess and still less embarrassment (he, too, carried a lot of anxiety), roared at me, and I broke into tears.

"Don't be sad," said Tante Denise, putting an arm around my shoulder. "Accidents happen. They can happen to anyone—even to grown-ups." (She spoke in French, of course, and so the words she used were deliciously literal to my childhood self: *grandes personnes*, big people.) She grasped her full wineglass by the stem and turned it over on the table, so that the red wine mixed with my water on the textured white paper cloth in an expanding red swirly sea. "See?" she laughed, "it doesn't matter!"

And my mother, Margaret Riches Messud: her gentle soul, even to the end, before and after the bitterness and disappointment. She stood, or rather teetered slightly, in our kitchen, in the last year of her life, beatific while I, in my turn, fumed: I'd taken her three times within an hour to the bathroom because she kept forgetting she'd already been ("Are you sure, Mama?" "Yes, I'm sure"): each trip was a lengthy ordeal on account of the Parkinson's; she couldn't manage any of the practicalities herself.

"Isn't it wonderful," she whispered, eyes alight, apropos of nothing. I was aware that she spoke in all sincerity and yet, at the same time, that she perhaps didn't know entirely that she lived with us, nor perhaps quite who I was, that I was her daughter. "I just love being here," she said, "and I just wish I could spend all my time with you." And she smiled at me, at the world, like a blessing, and she reached out to hold my hand.

DUBLIN, WE WERE

The curved glass window of a jewelry store on Wicklow Street throws back forms and countenances and in them, diamond rings and necklaces, heavy metallic wristwatches with their crystal faces, taunts to those, such as I, who might hover a body away, hoping not to be bumped, or collided with, to be talked to or passed through.

There are countless pasts here: living, half-living, dead. Worlds that are unattended in the present, unselected for words, straining for sounds that never quite rise into utterance, or become a lasting sign as a mark on paper, or a sense that can, with a touch, be called back to light from digital darkness. For all, there are names but for many, no voices to speak them.

This is my home. I can go anywhere. See anything, as long as it is that which lies on the surface. Who else is here and where?

Kenneth worked the buses in St Helens and did evil by night. Marie was a contract cleaner in Hounslow with her sister Chrissie. They needed to think they were free and to believe in hope. Mick was laid off from the ball-bearing factory in Letchworth and took to driving a taxi, but he didn't have a cabbie's temperament. Conor worked for a large reprographics company in Bonn. His spectacles were always too small for his face. Liam tended bar at Cloagh's Tavern on East Tenth Street in New York City. Eggs Benzedrine was the perfect start to his day. Catherine was an undermatron at the Melbourne Orphan Asylum. She enjoyed a long and happy life. They were here at different times, in the street and on the glass, and now they are not here.

Those who are gone do not know what they want, except, perhaps, because they do not exist, that they desire to be. Their animation into shadows from nothingness is my failed attempt to reach for a story. There is nothing human here. I am bloated with words. I am seizing with the unthinkable. I am not on the street but I am there, warped on the window's surface, where, if you are passing, you can wave to me and say hello before I move along to become another reflection.

Lives and nonlives accumulate in the glass. There is a dirty pane a few feet down from the entrance to a bar on Exchequer Street that has captured glances for decades. The dark rectangle is crowded with us. Peer in. But not too close. Kevin has what he needs hidden in every room in the house—behind the cistern, on the top shelf of the hot press, in the bits-and-pieces drawer in the kitchen. He has what he needs in the glove compartment of his work's piano van. What he needs killed him, which was what he needed. Vad and Kez are pressed together, smiling, turning slowly around in their world of smoke. Florrie stands still, leaning on a blackthorn stick. He's still got the moves. They're behind his eyes. You're a lovely dancer, mister. Ella chugs her lemonade and blinks the white sunlight out of her eyes. She can feel the kebab grease on her fingers, the streaks of chili sauce. There's a big smile coming, she knows it. Dani's string bag is bulging with half a dozen cauliflowers. It nearly has the socket out of her shoulder. And where'll the gratitude be? Where? Nowhere.

The Jervis Centre is empty, the lights are down and somewhere Yonas, the security guard, is stretching his legs. Faintly on the glass of the first-floor atrium barrier, in the long-gone hospital, Annie checks the fob watch that hangs over the left breast pocket of her uniform and settles back in a black vinyl chair. There's time to finish her tea, time for a second fig roll before the 3:00 A.M. ward tour. The hum is continuous and comforting. Nights are good that way.

On the surface of an oily puddle that comes and goes on Capel Street there are shimmering images of purple Doc Martens; of regulation Garda lightweight operational safety boots; of high-polished Tutty's brogues; of raggedy old runners; of white sandals decorated on the straps with plastic daisies; of thigh-high, high-heeled scarlet PVC boots; blue, round-toed Start-Rite shoes; immaculate Altra Lone Peaks; and a pair of feet, cracked and yellow, bruised and cut, the left big toenail missing.

Andy's bit of a face, no more than a smudge on the tough Perspex, and behind this, the mute energy of the artist's studio: pink, orange, scarlet, and tan dabs; a rusty radiator; a withered copy of *Viz* magazine; pots of dried-up brushes; a stack of books, titles obscured. Andy was poor and fearful and so treated like a prick wherever he went, but in the Hugh Lane it was generally quiet on a weekday and the security guards seemed to understand the necessities attendant on having nowhere to go, no one to be. Or maybe not that last one.

We are where we are but only, and always, approximately. The vastness of insignificance is all around and within. The eye has no corners, but there in the fuzz and blur is where the deep mind seeks patterns; the nothing doing, the entwisted fibers of what is felt, the scale of time and its materiality. We are where we are, again. Test the eye on what is found there. The image confined. The inapprehensible. The entanglement of selves. That which denies the line; the plot; the parsable, clear retrospection; the story. Come here while I tell you. Nothing.

A fringe and eyes—Anna's—on the streaky monitor, and underneath a scatter of open windows, files, and emails, and through a glass wall the Grand Canal Dock with the failing light all around and people headed all ways. On the surface of her eye, Anna catches a recursion of self and office and world and presses her eyes closed, trying to crush out all that there is and was and might be. "Good night." Melanie has spoken. "Good night?" she says. "Oh, yes. Yes," says Anna. "Good night."

Pressing his body against the low stone wall, Mike stares into the Dodder with no expectation of seeing himself, and indeed there he is not, and there—*there*—is the river's thick flow and gently corrugated surface, with a warped piece of blue-and-white sky, a margin of shimmering green, and no discernible end. Mike's better self is at the summit of Hungry Hill on a summer's day with a packet of beef sandwiches, a thermos of tea, and his boy Darragh. Darragh smiles and Mike smiles and Darragh smiles back, the same smile but different, and so does Mike. There is no discernible end.

In the midafternoon sunshine, there is no one waiting at the bus stop in Coolock but dimly on the scratched white surface of the shelter's plastic are the shapes of two sisters.

"They emptied me out."

"They butchered her."

"They emptied me out entirely."

"They butchered me entirely."

"They butchered her."

"What was pain to them?"

"What is pain?"

"My life was saved."

"What life was saved?"

"The life for nothing."

"Didn't I love you?"

The shades pull together and a bus goes by without stopping.

A painting takes up most of the wall in the enormous new kitchen on the second floor of the house on Leinster Road. There are heavily palette-knifed ridges and waves of black oil paint mixed, in places, with horsehair; shivers of faces made out in quick, sure dabs and lines of metallic white; irregular swirls of black make a night sky or a dome of thoughts or other sublunary presences. The canvas is covered with a heavy sheet of reflection-resistant glass, held in a neutral gray, metal frame, but, nonetheless, if Cara was to look up from her midmorning poached egg on toast, she would see some soft surface of herself and, to the side, in a much smaller kitchen from an earlier time, Eileen. Eileen mashing a banana, spreading it on slices of buttered bread and carefully scattering a little sugar over the top. For the kids' tea. They'll want a glass of milk but they can't have one, 'cause there'll be ructions if there's none left for the old fella's cuppa.

Cara does not look up. She turns over the page of a magazine that she has not really read, to another page that she will not really read. The egg is good but she will not finish eating it. She puts the fork down. There is work to be done before the children come home.

Two bodies drift together on St Andrew's Street and pass in front of a small frame at throat height. They follow a line of custom: the steps of others not known, for whom there are no maps, or memories, maybe. Behind the glass is a menu for a Lebanese restaurant. Each night, every few minutes, Dáithí and Lara move across this surface, not touching each other. The words they might have spoken are permanently separated from this repeating moment. All there is to be known about them is here, if it could be read.

Minutes past the commencement of a summer dawn, on the drive opposite Brickfield Park, Amy leans over the bonnet of a bottle-green Merc and checks her fringe in the windscreen. Ray is asleep upright, but tilted back slightly, in the front passenger seat, his good suit on, with the gold silk tie he got for Christmas from his brother JJ, done tight up to the top button. Amy is happy with what she sees and walks on to the bus stop. The mobile on the driver's seat rings and keeps on ringing, until it stops. Ray does not move. A moment passes and the phone rings and Ray startles awake. He glares ahead into the sunlight and a green blur and the hovering face of a woman he does not know, who is touching her cheek very gently. He blinks her away. The job is on.

The slick, hard surface of the vitrine shows Lisa to herself: in her smart suit; in a hospital gown; in her blue overalls, streaked, smeared, blobbed, and ragged with paint; in a tight white T-shirt of the kind she would have taken pleasure in wearing on a summer's day back when she had two breasts. The lights are low in the gallery. Lisa watches Bahram Gur, dressed in gold, head swathed in blue cloth, on horseback, kill a dragon with a single arrow. She feels the point go into the heart of malice. The bad flesh would have sunk into the earth but a dragon might grow back from a single seed. The hero might vanish, or she might triumph, on a single day, in a solitary reflection, with the test results in her handbag that read "All clear."

Down the Coombe, there is a group on the pavement, four particles standing before the yellow-framed window of a bookshop. Books that each has abandoned through life or death are behind the glass, joining them together in reflection. The green morocco binding of a pocket edition of Carleton's *Traits and Stories of the Irish Peasantry*, that was Carmel's, and before that, her grandmother's. The soft green cloth of Patrick's copy of James Stephens's *The Crock of Gold*, withdrawn from the library of Holyoke Community College. Annie's paperback of *Night* by Edna O'Brien, the paper crumbling orange. Neasa's Left Book Club edition of *The Irish Republic* by Dorothy Macardle, with the maps still intact.

The readers draw closer to the glass, but they do not touch.

Pictured on the glass of the tearooms, between the hazy late summer, late afternoon light behind and, outside, in the Phoenix Park, shifting arboreal greens and browns, in a moment of permanent radiance and joy, is the face of Orla. Standing, naughtily, on a chair, god bless her, in her raspberry matinee coat knitted by her grandma, the left arm slightly longer than the right, with an ice cream cone heaped high with a great immensity of cold, creamy happiness. Across a cluster of dimmer, higher panels is her daddy with his cappuccino, the possessor of the sudden knowledge that there is nothing better and the hope that, if he tries hard enough, this perfection will never end.

I could be anywhere but I am standing opposite the house on Griffith Avenue where I lived for two summers with the good, close friends who no longer know each other. I look down. The lights go out in my hand. I stare into the flat black surface and see no one.

Ibrahim's gaze passes from the spire of Findlater's Church to the pool of the Garden of Remembrance upon which he sees all his many faces from infancy to now. He smiles and says, apparently aloud, "Who has placed me here? I am a composite apparition. The blue, the green, the white waves in their tesserate tide. What do they recall to the people who visit this garden? I remember my mother. Not a particular time or place, but the whole of her, the whole of our love."

The net curtain is down in the front room of the house in Oaklands Terrace and I stand still, as a much younger man, with long curly hair and a full goatee. The sun shifts behind a cloud and I disappear, and in a mirror over the mantelpiece a man's arm is raised, in the hard knot of his fist, a belt. I don't turn away and the hours pass, and the arm, the belt, the fist hold there until the dusk comes on and the night draws in and I can no longer see into the past.

Most of my life was spent in other territories. Imagined versions of this city were told to me in childhood as home, and I grew and wandered, and, wherever I was, this birthplace rose up under the present one, shaping and shadowing, impressing on my eye with pictures out of time, imposing on my ear the tones and echoes of the voices of a more real place. When I returned to this habitation, as often I did, I found much there I had been told of, a world of familiarity that was at once strange to me, and I to it, and for this I was thought plastic, instead of what I was to myself; a not-dead ghost of light and dust.

I stand where there is all the time and, in the fullness of time, no time at all. The shapes of the hours, the days, the years, are thrown back to sight or no sight. The lives of cities, of countries, of continents, of islands, can be thought of as proceeding in lines, in nets and weaves, in deep continuities and discontinuities, of well-worn narratives, some of them true, and of immensities of the forgotten. Who we were—the someones, the no ones, the anyones—fold back onto themselves in the reflected moment. I am here to catch the image, the motion, the stillness, the gatherings. I am here for the return, for the depthless flavor of loss, for the return and nothing else.

This is my home. I can go anywhere and come back to myself on these many surfaces. We can return home in our reflections, even when the city we knew, the city we were, has gone forever.

CATS ARE HUNTERS, AFTER ALL

Imagine:

You are building yourself a home. You have found a piece of land on which to build it. The land faces east, and so the family you imagine having will be woken, softly, by the morning sun. With the current owner of the land, you have agreed a price that leaves you enough for bricks, for labor, but also for roses to greet your visitors by the door.

You have, into the walls, imprisoned a living thing. It is a cat. (It could have been a baby, unwanted. For this reason, you consider yourself merciful.) This is considered lucky, by others. Not you. Why are you yourself not sufficient, as guardian of this home?

While you lace roof tiles together, you hear the cat. You hope your timing is good: that by the time you move in, the cat will be dead, no longer pacing tiny circles in its alcove, mewling cat-dreams while your new wife tries to sleep in the bed she has been covering with finely worked roses while you have been building this house.

Fool.

Your timing was good, but that will not matter.

The home is a good home, built well. You are happy in it. The unpleasant smell fades. At night, you fall asleep listening to the creaks as the house settles into its foundation. In the mornings, you wake up to the sun slanting across your pillows. You do not talk about the cat. It is a thing that has been done, and does not need mentioning. The roses bloom, the evenings lengthen.

The more you do not talk about the cat, the more you have the sense the house is playing with you—hiding pins, tossing single socks into surprising cubbyholes when you're not looking, seizing you at doorways with a sudden inability to remember what propelled you through them—but you cast this from your mind, sternly. A house is not a living thing. It does not have a personality.

As you make friends in the village, you become less convinced of this. The personality that your house does not have is unavoidably different to those of your friends' houses. The home of your neighbor is suddenly and unexpectedly vicious: the heating system seizes up on the coldest day and refuses to be fixed; the roof collapses into the bedroom, and then again into the kitchen, raining splinters and plaster dust into a newly iced birthday cake. You are certain this last was a fit of spite, although (of course) you do not say this. Nor do they.

Neither do you mention to your wife that, every time you visit the home of her oldest friend, you feel compelled to bring a gift. You sense that it prefers soft things, scarves, plants with trailing, battable leaves. You do not think too carefully about what "it" is. Her friend has painted the walls with matte, chalky paint, and your wife is not the only visitor to run her hands along them as she enters, before she takes off her coat and drapes it carefully wherever something—a chair, perhaps—looks cold.

You find, tucked beneath the dresser, a bundle of tiny bones. They are ancient, dessicated and crumbling, but you remember with certainty sweeping this room no more than two weeks ago. You have a very definite memory of moving the dresser then, too, retrieving more hairpins than you felt it was possible for one piece of furniture to need.

This time, you do ask your wife: Can she think of how they might have got there? She purses her lips, no, and suggests that perhaps they blew in while the door was open. Neither you nor your wife opens those doors in November. You get halfway through a question about this before she changes the subject abruptly. You suspect that she has been opening them in order not to be alone in the hollow-feeling house while you are not there.

This is another conversation you do not start. You, too, have noticed the unsettling emptiness. You have wondered whether your childlessness is responsible, but you are not confident of being able to adequately express your horror at the idea of gifting a child to the void. It is not an argument you are willing to lose, so you say nothing.

The bones in the bundles get larger. From voles, tiny birds, to what you manage to convince yourself must be rats. When you find bones as thick as your smallest finger, you start to bury them in the garden. You try not to think about what creature hunts things this size, and what it might be doing in your house.

———

The bones continue to increase in size, and in frequency. You find yourself burying them in the vegetable patch early in the mornings, before the sun is quite up. Hoping the neighbors don't see.

Your neighbor's dog goes missing. You—of course—join the hunt for the missing dog. You knock on doors, ask people to check their sheds, barns. You search each face for the disquiet you are certain must show on yours. Several times, you draw the kind of breath that starts a sentence. Each time, you lose your nerve.

The dog is not found.

You jolt awake before sunrise, white-cold with fear. Sleeping, your subconscious has provided you with the notion that those things with personalities must also have appetites. In your imagination, you nudge awake your wife for comfort, for a reasonable explanation to this. Instead, you remember the dresser, the bones, the silence. You spend the remainder of the darkness awake and alone, trying to think of anything for which this rule might not be true. You fail.

The greengrocer's youngest daughter disappears. Their garden backs onto a wooded area, and it is here that the month's second search party concentrates its efforts. But a group of thirty can comb through a smallish, well-managed coppice in less than an afternoon, and it does not take long before you feel the collective waning of hope: this is not a search party that will find a living child.

You realize, then, that you are not the only one who has been up before sunrise, shovelling damp earth over makeshift graves.

One of the less haunted among the party suggests a search of the buildings in the village, in case the girl is hiding in a shed, or an attic somewhere. You all agree, yes, an excellent idea. Of course.

You find the familiar bundles in the corners of the less tidy homes, those belonging to large families. To single men. You feign surprise. At the first uncovering, the doctor is consulted, and offers her expertise: nothing the size of a human child. (You are relieved. You lack this knowledge, and you have been unable to ignore what that means for your assessments of your own findings. But who could you have asked? Not your wife, who will not discuss bones of any kind. Nor your friends, with their studied indifference to the peculiarities of their homes.)

Twelve houses later, and the doctor has been consulted so frequently that she has joined the search. This latest is a house that does not like strangers: doors ricochet off walls, endangering noses; banisters leave splinters in the soft parts of hands; twisted floorboards catch toes on the way past. It is in the midst of this swearing that the cry goes up: bones—a rib cage—human. Unmistakably.

You have seen death before. If the child disappeared this morning, these bones are not hers. Nothing natural causes such efficient decay. You start to raise this, but you have misjudged the momentum of the group, ahead of you already, someone shouting for the keys to the village lock-up, others stalking down the stairs in hunt, silent and determined. You catch the eye of the doctor, likewise halted mid-sentence, and share a moment of disquiet. This will not bring you comfort.

Another dog. A heart-stopping morning, at the end of which a friend's daughter is—eventually—found, entangled with one of the village boys behind an outbuilding. The search, though, unearths yet more bones, confirmed not-human but too large to comfortably ignore. Friends are avoided on the street, refused service at the butcher's. You display sympathy, and wonder at the recklessness of not sweeping under the kitchen cupboards while there is a man locked in the windowless holding cell awaiting what may still be a lynching. You wonder at your garden.

Your wife asks you to leave. It turns out that the mutterings on the street corners have tried you, in your absence, and decided on your exile. Just for a while, your wife says, until all of this. She waves her hands in a direction that you interpret as meaning "goes away" or "is forgotten," neither of which seem to you like a resolution. You perform indignance: you are not to blame for this, nor your friends, nor, even, the owner of the house where the remains were found. She shrugs, silent, resolute.

In truth, a part of you is relieved. The gnawing emptiness of the house has become less acute, but you cannot think of the vegetable patch without the familiar wave of horror. You do not want to leave your wife in this village of strange hungers, though. You suggest to her that she might come, too, but no: she loves the house, the roses, the morning sun. She will stay, and you will come back. You cannot think of anything to say that will bring her with you, so you say nothing.

You ask around. You seek out your blameless friends, those above suspicion. Those—now that you hold the list of them together in your head—with strangely characterless houses. You learn that even these friends have had the same request from their wives. You begin packing. You are given the keys to the lock-up as you leave.

From your new home, you listen for news. It is difficult to come by: no men are permitted to enter the village; no women leave it. Your wife writes to you, for a while. She does not mention bones, or disappearances, and you do not know if this is because there aren't any. You don't ask.

On market day, you hear that another child has gone. A boy, this time. You feel vindicated, then appalled.

Carefully, you compose a letter to your wife. You offer help to search for the missing boy. You ask if she might consider coming to join you. It is not safe there, your measures of protection inadequate at best, you too far away to be anything other than helpless. You describe the new home you have found, the emptiness of it without her. You receive no reply.

The snowdrops appear, then the daffodils. More letters go unanswered. By the time the fields are stubbled green with the season's first growth, you have stopped alternating abandonment with fury. Instead, you have settled into an indignation that clenches your left fist whenever you are not paying attention to it, and wakes you up with an aching jaw.

On one such morning, you decide. You will go back to the village. You will bring back at least the books you have been missing, the summer clothes you'd thought you wouldn't need, your most comfortable shoes. At most, your wife.

You return with none of those things, and an expression on your face that means concerned questions, later. No, you say. No one. Yes, completely. No sign of where they might have gone. And already stones missing. Whole walls, of some houses. No, you don't know. For some other building, maybe?

You ask around, discreetly. You find it difficult to disagree with the economics: much cheaper to disassemble those houses than hew new blocks from rough stone, and savings must be made where they can. Yes, there are some disagreeable findings in some of the walls, but progress must be made. Those working on the dismantling report some feelings of unease, yes, but this is only to be expected in a ghost town like the village has become.

You learn which building this stone will raise. A block settles, a small one, behind the top half of your rib cage, and stays there. You compose the beginning of several letters to the firm undertaking the construction, but there is no tone, no combination of words you can assemble that sounds like anything other than lunacy. These half-coherent words—bones, hunger, children—may be condemnation enough once the disappearances start, and you know well the consequences of suspicion. Instead, you stop walking past the schoolhouse and its new classroom, choose a route that means you don't hear the laughter of the children. You tell yourself you need the exercise.

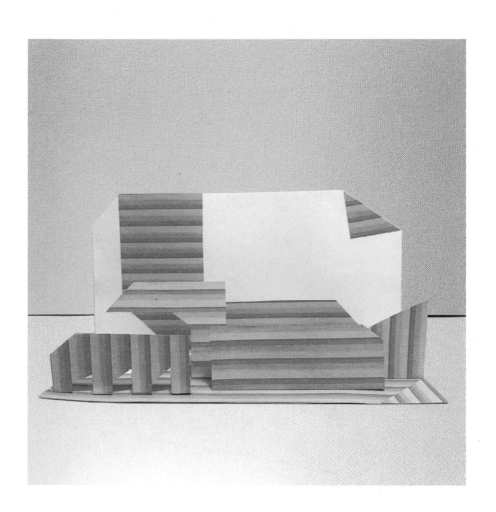

Jena H. Kim

Jena H. Kim

INTERVIEW / ROBERT KIRKBRIDE

THE SYNTAX OF SPACE

*The following interview was conducted at
the Parsons School of Design, in a small
room with two chairs and a small table.*

*The interview with Robert Kirkbride
was to cover the historic asylums that
housed patients with mental illness, which
were conceived in the nineteenth century
by another Kirkbride, a relative, Thomas
Story Kirkbride. But the conversation, as
was its hope, set out past the confines
into a peripatetic expanse that included
Roman walls, superheroes, wood joists,
Abraham Lincoln, and French museums. A
marshaling of complexities and influences
that shape the constructed space and the
currents toward its potential erasure.
—Mark Hage*

RK: In the 1840s, Thomas Story
Kirkbride and his colleagues banded
together to develop an ethical approach—
an architectural typology, a physical
infrastructure, a social system—to support
mental illness. They were working against
the tide of mesmerists and charlatans,
against the grain, to establish confidence
in a medical practice. The word psychology
was not yet widely used. The United States
itself was a fledgling nation. The social
fabric of hospital systems, penal systems,

all of these different social infrastructures
were sketchy at best. It's a remarkable
time, in a nation that was brand new. The
pursuit of happiness, inalienable rights, all
men created equal: All of those wonderful
statements had no infrastructure to really
hang on to, be attached to.

MH: *What was the condition of mental
health patients before the Kirkbrides?*

When Kirkbride was hired to lead
a new hospital dedicated to mental
illness, located west of Philadelphia—
this was 1840, he was hired as the
first superintendent—the Pennsylvania
Hospital had previously had a cellar-level
location for patients and the hospital had
had to build a fence to prevent onlookers
from gawking.

A cabinet of curiosities.

A strange form of entertainment and
spectatorship, although that was pretty
much standard wherever the mentally
ill were kept. They were oftentimes just
mixed in in jails or kept in basements or
attics of private homes, under real stigma,
and tucked away. Think of Bertha in *Jane*

Eyre (1847). Or they had no place to be. That was the other reality. That is a far more prevalent reality now. Homelessness.

Dr. Kirkbride was a Quaker. What influenced his ideas?

The Kirkbrides had come over in 1681 from Cumbria, which is on the border of Scotland, at the westernmost part of the Stanegate, alongside Hadrian's Wall. The region of Cumbria wasn't included in the Domesday Book of 1086 after the Battle of Hastings and the Norman invasion, meaning that it remained affiliated with Scotland until eventually being absorbed into England. Yet even after, Cumbria was always a place that was resistant to English rule.

Indomitable.

Indomitable. It was always a free, liminal, zone. Many Quakers came from that area, sharing the fundamental belief that each individual is a source of light. Light and silence were critical to the Quaker belief system. The belief that each soul is a light is the fundamental reason there is such a commitment to the value of each and every person: because there was a potential for renewal, regeneration, rediscovery. Thomas Story Kirkbride was interested in how one creates an environment for well-being that supports that inner light and the

opportunity to find oneself.

That's also, in a parallel story, why Eastern State Penitentiary (1829, Philadelphia) is a penitentiary, not a prison. The belief was that you would become penitent and return to society as a recovered individual. In the penitentiary they believed all you needed was absolute silence and separation from people. You were on your own with the Bible. The aspirations of the penitentiary founders were, however, overly optimistic. We know now that solitary confinement is not a healthy condition for cognition, for the mind.

When Kirkbride took over the West Philadelphia hospital in 1841, he immediately started to theorize on how to modify that facility into what became the Kirkbride plan. He published several articles and then published the first edition of his treatise in 1854.

Is his book still available?

Absolutely. There were two editions. 1854 was the first, 1880 was the second, which included revisions featuring new technologies, gaslight, all sorts of new boiler systems—because they were washing the sheets for, and feeding, hundreds if not thousands of people. By the second edition we're in a time period where occupant densities exceeded Kirkbride's desire. The limit on the number of occupants were critical. The ideal

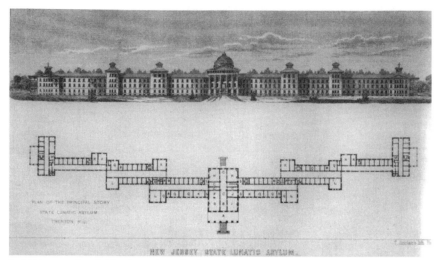

A lithograph of the batwing design for Trenton State Hospital

maximum capacity for a state asylum, for Kirkbride, was two hundred fifty patients.

It is said that patients and staff were so integrated that the only way you could tell them apart was by the keys that hung on the staff's belts. Can you comment on the interaction between staff and patients? There is something about Dr. Kirkbride paying people well, taking care of the workers who were most exposed to outbursts, by giving them frequent vacations. It's a very different model from the current for-profit optimization. It's more about an entire community that's in balance.

It's consistent with Quaker values—recognizing the humanity of the patients and the workers to promote a healthier environment for everyone. Kirkbride was focused on the daily ritual of the building and how you used the architecture of the building and the distribution of the building to help structure the day. You tried to provide zones in the building that never got too large, so that the doctors and the visiting physicians would know the names of all their patients. And for the day-to-day correspondence and interactions to be respectful.

Can you describe how the buildings were used and what was unique about them, and go over the design with the batwing idea?

The "echelon" plan includes a central main administrative building, in which the superintendent often lived with his family, with symmetrical wings that extend

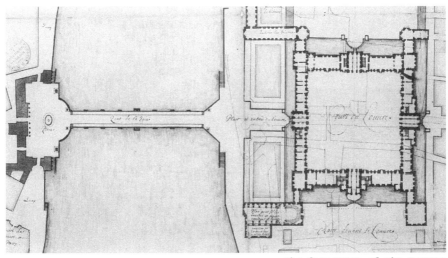

The forecourt of the Louvre

backward—rather than into a forecourt like the Louvre or many European-style court buildings where the arms come forward. Usually each wing included three segments stepping back, with many variations. Patients who were closer to returning to their lives outside resided closer to the central main and attended dinners with the superintendents as part of the process of normalization. The more severe cases were at the extremities of the arms. On a very pragmatic level, one of the critical things that Kirkbride emphasized was generating confidence through the building, and through day-to-day life. He called it a generous confidence.

Why does this matter? If the arms came forward, the most extreme cases would be in the first spaces you would encounter, so someone hanging out

the window, or screaming, would be the first impression on arrival to the asylum. Kirkbride recognized that superintendents had to instill confidence in the family to part ways, to give that family member over to the institution at a time when the United States did not have an established medical profession. You were asking for a lot of trust for people to believe in the state.

These massive buildings were deliberately awe-inspiring in scale and workings. The power of the state to build such a facility would instill confidence. That trust, and that confidence, were essential to Kirkbride. It wasn't just the building, it wasn't just the treatments or the medications, or the practices or the rigor or the behaviors, it was the confidence in the relationship between the patient and the establishment. They were building a code

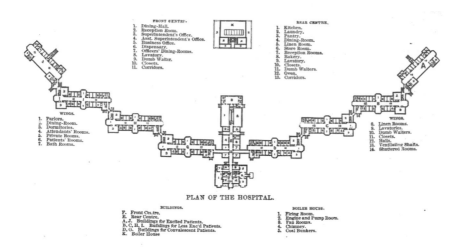

PLAN OF THE HOSPITAL.

Floor plan for Danvers State Hospital

of respectful conduct for patients and staff, embodied through the buildings.

The grounds of the hospitals also provided respite and occupational therapy for patients, a specific mode of treatment advocated by Kirkbride, and were significant in the emergence of landscape architecture practice in the United States. Several asylums—in Buffalo and Poughkeepsie, respectively— were designed by Olmsted and Vaux. There are really interesting roles that the buildings and grounds played as vehicles for promoting a more democratic approach to well-being. As an interesting sidenote, during the Civil War, Abraham Lincoln would take restorative walks through the park at Saint Elizabeths Hospital, in Washington, DC—the only federal Kirkbride Plan Hospital.

Are there records of the interactions between Dr. Kirkbride and his architects? Was it he or the state that hired them?

Kirkbride's plan was the driving force for about seventy-five asylums across the United States, including variations produced by John Notman, H. H. Richardson, and Thomas U. Walter. It was a real greatest hits of architects at the time. But Kirkbride's architect of choice was Samuel Sloan, who started as a carpenter at Eastern State Penitentiary. Sloan designed the prototypes illustrated in Kirkbride's treatise.

The state, however, hired the architects, not Kirkbride himself. Many of these hospitals were built where they are as a result of winning proposals submitted to the respective state government by young towns that had aspirations to become cities, such as Traverse City and Kalamazoo in Michigan; Warren, Pennsylvania; Fergus Falls in Minnesota. They won the contracts in competition with other small cities in order to grow themselves. As you built the brickworks and felled the timber to do the framing and the beams and joists, you were simultaneously building the local industries to build the fabric of the town. These buildings grew up symbiotically with towns across the nation. So when you look at the doorknobs, the handles and hinges, the light fixtures, all of these things were part of a nation generating a whole new building industry. The asylums are three-dimensional documents of local and national histories, committed to social justice on behalf of people who had been perennially overlooked.

It's really important to be cognizant of that historic value when communities are thinking about tearing down their local Kirkbride because the developers are pushing on the bruises of local stigmas and family histories. Those histories may be very difficult and not to be dismissed or forgotten, but those become very easy buttons for developers and lazy politicians to push with the aim of erasing the buildings.

Kirkbride did two years of research before he started the detailed plans.

Kirkbride had traveled in the northeast to visit existing asylums and developed his own gentleman-architect approach to defining and specifying the materials, including wood floors, and for tending to sound and acoustics, and providing direct ventilation and light. For maximum lighting, he called for high ceilings, with transoms above the doors. The steelwork, covering the windows to prevent escape, were designed to be discreet to prevent the sense of imprisonment. He got into the nitty-gritty on all of these details. He was thinking about it from the perception of the user, which we still are challenging architects to do—to think about users and not have it come from the willful, formal decision-making. The forms Kirkbride specified embodied the principles of treatment. Correspondingly, Kirkbride laid out the specific hour-by-hour regimen of how the day happened. Early to bed, early to rise, with carefully planned activities, meals, and entertainments. And in the evenings he himself would offer, multiple times in a given week, magic-lantern shows. He was the first, reputedly, to use photography in psychological treatment. Working with a photographer in Philadelphia, he developed these incredible slideshows about places of interest and scientific wonder.

Were the Romanesque and Gothic styles used just because they were de rigueur at the time, or did they have an added message or import?

It was largely taste, but each one had its own appointments and localized flavor. But it's interesting how stylistic references and cultural perceptions cross-pollinate and even muddy one another. Although Samuel Sloan tended toward Italianate detailing for his hospitals, and the Buffalo State Asylum was deeply imbued by H. H. Richardson's Romanesque, many might view asylums of this period through the hindsight lens of the Gothic. In the 1970s, after the public view of psychiatric hospitals had darkened considerably, Batman cartoons borrowed heavily from Buffalo State Asylum's signature towers for the dark imagery for its Arkham Asylum, which housed the Joker and other members of Batman's rogues gallery. It's worth noting here that Batman's Arkham Asylum is itself a reference to the Arkham Sanitarium in H. P. Lovecraft's gothic stories, modeled after Danvers State Hospital, in Massachusetts. Italianate, Richardsonian Romanesque, Gothic—they flowed together in a darkening public view toward the institutions of psychiatric care. This is a direct result of overwhelming asylums— Kirkbride plan or not—with populations they were never intended to support, as a consequence of warfare and also abuses by American citizens. In visiting

communities with Kirkbride Hospitals and talking with them about their local histories, I've learned of larger, unfortunate patterns that played out. Women would commit themselves to escape abusive husbands. Husbands would commit wives after postpartum depression.

Or to get rid of them.

In one case in Fergus Falls, a husband committed his wife, placed their two daughters in foster care, and then remarried within the year. Older siblings committed younger siblings in order to prevent subdivisions of family inheritance. There are legacies of abuse of the original intentions of the asylums, not only by malevolent doctors or head nurses, but by everyday citizens. In many cases these are traumatic family histories, producing stigmas that are being pushed at knowingly by developers and others, by scapegoating the buildings. "Let's erase that bad memory for you."

The other thing I would say, having just been out at Athens, Ohio, at the Kirkbride there. Levi Scofield was the architect. Just twenty-four years old, fresh from the Civil War. What Scofield did was to incorporate detailing from his regiment. Details are embedded in the building itself that speak to the history of a war that created a whole new level of need for these buildings. If Kirkbride's specification was that you should only have two hundred fifty patients in a state asylum, by 1876 in Greystone, in Morris Plains, New Jersey, it was eight hundred patients.

Over six hundred thousand square feet, right? To give it scale, that is the size of the new MoMA. It was gigantic.

Enormous. The Civil War atrocities plunged people into a whole new category of experience for which there was no reference. The Civil War created both the need to house traumatized people and the well-oiled machinery of industry that the Northern Army had become. The bureaucracy had been established and was simply redirected to build all of these buildings at an epic scale that would otherwise not have been possible. The history of these buildings is so rich because it crosses over into so many difficult, delicate areas. We as a nation put a lot of people in harm's way; and then we had to build the physical infrastructure to compensate for that.

On a personal level, given the fraught history, what tilted you to become actively involved in protecting the buildings rather than wanting to dissociate from them as a member of the Kirkbride family?

Well, I was never shy about being associated with them, despite their problematic histories. I have a mini-family history that has centered on the constructed environment and infrastructures, including Quaker infrastructures, in particular. In her midfifties my grandmother, Beatrice H. Kirkbride, a thee-thy-thou Quaker, became a researcher—a tenacious detective, really—for the newly formed Philadelphia Historical Commission. One of her targeted projects, working with Dr. Margaret Tinkham and Charles E. Peterson, was to protect the Southwark neighborhood and its black community against the midcentury urban encroachment of Federal Highway Systems, a recurring theme that was playing out across North American cities. It's remarkable to read that correspondence. To inform her work, Bea took history courses alongside my father, who was studying architecture at the University of Pennsylvania, where I would also study architecture, twenty-five years later. While completing my master of architecture, I became fascinated by T. S. Kirkbride's treatise on asylum management, and I also had an ongoing debate with my grandmother about how to best adapt and reuse abandoned Eastern State Penitentiary, a project that was especially important to her. But it was the fall of Greystone that brought me into contact with nationwide preservation efforts that converged at that moment

This page, clockwise from left: Hudson River State Hospital. Greystone Psychiatric Hospital. St. Elizabeths Hospital. Buffalo State Hospital.

This page, clockwise
from above: Fergus
Falls State Hospital.
Thomas Story Kirkbride's
*On the Construction,
Organization, and General
Arrangements of Hospitals
for the Insane*. Trans-
Allegheny Lunatic Asylum.
Bricks from the Athens
Lunatic Asylum. Northern
Michigan Asylum.

to form PreservationWorks. This shared energy provided agency for action.

So a long history of knowing where you come from. You had said in one of your lectures that Americans are not comfortable with timelines and that we have a fraught relationship with history and vestiges.

We still have a mythology that we're a young country. We're not. We have one of the oldest continuous constitutions in the world. We also constantly portray ourselves as underdogs, but we've not been underdogs for… ever. It's just amazing the mythologies and narratives we tell ourselves. How we oversimplify history, as a specific moment in time.

As a product.

Philadelphia is a perfect example. To promote colonial tourism in anticipation of the bicentennial celebration, planners cleaned up the area around Independence Hall, weeding out the higgledy-piggledy buildings that had accumulated over time to present a purified, if entirely fictional, image of 1776.

In the process of doing that, they erased several Frank Furness banks and buildings, which now we would adore to have back. Generally speaking, in the United States we tend to deliberately purge a constructed environment rather than embrace a layering of history.

We go to Europe to experience their deeper histories. And we love architects like Carlo Scarpa who weave together the old and the new fabric so they live side by side, providing juxtaposition, or a complementary narrative. And yet, in the United States we reduce time and complexity into an oversimplified elevator pitch: This is Philadelphia, the colonial town. It's so superficial and shallow that it also puts an unnecessary polarity between historic preservation and architecture as either/or, rather than both/and.

It cost fifty million dollars to demolish the Greystone building in New Jersey. It could have been repaired for fifty million and made into artist studios. At par, we have a void instead of a beautiful building.

Not only that, the tragedy behind Greystone is that it was a personal, political vendetta of the local politicians who made a deal to tear down that building no matter what. One company was willing to refurbish the entire building at absolutely no cost to taxpayers, yet state and local leadership had already made up their minds to spend tens of millions of taxpayers' dollars to erase history.

To go back to the distrust of history, could this be related to hyperconsumerism that needs to devour the old to put new things

on the shelf perpetually? Intellectuals are not
trusted in this country because they speak of
"useless" things? Is it sort of a continuum, a
consumerist world that aims for end result in
all facets, now influencing all facets?

There are a few facets to what you're
asking. One is that I think what we're
finding in the current political climate is a
historical mistrust of higher education. As
a culture, the United States has always
been very much DIY, or at least the
illusion, the appearance, of pioneerism,
of do it yourself. So we don't trust the
authorities, the scholastics.

Abstraction.

If you go to the roots of Quakerism, for
example George Fox, many early leaders
were not book learned. Many of the
utopian religious groups that settled the
United States came as boot-strapping
communities. There were remarkably
powerful rhetorical speakers, but that was
not necessarily from book learning; and
they were very proud of being antithetical
to book learning. So that's a very strong
undertow to the United States.

Which could be misused.

Which is easily triggered. The dog whistles
that are blown currently activate this kind
of off-road, rogue behavior. I'm going to do

it the way I want to do it, I don't need to fit
in, you're just telling me who I have to be.
A kind of libertarianism but on steroids,
devil-take-the-hindmost. But there's a
distinction with the Quakers, with their
version of that willful desire not to fit in—
which founded our banking system, our
legal and penal systems, and all these
social systems and infrastructures. Those
current politicians with the dog whistles
would call them Communist or Socialist
and they would have been calling Thomas
Story Kirkbride a Socialist or Communist
for his commitment to people who had
nowhere else to be.

Where do they go when you willfully
undermine the social fabric? They go on
the streets, they go into prison; and we
are paying for them anyway, you are just
shifting the way you are paying for them,
as lost causes versus as people who have
an opportunity to find a new way into the
world. That's one part of the allergy to
the social fabric and the intellectualism of
understanding these histories, however
complex they might be.

But also, think about the built fabric.
These buildings were sited strategically
on the highest ground, with the best
view, the best vista, the best breezes.
Ventilation and solar patterns, vistas,
adjacency to water bodies, rivers—
they were sited strategically on choice
landscapes as part of their function to
treat the mentally ill. They were not on

the cheapest land per public housing, as is often done. When you look at them on Google Earth, you see they are on ideal pieces of land. Of course developers want to tear them down.

Circling back to the idea of common history and this new trend of the world becoming about the person, the person becoming the center, rather than the person caring for others, what are the lessons of the Kirkbrides in terms of combating this present attack on history, which in a way is an attack on language, which is our shared history. If you dismantle language, you really can get away with saying anything. To me what makes us human is our ability to have a common agreement, and it is related to language and history. The speed at which it is being dismantled is remarkable. Is there something in the history of the Kirkbrides that allows history to be something beyond trauma and dark, dusty hallways?

These buildings are three-dimensional documents. They embodied and documented the physical infrastructures that created a community. In Athens, there are multiple types of bricks incorporated into the roads, as well as the facades and the built fabric. Those brickworks were from different parts of the town. Athens was creating the physical commerce to constitute itself as a town where democracy is practiced and capitalism is practiced. All of these things were knit together. The building embodies that history.

Look at Traverse City. The joists are northern Michigan pine that was all but deforested by Sears and Roebuck and the creation of balloon-frame housing— those trees were living, breathing creatures as the nation was being formed. It's the language of our understanding of our landscape.

When you look at Greystone in New Jersey, and you realize its construction was in the 1870s, you have Italian and Polish masons and Irish workers who are building that fabric. The carpentry, the materials, the care of construction are the marks of the hands of people building it. Those are human relationships. It's not just stuff people made. The value is the human language and human relationships translated into stone and wood and space and light and systems that were innovating to improve the human condition. It wasn't just jobs people did to put buildings together. The asylums are irreplaceable in their tectonic knowledge and embodied knowledge and embodied energy. Unfortunately, the banking cycle that drives the United States and the industry it has become, the thirty-year mortgage cycle, means that the land is always worth more than the building on it. So of course the developers want to erase the asylums.

They just want to put up their new building because that choice land is worth a lot.

It feels like in New York City these days the forces that want to tear things down are a little stronger, much stronger in some instances, helped by the forces that are supposed to oppose them. Is there a lesson of the personal connection as a tool for preservation? In maybe not having aims and proclamations that are huge, but finding something small and personal that is difficult to overcome by bigger forces?

We tend to always be thinking about ye olde architecture, but brutalism and midcentury modern are also subject to destruction. The loss of valuable Paul Rudolph structures, among others. It's not just old stuff anymore. But there's a real bifurcation in the way politicians, developers, preservationists and citizens negotiate that space. A binary condition has emerged where historic preservationists see the down cycles economically as the breathing periods where they have the chance to establish protections, in contrast to the cycles where the things are just insane and expanding, which is of course what architects prefer. Understandably, architects become intoxicated with the opportunity to build: just keep the machinery going as long as possible. It is a problematic cycle.

Another part of the conversation that is important here is that of architecture and ornament. Ornament has only in the last couple hundred years been viewed as a matter of style, and a matter of superficial cost, as Durand had argued. The science of building is more important than the art of building. "You don't need no stinking venustas, you don't need Venus."

You need utilitas.

You need utilitas and firmitas. You don't need pleasure. That's all you need to have in architecture. Ornamentation becomes just an added cost. But every decision, whether it is a reveal, the joint between the wall and the floor that we're looking at in this little room right here versus a molding that covers that joint—regardless of how you attenuate, treat, approach that edge condition, those are deliberate decisions that reflect the relationships of human beings and building trades with one another. You are articulating how those trades, the conjunctions in the grammar and the syntax of how you make space in the building and construction trades, and through those traditions, and how you articulate the decorum of behavior in those spaces, through the appointment. That is as ancient as the hills, that is the underpinning of the architectural profession and practice.

The diminution of ornament to being just about frippery or style is really a denigration of a much older tradition. The

Roman republic, the Greek republic—they were founded on the public forum as the space of protest, the space of debate. In these traditions, architectural ornament was literally ornare, to prepare. It prepares you for rhetorical persuasion. That is what happens every day in the congress, in the public realm, in the United States. When we simply undress the constructed environment from thoughtfully articulated spaces and places, surfaces, seams, then we undermine our cognitive capacity to hold arguments.

And to create a story.

To create a story, a sense of personal and communal identity. We as designers are constantly working with, challenging, manipulating the materials of rhetoric about who we are—and who we present ourselves to be, to ourselves and to one another.

The excuse for demolishing buildings has been their deterioration and that they're unwieldy for new spaces. But those systems and materials that were used in tune with their natural limitations created spaces that are of a human scale. With current advances, buildings are creating artificial constructs that have no relation to natural laws. It's a fake sense of majesty.

It's a very convenient argument that it's difficult to utilize those spaces. You said

it quite directly. It's demolition by neglect. That certainly is what happened at Greystone in Morris Plains, of just saying that there's no way we can replace it, the roof is too expensive.

You can repair anything.

There are several successful renovations and adaptations of Kirkbrides. In Tuscaloosa, the University of Alabama is revitalizing Bryce Hospital as a performance and arts center, an entryway to the university, not a stigmatizing blemish. The argument that it's difficult to utilize those spaces is just simple laziness. It's an absolute disrespect of history and of those who lived and died and worked in those spaces. It also does not value the idea that we can continue, and need to continue, to learn as a society.

What were some of the failures and successes in preserving these buildings?

I think Greystone and other demolitions, including the central back buildings at Fergus Falls, which happened just recently. At Fergus Falls there were service buildings behind the central main—a gymnasium, kitchen facilities that fed five thousand patients, and electrical power supply to the whole site. There is no reason that couldn't have been a regional makerspace. To take the power supply and the kitchen and have communal cooking. To give cooking lessons in the kitchen. The failure I'm getting at is a failure of the imagination. That is where the failure tends to be. The lazy politicians, the payola, all of those kinds of relationships, are perhaps predictable in local politics, along with the personal vendettas. But I think the large problem is the failure of the imagination. That's shared. We don't find, or make, a compelling enough argument to convince ourselves how these buildings can and might serve in new and different ways to help us address the difficult realities we face.

Raymond Minervini, a developer, had the vision to buy Traverse City for a dollar. The first thing he did was to put a new hat on it. You fix the hat and the bones will stay dry. Then you can do very simple things to redevelop and adapt one bit at a time. You do not need to do it all at once. That is not even the appropriate way to restore, revitalize a building like this.

Raymond turned certain parts of the building into condominiums. Some people raised the question, Who is going to want to live there? That is a very convenient argument about the built fabric—that it's very difficult to utilize those spaces, and who would want to use them, anyway. Well, there's a wait list for the condominiums. Because a younger generation grew up wanting to know about Traverse City. About their uncle who was a patient there, or their mother or father who worked on the property, drove the bus on the campus.

Is any kind of preservation a good thing? Is turning something like this into a high-end hotel a sort of erasure of the history? Or as long as we keep the edifice...

I think there's an easy polarity between saying either it's going to be a fossilization of history, and that is being more "truthful"; or, that it is going to be something entirely different from its original use. The truth is we must be far more sophisticated than we often allow ourselves to be. We can and we need to be able to entertain multiple layers of history because there are multiple layers of our identities as a nation and as individuals. Neither you nor I, when we walk out of this room and talk with another person about a totally different topic, are the same person that we are sitting in this room at this moment. We enable ourselves to surf on different identities to negotiate our daily lives, and we wear many clothes, many hats, and entertain being many people.

We need to be able to sustain and nourish that approach to ourselves, and our built environment. How we treat the built environment is very much how we treat ourselves, whether we fully realize it or not.

COMPROMISE

My name is Sui and in June I'll be turning sixty. I have three adult children; their names are Charlotte, Pam, and David. My husband died in October, while the leaves were still green and clinging to their branches. Now it is spring and there are new leaves, and I am a widow. Such are the major facts of my life.

I live alone in the house my husband left me. I work as the secretary at Royal Dental on Lamar Boulevard, a job I've had for about as long as I've been in the US, long enough to watch the practice pass from Dr. Baker, the original proprietor, to his son. I take in the mail and water my plants. On weekends I prepare a meal whenever I get hungry, which is sometimes twice and sometimes four times a day, indulging a little in the absence of structure. I talk to my children on the phone whenever one of them thinks to call. I say hello to my neighbors, who are comforting to me in the same way that my house is, as guideposts in time, reminding me of who I am. I have known most of them for over twenty years. They're the closest I have to friends. When I wave to them from across our yards, I think how lucky I am to be standing at a distance, oblivious to the details of their lives, how they move inside their homes, and to not have to see their faces up close. A person's face is like a house, I think. The marks and stains and sunken places are proof of what has happened, but they cannot tell the whole story.

Even before my husband died, I was treated like a widow. That was eighteen years ago, when he left. I was not young, but I was younger. My neighbors are Christians. Most of them go to Hill County Bible just a couple miles down the road, next to the Korean grocery store where I like to buy fruit. They brought casseroles and brownies to my doorstep, sending their small children sometimes for extra sweetness, and I was not charmed or annoyed by this so much as I was amused. When Mrs. Wilhite, the very old preacher's very old wife, had asked me on the sidewalk one evening how my husband was, only a week after Huayu told me he was staying in Beijing—he wasn't coming back, I'd told her the truth, because I saw no reason not to. "He's gone," I'd said. Her blue eyes bulged out of her powdered white face. "Another woman," I explained. "In China," I added, to calm any questions about who she might be. "*Affair*," I said slowly. It was an English word I'd practiced for the sole purpose of explaining my situation.

Back then, David was only five and running around in his underwear, aiming dart guns at his older sisters. Now he's a year out of college. I don't know much about the Christian faith but I do know something about people, and I think they treated me like a widow in order to preserve my dignity, because out of the myriad ways to experience loss, death is by far the noblest. A month after I told Mrs. Wilhite the news, she showed up at my doorstep holding an envelope. By this point the gifts and pasta salads and people "just checking up on me" had subsided somewhat. "For you," she'd said. "From the congregation." Inside were ten one-hundred-dollar bills. "Just something to tide you over." I took the money. Why not? As the Americans say, I had three mouths to feed. I traced the lines in Mrs. Wilhite's face, moving from her eyes down to her pink neck. Then she said, "She wong," and it was like when I'd said *affair*, it sounded tentative. *Xi wang*. Hope. "She wong," she said again, just before turning to leave.

Mrs. Wilhite has since passed away and so has her husband, the preacher. They weren't alive to witness my husband's return—his rebirth, one might say—this past fall. He had pancreatic cancer. My sister-in-law called me from Beijing in July, just after I turned fifty-nine, and I had to ask her to repeat her name, it'd been so long since I'd heard from her. She claimed that hospice care was better in the US than in China, and I didn't ask about the other woman, the one he'd left us for all those years ago. Instead I asked how much time. "The doctors say half a year," she said, her words choppy over the phone. Later, when I told my kids, they warned me that it could end up being much longer than that. They said these things are unpredictable, and you never know when someone might live longer than expected, although in my husband's case it ended up being shorter. When I didn't respond, my sister-in-law said, "He's still his children's father." She whispered it, like it was a secret. Like I didn't know. "They should see him before he goes, right?"

I didn't tell her that my children hated their father, and that to them hate was as much a virtue as love. They called the idea "absurd" and "unfair," and for the three months that Huayu lived here in his old home, Pam was the only one who visited.

"The others don't know I'm here," she said, after I swung open the front door. I'd thought it was going to be the nurse, Toby. She stepped around me to get inside. When had she arrived in town? I wondered. And how long was she planning on staying? What made her decide to come? I stayed standing with the door wide open, blinking at the street. It was September and the weather was sunny and mild with a delicious breeze. My neighbor saw me and waved. I waved back.

"Is that him?"

I closed the door. She gestured with her head at the bed in the living room, which sat facing the windows to the backyard. The blinds were drawn. It was afternoon and dark in the house. Who else could it be? Huayu was asleep. I realized that I was more nervous for Pam than I had been for myself. When I saw Huayu in the airport for the first time in almost two decades, it was as I had predicted—shocking, not because he was someone I once knew, but because he was a person I did not recognize. The sickness had altered him. It was like receiving a new man, a new husband, and to me this was a relief. I'd agreed to do this because I know that death is the greatest simplifier. It covers up old wounds, which is basically as good as healing them. At the airport a woman in a vest was pushing Huayu in a wheelchair. I spotted him not by searching for my husband but by searching for anybody who looked sick. Then he pointed at me, and it made me wonder what he'd been looking for, what gave me away. He was amazingly thin. His hair was white and sparsely laid. His coat was a gray shell, and he curled himself deep into it, the flesh around his mouth and eyes like wax that had dripped and hardened again.

I followed Pam to Huayu's bedside. The living room had remained unchanged, aside from the bed and the PCA machine, which was connected to the IV in Huayu's hand. I tried to recall the last time Pam was here. My kids have stopped coming home for the holidays. They prefer going to Charlotte's in California, and I can't complain because they always buy my plane tickets. It was only some years ago, I remembered, when David graduated from high school. There was still the brown leather couch and the matching one-seater. The same glass coffee table. Pam looked down at her father's sleeping face, the jowly skin. "How dare you come back to us," she said, like she was reciting a fact. I watched them from behind the headboard. Huayu's mouth was open. His breaths were strained, as though the air were passing through a grated barrier. "How dare you come back to us like this."

She stayed looking at her father until the hum of the machine grew loud, the chirping of his vitals sucking up the quiet in the house like insects in the night.

"He won't wake for a while," I said, to break the noise. Of course, now I wish I'd said something else, something that would have validated what Pam was feeling, even though she didn't understand that her father could only come back like this, only with death as the circumstance. "The morphine puts him into a very deep sleep."

It turned out that Pam was only staying for one night, and even so, she booked a hotel. "I changed my mind, I don't want to be here when he's up," she said once we were back outside. In the sunlight, her hair took on a matted sheen. I noticed that her face looked sharper, like someone had pinched her jaw toward the tip of her chin. She'd lost weight. Or maybe she was just getting older. "I mostly wanted to check on you anyway. I fly back in the morning."

"You're sure you don't want to talk to him?" I said. I thought that she should, if only to save herself from regret in the future.

"Don't tell Charlotte and David I came. I'll tell them myself later."

"I won't," I said.

"Don't tell him I came either."

At this I felt myself frown, but I promised.

It is astounding to me how my children have turned out. I suppose it is always this way between children and parents. Charlotte, for example, my oldest, has a completely different view of our neighbors. "They were trying to convert us, obviously," she said at the table one night, during Christmas dinner. This was some years ago, when David was still in high school. We were at my house, which I still thought of then as mine and theirs. A discussion about capitalism and Christmas, which we only ever celebrated secularly, had turned into a discussion about religion. I could hardly keep up.

"Was it obvious?" I said.

Charlotte had prepared steaks on the grill, and I'd asked for my mine well done and was having a hard time cutting into it. Only in Texas was it warm enough to grill outside in December. David had asked for his medium rare and was using the blood on his plate as a sauce, swirling his fork around in it to wet every bite.

"They gave us a thousand dollars," said Charlotte. "No one does that without expecting something in return."

She worked her fork and knife against the meat with great precision.

I didn't tell them that nobody—not Mrs. Wilhite or her husband or anybody from Hill County Bible who stopped at my house during that month—ever asked me if I would like to join the church. Charlotte would've just said that the money was invitation enough. She'd grown suspicious of people, and who could blame her? She was sixteen when her father left.

Pam reached for her wine. Pam is a vegetarian and was eating a medley of root vegetables, carrots and daikon and beets. "I don't remember any of this at all," said David with his mouth full, and then the conversation moved on to something else.

In the three months we spent together, Huayu never asked if the children were coming to see him. I think he was afraid of the answer. "A real musician," he said once, after I told him that Pam plays the cello in the Berlin Philharmonic. This was before she visited. "She wasn't even playing the instrument full size when—" He coughed, an unwieldy sound, like the top notes of metal slicing into metal, and he never returned to that thought.

Was it awkward between us? My children asked me this over Thanksgiving at Charlotte's, a month after their father had passed. I told them it wasn't. "But how could it not be?" said David. The four of us were sitting on Charlotte's couch, drinking chrysanthemum tea. "Did he at least say he was sorry?"

Their mugs were paused in midair while they waited for an answer, hovering around their necks, and the synchronicity made them appear momentarily childlike. When they were little, I had gotten used to things happening in threes. It happened despite the age gap between the girls and David. Three people tying their shoes. Three people throwing rocks in a lake, three plunks as the rocks struck water. A few times the occurrences were more eerie. Three people scratching an itch that happened to be in the exact same place on three separate bodies. Perhaps it was this maternal omniscience, felt rarely now, the ability to see them as they could not see themselves, that empowered me to say what I said next.

"There was a funeral at the church."

I took a sip of my tea. It burned my tongue. Pam set her mug on the end table.

"Some of the neighbors still remembered him. He was baptized."

"They'll do anything to take part in another person's misery," Charlotte scoffed.

"He was in a lot of pain at the end."

"He made choices," said Charlotte. Her voice was loud, and it reminded me that I was dealing with adults. "He isn't redeemed just because he got sick." She spoke of redemption with such confidence for someone who doesn't believe in religion. Again I was astounded. Where did my children get these ideas?

"Did he apologize?" said David.

My son never really knew his father, doesn't have clear memories of him. Does that give him more to begrudge or less?

I said, "Yes. He did."

I lied to my children that night, and it was not the only lie I told over the entire ordeal. There had been an unspoken agreement between me and Huayu that we would not discuss his eighteen-year absence. With those years struck from our history, there was nothing to be sorry for. I was the one feeding him and washing him, and later, dispensing his medicine to relieve his pain. If I wanted to talk about it at any time, he would've had no choice but to listen, being as he was captive to these needs and therefore captive to me. But I wasn't interested in moving backward in that direction.

At first we didn't talk at all. To Toby, the nurse who came by every Monday and Thursday, it probably looked normal enough, like one of those marriages where the talking had petered out and now companionship functioned best without it. Then one day I was giving Huayu a bath using a washcloth and a basin of warm water. We were three weeks in. I was taking leave from work indefinitely, having been guaranteed my job back whenever I wanted it. A gift from the Baker family, the young Dr. Baker had expressed demurely the last time I was in the office, for my thirty years of service to him and his father. The dentists are Christians as well; there's a decal on the waiting room wall, a quote from Corinthians that says, "Love never ends. But as for prophecies, they will come to an end; as for tongues, they will cease; as for knowledge, it will come to an end," which I've always found harsh for a dentist's office. I figured the Bakers' generosity had to do with their being afraid of death and not wanting to play a role in hastening it. Huayu was lying on his side so that I could do his back, where the skin was looser than it was on his arms and legs. It bunched as I dragged the cloth across, reminding me of the film that forms on top of cooling rice porridge. A faulty cover for what lies underneath.

He said, "That stain."

There were holes in his voice. I wrung the cloth into the basin and looked at where he was pointing, at a corner of the ceiling above the couch.

"That wasn't there when I left."

Somehow the stain, which looked like a brown storm cloud, bridged the gap between his leaving and coming back. Perhaps Huayu had been trying to make himself vulnerable, give me the opening for the conversation he thought I wished to have, but his acknowledgment was enough for me.

We talked a little more after that, usually when I was bathing him or spooning rice porridge into his mouth. I told him the facts of his children's lives, like what each of them does for work, but I did not delve into the truer qualities that make them who they are, that make them real and foreign to me. I stayed with my children and yet I don't fully know them, so I could only imagine how it might feel to suddenly see Charlotte, Pam, and David as people with attitudes and tastes.

We took a vacation to Port Aransas once when it was the five of us. The beach stretched for miles and miles. The tide rolled back, and the wet sand caught the light from the sky and made a glowing path on the ground. Huayu asked the kids to build a sandcastle. David was a toddler and couldn't be bothered with anything beyond sensation. He flapped his arms as the tide came in and water frothed between his little legs. Charlotte was fourteen and serious. She packed sand into pails and turned the pails upside down, patting them all around so that the shapes came out whole. When they didn't, or when a piece fell off later, she started over. Pam, who was nine, couldn't match Charlotte's intensity for the project, so she eventually wandered off on her own, collecting shells. Huayu and Charlotte worked for hours. Focused and quick, Charlotte was the perfect fit for Huayu, to impress him, even though he'd wanted his firstborn to be a son. I watched them while keeping an eye on the other two, occasionally offering someone a piece of fruit. They crawled on all fours and kneeled, etching ridges in the castle walls. They dug a moat around the four towers and filled it up with water.

My children think it was a kindness that bordered on stupidity—one that resembles martyrdom—that allowed me to take care of their father, my husband, when really it had nothing to do with kindness at all. We get so few chances in life to be of real use to another person, to make their life more bearable, and meanwhile the chances to do harm are everywhere and often discreet; you don't fully realize what you've done until it's over. My kids are somewhat estranged from me now because they don't understand. It is my hope that they will always be clear-sighted regarding what's right and wrong, so that their lives will remain straightforward.

Charlotte hates her father even now, even though he's dead. I never told him how she felt, partly to spare him and partly because I was jealous. I don't think any of my children find me worthy of such strong emotion, not even Pam, who came to me in Charlotte's guest room the night I lied to them over tea. She apologized on her sister's behalf, and I thought of that day on the beach, when she had drifted off by herself.

"She's not angry at you," Pam said. "She's angry at him."

"I'm actually fine with the fact that he left, to be honest," she said when I didn't respond. We were sitting at the edge of the bed. The lights were off in the room but there were no blinds or curtains on any of the windows in Charlotte's house. Cold light from the street came pouring in, casting shadows across Pam's face. "What I'll never understand is why he had to cut us off completely. He didn't visit once. All those years, I kept wondering whether he thought about us. Whether or not he missed me."

My children had all been looking to me to match them in some way, Charlotte her anger, David his confusion, to reflect what they felt back to them. Pam was devastated, maybe more so because she had seen her father. She wanted me to be too, but I knew my own devastation couldn't console her.

"People deal with things in the way they know how," I said, reaching for something solid. "He had the decency at least to tell us the truth about why he was leaving. He gave us the house."

Pam smiled. "You know, Mom, sometimes I think you're a good person, but then I think you have no standards for people at all, and what good is that?" She stood up from the bed and said good night. She shut my door gently, and then I was alone.

Pam's surprise visit came at the six-week mark, right in the middle of Huayu's stay. I remember it wasn't long afterward that he asked the question I believe he'd been building up to ever since he pointed out that stain. Recently, a maintenance person came by and said the stain was a result of condensation in the attic. The old pipes have since been replaced, but I've decided to leave the stain, to not paint over it.

I was telling Huayu about David. "He's been into lifting weights. He's trying to get his sisters into it, too." Was this awkward? Maybe this was what my children had meant, but to me it felt easy, like talking to a stranger or myself. Huayu accepted it like a stranger, with detached interest, nodding and swallowing his porridge. I scraped the bowl to collect the dregs, the sticky white starch. By this point his pain had gotten worse, and Toby had just upped his dosage. Some liquid leaked out of the corner of Huayu's mouth. I caught it with the spoon.

"I want to ask you something," he said. "You might find it strange."

I feared he was going to ask about the kids, about why they hadn't come to see him. I set the bowl down on the counter behind me. He picked up the morphine pump, holding it loosely as though it were a candy bar or a TV remote. It was a simple handheld device, gray with a green button on top.

"I hate this," he said, "having to do this for myself. I'm wondering if you would be willing to do it for me. Push the button."

What he was asking of me was strictly forbidden, and I said so. Toby had said only the patient was allowed to administer his own morphine.

"Who will know?" said Huayu. "In return, I'll give you something as well."

I laughed, quietly to myself at first but then I couldn't stop. What could he give me in his current condition? The laugh came from the bottom of my stomach. I threw my head back and let the sound hit the walls. It spread throughout the house.

"I'll listen," he said after I was done. "I'll listen to whatever you have to say, whatever you want to tell me."

I felt exposed all of a sudden, defensive. "What is this? Some kind of deal?"

"Not a deal, an exchange."

"What could I possibly have to tell you?" I said, even though by then I must have already been thinking about his offer, accepting it. Some part of me wonders whether I had planned this moment all along.

"Everyone has stories they've kept to themselves."

"And why would I tell you?" My heart was pounding.

"Because I'll be dead soon."

He let go of the device. He brushed his knuckles briefly against mine before letting his arm flop back onto the bed, hardly making a sound.

"Whatever judgments I have, I'll take them with me."

Our time together had been a careful game, where all the pieces were things left unspoken. The children. The absence. He'd broken an essential rule. It was as though glass had shattered on the floor.

"You don't know how much time you have," I said, staring out the window. I was startled by his touch. I'd stopped raising the blinds as often after the pain increased and Huayu fell into a more or less permanent fatigue, but Toby said even a few minutes of sunshine each day could be beneficial. The grass was yellow, the day was overcast and bright. Birds hopped along the fence between my backyard and my neighbor's.

Huayu said, "I can feel it."

When I lived in Beijing and attended university, I fell in love with my best friend's fiancé. "He might have loved me too," I said to Huayu. "No matter what we tried, we couldn't stop seeing each other."

This was days later, after I'd had time to think. I was sitting in a chair next to the bed, between the bed and the old coffee table. We kept our gazes forward. I was holding the device, and it felt solid in my grip, even as my palm began to sweat. Through the window from outside, we might have looked like a couple admiring the view, but the blinds were closed, and even though Huayu was awake, I chose not to open them.

The dark house created a sense of timelessness. Days began to blur. I told my husband bits and pieces until eventually he had the whole story.

Stripped to its bones, my story is ordinary. The guilt over the affair was painful but I couldn't stop, so eventually I dropped out of school. I married a man, Huayu, who took me to the States, where I could count on never seeing my friend again.

"Did you ever think about running away together?" Huayu asked. This was toward the end. A week later I would walk into the living room to find my husband stiff and slack jawed, not breathing. He'd called me over to do the button. I held it down with my thumb. There was an ease between us now that wasn't there before, when I was filling his head with my children's hobbies and credentials. I lowered myself into the chair next to him.

"He suggested it once. I said no. What we were doing was wrong, but in my mind it was not as wrong as openly breaking an innocent person's heart."

"She would have forgiven you eventually."

"What makes you so sure?"

He didn't answer. Then he said, "Why did you let me come back?"

"Not because I forgive you," I said, and I told him what I thought about death, how it is its own morality and doesn't have to compromise with whatever one's life has been. Something about that had always attracted me. "You can say no to love," I said to him, looking at him. "You can't say no to death."

Huayu nodded. "A simple morality."

"And pure," I said.

"What if I asked you to forgive me?" said Huayu. "What if I told you a story from my life? Would you have sympathy?" The morphine was working. He was struggling to stay awake.

"That wasn't part of our deal. Besides, it's not my place to forgive you, just like it's not your place to forgive me."

"Whose place is it to forgive you?"

"My friend," I said, "whom I betrayed and then abandoned."

"And me?" he said.

I sighed. "Our children, but none of them want to see you."

I considered telling him about Pam, how she'd flown all the way from Berlin just to say two sentences to him while he was asleep. He could count that as forgiveness. But my loyalties were to her, I'd promised her, so in the end I stuck with my lie.

"I want to be baptized," he said. "Before I die, I want to be forgiven."

"I'll arrange it," I said, feeling as though we were always headed here, like we had finally arrived.

A crew came by to pick up the equipment. The bed, the machines, the various cords that connected to various ports, all taken apart and packed into a van returning to the hospital. Toby was there. I realized I would not be seeing him anymore, and I felt a small shock in my heart, like I would miss him, even though that was ridiculous. I think a lot about meeting Toby. In my house that first day, he'd placed an IV in Huayu's hand. He connected the PCA tubing to the morphine and attached the maintenance fluids through the Y-port— explaining each action as he did it in a kind of running narration. For whose benefit, this wasn't clear. There was a melody to it though, which made it nice to listen to. The liquid moved in spurts down the tube and disappeared into Huayu's hand.

Toby was a good nurse, but he'll fade from my memory eventually, just as more important people in my life have. But I'll never forget what he said.

I was showing him to the door. "How long was the flight from Beijing?" he asked.

"About fifteen hours." Doctors had approved the flight, but suddenly I was worried. I asked if it was bad.

"No, no," said Toby. "The cancer has done its damage. There's not much that can make it worse." He looked back at my husband, even though from where we were by the door, you could only see the headboard.

"It's painful, that's all." He stared into my eyes. "It's a terribly long time to be in pain."

After my living room was restored, Toby said goodbye and that he was sorry for my loss. I told him thank you. He's a kind person, just like the young female pastor who dabbed water on Huayu's forehead, and like my employers the Dr. Baker's and my neighbors, who brought all kinds of gifts and flowers after my husband died for real this time and also attended his funeral at the end of October, when the leaves were crisp and finally falling.

In June, I'll be sixty. I'll have been a widow for eight months, but it already feels like much longer.

GREEN

One morning toward the middle of April, John D. Ewing, a retired investment banker who lived in one of the better neighborhoods of our town, decided to solve his backyard problem of patches of dead grass by hiring a local firm, Backyard Answers, to pull up his lawn and replace it with flat-topped cobblestones in brown and red, arranged in a pattern of intersecting arcs. To celebrate his new yard, Ewing invited some dozen friends and neighbors to a grilling party, where guests praised his handsome cobblestones, inquired about cost and upkeep, and turned their attention to local politics. Two days later, one of the invited couples, the Hathaways, hired Backyard Answers to replace their weed-grown back lawn with porcelain tiles on a base of mortar. When another couple, Alan and Rose Perlstein, converted their backyard to alternating squares of dark and light granite, people in the neighborhood began to take notice. Was there something to be said for the new style? In a different part of town, on a street of older houses behind high hedges, two sisters replaced their back lawn with hexagonal tiles and rows of pebbles. After three more backyards—in less prosperous neighborhoods—were transformed into tile and stone, it was clear to us that something had begun to happen in our town, something that appeared to be more than a mere inclination to imitate one's neighbor.

I observed it all with the mixture of amused interest and vague disapproval that is my habitual response to changes in fashion, but when my fifteen-year-old daughter began pleading for backyard cobblestones, I gave way without protest. No more weeds springing up between the back porch and fence, no yellowing grass requiring my anxious attention, no mowing, no edging, no seeding, no raking, no fiddling with the sprinkler and shifting it from place to place: the benefits readily justified the expense and far outweighed the loss of green in one small part of our quarter-acre property. Up and down our street, neighbors were replacing back lawns with tile and cobblestone and brick. You could feel an excitement in the air.

As the fad for grassless backyards swept across town, many of us were struck by an event that took place toward the middle of May. In the front yard of a Victorian home not far from the town library, a broad lawn shaded by two ancient sycamores was torn up and replaced by three colors of travertine tile on both sides of the flagstone walk. The sycamores remained, surrounded by curved wooden benches. By the end of the week, patterns of brick and tile had sprung up in the front yards of some two dozen homes in different parts of town.

When my daughter and her friends expressed enthusiasm for the new look, I found myself stirred into opposition. Lawns, I pointed out, were refreshing spaces of green, welcome contrasts to sidewalks and streets. Their loss was something to be taken seriously. But more than that, any lawn, however trim and orderly, was an expression of natural growth within the artifice known as a town. A town without lawns was like a city without parks. The teenagers would have none of it. Lawns, they argued, were all alike. The new yards had different kinds of stone, different designs and patterns. And besides, there were still trees, bushes, hedges, flowers. Nature was everywhere, if you wanted nature. And what about water? Lawns needed a lot of water. Wasn't it eco-friendly to save water? Surprised by their passion, I became thoughtful but held firm. Within two weeks, front yards all over our neighborhood were being transformed. Under protest, sighing mightily and shaking my head, I gave way. We chose brick in three shades of red, reaching to the front sidewalk and around both sides of the house to the cobblestoned back.

By the end of May, more than half the yards in our town had done away with lawns, including those narrow stretches of grass between sidewalk and curb. By mid-June, only a scattering of green yards remained. Homeowners unable to afford the expense were sought out and generously aided by the recently formed Society for the Yards of Tomorrow, which raised funds vigorously for that purpose. One stubborn owner, who ran his own plumbing business and loved taking care of his yard, refused to give up his lawn for any reason. He was paid a visit by twelve concerned neighbors, who after three hours of discussion were able to persuade him to sell his house to all twelve of them for double its market value. The new owners quickly transformed the grass into elaborate patterns of many-colored tile and sold the property at a substantial profit to the assistant manager of a software development firm, who had been searching for the ideal home in the suburbs.

Even as our lawns were disappearing, we became aware of other changes. Many of the new yards still retained borders of soil along the base of the house or the bottom of a fence, where rows of bushes and flowers flourished in sun and shade. Owners now began pulling up their plants and filling in the strips of earth with brick and tile. Hedges vanished; window boxes stood empty. Stalks and leaves once visible in the latticework spaces of porch aprons were cleared away, leaving only darkness. You would have thought our town was ridding itself of some harmful invasive species. Flowerpots on porch steps sat upside down or held nothing but a squeegee or a paintbrush. On the dark-red walls of the public library, green vines no longer climbed along the bricks.

One morning toward the middle of July, as I stepped out of my house to drive to work, I saw at the end of the block a section of beech tree moving slowly through the air, clasped by metal arms at the back of a transport truck. I learned that a neighbor had hired a tree-removal company to cut down his beech tree and extract the roots from their circle of earth in his tiled front yard. It was no exception. All over town, trees were beginning to disappear. It was as if their green-leaved branches were perceived as upper lawns, hovering above our heads. We were scarcely surprised when the Department of Public Works voted in August to send out crews to our curbsides to cut down town-owned trees and extract the roots. This official elimination of our street trees seemed to me the definitive sign of the destructive passion that had overtaken our town, though at the same time I recognized the chain saws as the logical culmination of a desire for change that had begun innocently enough.

By Labor Day, our town had been stripped of green. No leafy branches shaded our sidewalks, our yards, our paved-over park with its picnic tables and duck pond. No blades of grass thrust up between cracks of stone. In what might have been a touch of nostalgia for our absent trees, statues began to appear in front yards. Rodin's *Thinker* rose up in various neighborhoods, along with Greek gods and goddesses, an occasional Abraham Lincoln or P. T. Barnum, and twisting abstract sculptures in steel and stone. On a property near the town hall, a massive oak tree of granite was erected in a tiled front yard, with precisely carved leaves and hundreds of elegantly sculpted acorns. After numerous protests and a visit from the town planning commissioner, the owner ordered the oak to be removed and replaced by a twenty-foot granite Statue of Liberty with a winding inner stairway leading into the torch. Window boxes once filled with petunias and snapdragons now contained colored glass pellets, playful elves, or rows of pinwheels. People swept and washed their tiled yards, wiped bird droppings from the faces of statues. Was I the only one who missed the turning of the leaves?

Snow fell, covering our yards in the old way. The question of Christmas trees was addressed at a town meeting, where it was decided that banished conifers would be replaced by locally built structures reminiscent of hatstands, with arms that lengthened as they descended the central post. On New Year's Eve we clinked our glasses, resolved to lead better lives, and wondered what the coming year would bring.

Spring came, and with it the familiar sense of awakening, of a world of hidden things about to burst into life. The absence of green confused many of us, as if we had expected the melting snow to reveal the old springtime hidden underneath. In the warm air, no green-leaved forsythias thrilled us with their promise of yellow blossoms, no green leaf tips sprouted at the twig ends of sugar maples. The few remaining birds poured out their song from the heads of statues, before returning to old nests crumbling in roof gutters or under eaves. As I walked the streets of my neighborhood, on treeless sidewalks exposed to relentless sunlight, I waved hello to neighbors kneeling beside soapy buckets and scrubbing their tiles with stiff-bristled brushes or repairing cracks that had formed under ice and snow. At home, my daughter and I took turns hosing off our cobblestones and bricks, while I dreamed of showers of grass thrown up by the lawn mower. Behind the garbage cans at the side of the house, I discovered an empty flowerpot, which had once overflowed with fern fronds, deep green.

The turn came quietly, a few days later. Mark and Carol Ackerman were next-door neighbors of Alan and Rose Perlstein's, up on the hill. He was a cardiologist, she a dental surgeon. A year ago, they had made a point of displaying originality by selecting brightly colored tiles and overseeing their arrangement in artful designs, such as mosaic images of heraldic lions, intertwined serpents, and spread-winged falcons enclosed in borders of white and red stone. They now employed Yard Makeovers Inc. to extract two square feet of tiling and mortar on each side of the front porch steps. In each empty space they planted an evergreen shrub, purchased at a garden shop in a nearby town.

Was it nothing more than an aesthetic whim? An act of showy self-assertion on the part of a couple who liked to draw attention to themselves? Was it perhaps a medical decision reached by thoughtful doctors concerned about the quality of our air? Whatever it was, neighbors gathered on the sidewalk in front of the

Ackerman house to stare. People from other parts of town drove over to see what the fuss was all about. By the end of the week, you could see green bushes rising here and there in the stone yards of our town.

Within two weeks it was difficult to find a yard without some touch of green: a bush beneath a living-room window, a bed of ferns enclosed in a rim of stone, a breast-high sapling casting its thin shadow over tiles. It might have ended there, a minor variation introduced to bring out the subtle qualities of arranged stone, but one day a waist-high hedge appeared along the border of a front yard near the high school. In another part of town, a flowering dogwood stood suddenly in a small circle of grass. Three days later Alan and Rose Perlstein, with an eye on the Ackermans, hired Yard Makeovers Inc. to remove all of their granite tiles and to cover their entire property with fresh sod.

There was no stopping it now. Yard after yard was turned into new grass or richly seeded soil. Hedges and bushes took root again. Young maples and hemlocks appeared on sunny lawns. One afternoon my daughter sat me down for a serious talk and offered to contribute her weekly babysitting income to the uprooting of our cobblestones and bricks. In another part of town, the twenty-foot Statue of Liberty was carried off on a flatbed truck and replaced by a massive oak tree rumored to have come from a forest in Maine. The town board, responding to public pressure, ordered the Department of Public Works to begin planting young trees along curbsides: red maples, sugar maples, lindens, sycamores, beech.

By the end of June our town had returned to the old world of tree-lined streets and green lawns. Under new branches, strips of fresh grass rose up between sidewalk and curb. I hummed as I gripped the rubber handles of my power mower and guided the blades across the yard. My daughter and I planted a vegetable garden in back, with rows of sticks for tomato vines and corn. Together we tended the flower boxes on the front porch. When all is said and done, I'm the kind of man who embraces the normal without apology. I woke each morning happy to greet the smell of cut grass. After a brief diversion, a playful experiment, things had returned to normal in our quiet town.

Or had they? As the days passed, I became aware of a slight difference. People were working away in their yards, a familiar enough sight in the middle of summer, but what drew my attention was the uninterrupted planting of new bushes and young trees, even in yards well supplied with both. A crowding seemed to be taking place. It was as if households had made up their minds to prevent any future assault on their little worlds of green.

Large hedges, higher than my head, were replacing smaller ones. Tall shrubs overshadowed low bushes. In the neighborhood of John D. Ewing and friends, it was common enough for houses to be set back from the road behind lofty hedges and thick-branched trees, which prevented passersby from peering in. But now, in more modest neighborhoods, such as my own, porches were disappearing behind high rows of honeysuckle and azalea. Ivy vines wrapped themselves around porch posts. Wisteria and lavender-flowered hydrangea climbed past living-room windows and made their way up toward bedroom windows on second floors. From the sills of the same windows, lush vines spilled down. Chimneys vanished within swirls of green.

I could feel it myself, this restlessness, this desire to push beyond carefully defined limits toward unknown lands. I had longed deeply for the restoration of our green yards, but the return no longer seemed enough. Our neat lawns and clipped hedges now struck me as tame and meek, mere imitations of manufactured items for the home, like wool rugs and mahogany sideboards. At best they were decorative touches in a world aggressively dedicated to the eradication of natural things. I applauded the desire to fill yards with growing forms, with life. One July day, in a burst of energy, I lined both sides of my narrow front walk with ten-foot shrubs purchased at a recently opened garden center. My daughter and I laughed as we pushed our way through thick leaves and springy branches to the hidden front porch.

In the same spirit, people in many parts of town had become impatient with the slow growth of saplings. They began buying trees that were nearly full-grown. On street after street you could see transport trucks carrying great horizontal oaks and beeches and firs, the roots wrapped in burlap. In every neighborhood you could watch as metal arms tightened around trunks and lowered great trees into prepared holes.

Small forests, extending to the property line, were becoming popular. Homeowners refinanced to cover the cost. On my block alone, one backyard was filled with freshly planted Norway pine, which pressed against every window and rose above the roof, while a nearby front yard was given over to a dense growth of birch and beech. Driveways became woodland paths. Caught up in the fever, I took out a loan and hired workers to turn our vegetable garden into a copse of hemlock.

One Saturday toward the middle of August, a work crew in yellow helmets stood in the middle of the street not far from my house. A group of us gathered to watch as the men drilled into the center of the road, tore out chunks of blacktop, and left a broad hole surrounded by dirt. Soon a long truck arrived, bearing an immense sugar maple tilted on its side. The heavy tree rose slowly before being lowered into the ground. When we asked what was happening, we were informed that crews were at work in every neighborhood, tearing up streets and planting trees. Paved roads had been condemned by the Department of Public Works as undesirable throwbacks to our earlier town, old-fashioned obstructions to natural growth.

By early September, dense groves had sprung up in many of our streets. Despite some expressions of concern, the decision of the DPW was enthusiastically embraced by most of our citizens. Those of us who could no longer drive through the forested roads now rode bicycles or walked to the one remaining bus stop in town.

Though I vigorously supported all efforts to increase the number of trees in our town, I was startled at times by the sheer swiftness of our accomplishment, the daily evidence of lushness and rapid growth. It was as if the energy of our desire had entered the roots and branches themselves, filling them with extravagant life.

As late summer passed into autumn, there were no signs of letting up. In our tree-crowded yards, we stood on branch-pierced ladders and trained leafy tendrils to spread across bare windowpanes. Many of us took to covering our front and back porches with strips of sod. Indoor walls became sites for climbing vines. A few enthusiasts went so far as to carry buckets of loam into their living rooms in order to replace an end table with a cone of soil supporting an evergreen bush. Meanwhile, on block after block, town crews worked tirelessly to tear out any remaining sections of paved street and fill them with thickets of pine and spruce.

Extremists urged the destruction of all public buildings, those masses of brick and stone that did nothing but interrupt the designs of nature, but more reasonable minds prevailed: all school corridors, all town hall offices, and the main room of the post office were lined with bushes and trees in terra-cotta planters concealed beneath slopes of imported soil. In alternate aisles of the town library, rows of tall shrubs pressed against the spines of books. When we stepped into privately owned buildings open to the public, such as churches, banks, downtown stores, and car dealerships, we found ourselves pushing aside branches heavy with leaves.

Sometimes, in the deep hours of the night, a doubt came over some of us, but in the morning we were swept up once again in our desire to carry on with what we had so passionately begun.

Now, as the ground hardens and the air grows colder, we understand one thing: there can be no turning back. Our town is slowly being transformed into a deep forest. Some of our citizens, defeated at last, have abandoned their homes and moved to nearby towns, with the vague hope of returning someday soon. The rest of us remain in our mossy houses, where branches occasionally break in through upper windows. We spend hours each day exploring the surrounding woods, learning to identify and gather edible leaves, fruit, and mushrooms, though we can also purchase meals from food trucks that park behind the deserted mall at the edge of town. Half-hidden among trees, our schools, our library, our post office, and our downtown businesses have sharply reduced their hours. All are in danger of shutting down completely as they fill with foliage and small, scurrying animals.

My daughter and her friends spend most afternoons in the woods, returning with pine cones and sprigs of berries arranged in their hair. Owls sit on the edges of our roofs. Raccoons thump and scratch in our attics. There are rumors of prowling wolves, though that is nothing but ignorant gossip. It's true enough that some dogs and cats have left their homes to roam in feral packs. Far more worrisome are the notices posted on tree trunks by our diminished police department, warning us to guard our homes against break-ins.

When we try to recall our earlier town, with its neat rows of houses seated in little rectangles of green, the image seems to be that of a colored drawing made by a kindergartener with a box of new crayons. Some say that if we don't change direction, our town is destined to disappear entirely. They prophesy a time of smashed and decaying houses, with mighty trees thrusting through floors and bursting through roofs. Others feel that just as we once turned from green to stone and back again to green, so another change is imminent, though what that change might be, no one can say. In the meantime, we can only get ready for the long winter, storing supplies in our cellars and reinforcing our windows and doors. Already we find ourselves dreaming, at times uneasily, of the coming spring.

Bruce Goff. This page, Struckus House. Opposite page, Ford House.

Bruce Goff. This page, Bavinger House. Opposite page, Gryder House.

THE POEM OF THE BOW

AL-SHAMMĀKH IBN ḌIRĀR

TRANSLATED FROM THE ARABIC
BY DAVID LARSEN

Sulaymā's trace is gone from the vale of Qaww, and from ʿĀliz.
    The scrublands and rebuffing heights stand vacant [of her tribe].
For there to be friendship, some wrongs must be suffered.
    To brook no wrong is to be oppressive, or be alone.
Then there are slips with no reprieve, as on the high precarity
    where my forethought prevented rashness, and lives were saved.
I also recall a decisive matter in which the second guess
    · that inhibits action did not stay my hand! And I remember the camel
that strove beneath my saddle like a he-ass of the wild with the pale belly
    sought by hunters. Harried by she-asses in a herd,
their udders pinched at the dry zenith of the season
    ruled by Sirius, he frustrates their thirst, and the stone shimmers.
They wait a day at Yamʿūd. Like dry wells, their eyes
    look up at the sun as they wonder. Is it even going down?
Their bodies groan with thirst. They wait on why
    he's led them to this sunny slope. But the he-ass holds silent.
When they see the path to water he intends,
    they run ahead to find a track between the sands,
where he races them against the darkness he sees falling,
    like rivals in a race pitted by a dogged rival.
Away from the dell of Dharwa he points them toward Rumma,
    across the arid marches of Raḥraḥān.
But hunters' blinds sprout over Rumma's waters
    looking like domed litters with dyed tassels hung.
[So they run on,] shying from his temper and shrinking from him
    like pregnant pack mares shrinking from a stallion.
Night falls, and they traverse Dhu 'l-Arāk at its highest point.
    Then before they pass by Sharj they make a turn,
pining for the pools of al-Qunnatān, but repelled
    by rocky ground and tracts of stone impassable.

Obstacles abound. The camels of ʿAthlab the hunter
    and the Ibn Ghimār brothers fill their breasts with disquiet,
lest the herd fall into their hands and wear their blood
    like dyed curtains trailing from a camel litter.
No stopping at Dhu 'l-Arāka, where ʿĀmir, the archer of al-Khuḍr,
    shoots to hit the spot where camels' necks are cauterized.
Possessor of little more than his bow and some arrows,
    ʿĀmir fires at the live beast as if it were a dummy.
There are no survivors of the blue [tips of his arrows] and the yellow
    [bow] of aromatic wood and sinew when he takes aim.
Its maker hacked through bush and bramble to select
    a bole of jujube to be a bow.
It grew in a sheltered place and grew up straight.
    The thicket that concealed it was intertwined.
Through green and brown the bowyer chopped without ceasing
    until he and it were all that stood, and it was his,
and he put it to the bladed [ax], whose cutting edge
    is inimical to tree trunks and is called its *crow*.
When it rested in his hands, he saw he held a fortune.
    He gripped it tight and shunned the company of his fellows.
Two years he left its bark unstripped while it absorbed
    the sap, and he examined it and squeezed its bulges
and shaped it with the iron brace and the cane with notches
    the way a bronco's temper is corrected by the spur.
Then he took it to the seasonal market, where it drew a buyer
    with a practiced eye that recognized its value.
To this man the bowyer said, "What you'd pay
    for a prized possession is its price. Are you buying?"
The buyer said, "I'll give you one wrapper of Sharʿabī make,
    and four of Siyarāʾī. Or ingots [of gold]

weighed and measured from the forge—eight of them,
    red as embers glowing in a baker's fire.
Plus two mantles striped in the Khālī fashion, and ninety dirhams,
    and a rugged leather blanket tanned with acacia."
The bowyer demurred. In secret council with his soul and its ruler
    [which is the heart] he wondered. Might another buyer offer more?
"Sell to your brother," the people of the market said. "Let there be
    no obstacle to your profit from a sale today!"
The bowyer's eyes ran with tears when he gave it over,
    and painful passion shook his chest.
The bow draws easily when tested, far enough
    but not so far the arrow "drowns."
When the archer lets it go, it sings the keening song
    of a mother's anguish at the funeral procession
as the arrow merges with the dodging gazelle
    whose feet fail it when ʿĀmir aims and fires.
[In sheen and hue] it is as if perfume keepers
    of Yemen had coated it with oil of saffron.
The bow is kept apart when dews descend,
    dressed in clean cloth, never wrapped in rags.
So when the death-dealer lurks beside the path
    at al-Aḥsāʾ where water lies in view,
the asses turn tail, running in a column
    [uniformly spaced] like perforations on a bridle.
Their eyes, turned outward by fear, go before them. And when
    they arrive at rescue, they still hang back
out of foreboding. They strain to find out who
    is at the water but the hopping, flopping ones, [the frogs].
They touch it with their front feet and then submerge their chests,
    angled to the archer's disadvantage.
And then at last the asses drink. It is midnight.
    With twitching flanks they bunch together in the water.
Morning finds them at it still, their cheeks stretching
    like leather pails at Yamʾūd's wells,

gargling at times and barking air
    at others through windpipe and nostril.
And when from far-off Wāsiṭ yet unbuilt on
    the pebbled pools start calling,
rocky ground is once again the asses' shoe,
    holding up their hard and massy hooves.
The he-ass guides their steps toward high Qawwān
    on tracks that are no more than threadlike traces.
His bray resounds from snout to belly as he drives them on,
    cantillating like a camel driver.
In all paces of the asses his step is practiced.
    He brings the herd to lap Ḥamāma's source
by putting them through long, convoluted
    distances down twisting paths to water.
In spots where they are tender, he defends them
    from ambush of hunters and imagined threats.
High above Ḥamāma juts a rebuffing height
    with a level top where the ass can plant his feet,
and the asses rub necks with one another, no more
    budging now than spears jammed windward into the ground.

TOUGH NICKELS

My husband watches me eat cereal. He looks wonderful in the dark morning. His soul sparkly and rough as a geode, his sweatpants drooping. His hair, that of a lion who went down to hell.

He looks like someone I want to marry.

But I can't. "I can't marry you," I say. "I have to go to work."

"What?" he says, sleepy. The little green fires behind his eyes begin to smoke. "I just want to see you before you leave."

He kisses my ear and sasquatches back to the bedroom, blanketing his whole long body. His shift at the coffee shop starts at ten, so he can sleep as long as he likes.

I sigh. It's still dark. I put on my scratchy polyester things and head out.

I work too much at my new job, and I rarely see my husband anymore. I'm so tired, but I can't sleep. Each night around midnight, I creep across the yard to Larry's crumbling mansion. Larry is usually already outside, waiting for me, calling in the raccoons. Larry's our landlord. He's an old man, he's losing his marbles, and he has a way with all the creatures in the yard.

I come home in a tired rage, like a fifties dad in a gray suit unleashing resentment on his family.

Our dog, Beatrice, pleads with me to go outside and rub her belly. "I don't have time for your bullshit," I tell Beatrice in my gray-suit voice. She limps away. She is old, and when she dies, I will think back on this moment and be ashamed.

My husband stands in the doorway to his office. He's been working on a song, I can see the geode through the same T-shirt he wore this morning, and he starts telling me all about his new album. I can't bear to hear it. I want cheese, I want wine! I want a bath! I want to be left alone for eight hundred years. I want a giant soft-shelled sea turtle to lie on my back and flatten me into the wet sand. I want to be submerged into the prehistoric past. I want to open box after box of expensive makeup and put it all on my face. I've been at work since seven thirty in the morning and most of my organs have evaporated, leaving behind sugar dust.

I eat the pasta dinner my husband makes. I gnash my teeth, thinking about all the nonsense that happened at work, as my husband tells me more about his hopes and dreams.

After my bath, just when it's time for bed, I start to feel alive again. Whole, like an egg in a slotted spoon lowered down into simmering water. A crazed raccoon energy rises in me, roams out to join the raccoons in the yard. Screw you, I tell my alarm clock.

I read wild literature in bed, grinning with my teeth out.

When my husband begins to snore, I slip out of the sheets and go see Larry.

Larry is backlit by the lanterns of the historic mansion he lives in. The top rooms are rented by people who make a little money doing Reiki or bartending. I'm the only person on the property with a real job.

Larry hasn't had a real job since his hair was blond and his ears still worked. He's been landlording for decades, which, from my perspective, mostly involves shuffling around the lawn in flip-flops.

"Hey, Russian beauty," says Larry. Raccoon eyes glow at me from the bushes behind him. Larry is obsessed with my being Russian, like many men his age. They get aroused thinking about the Cold War.

Larry's arms are hairy and a little too long. He takes me by the hand and twirls me, checks me out top to bottom, pausing at my nipples. His smile exposes silver fillings.

I cross my arms to hide my nips and nod at the bushes.

"It's our little friend." The raccoon emerges.

The raccoon sniffs at Larry's ankles, then mine. The raccoon is young. His dark lumbering mother lives here somewhere and hates us, but the preteen raccoon is curious and almost kind. The three of us look at each other like wary diplomats. Larry scratches the raccoon behind the ear, then wipes his hand on his shorts like he's touched something radioactive.

"Well, kid, should we go watch *Tough Nickels*?"

Larry's got a huge bowl of popcorn waiting for me on the leather couch. Everything in his house is gorgeous, picked out by his art collector ex-wife. Little clay chickens with dull eyes on adobe shelves. Lacquer boxes shining like snakes. Colorful blankets woven by old women who knew things. Larry wraps one of the blankets around me.

"What the fuck is *Tough Nickels*?"

Larry throws his head back and laughs like I've really done it this time.

Turns out, *Tough Nickels* is a black-and-white TV show from the fifties about a cowboy named Nickels who just can't catch a break.

Larry puts one hand around my shoulder and eats popcorn with the other. He's entranced by Nickels. I look away. It's hard to watch him eat.

"You're just an old white man," I say to Larry. He can't hear much of what I'm saying, and he's concentrating on the closed-captioning on the screen. "Everybody hates you and your kind. And they're right, Larry. You don't care about sexism and racism or the other isms; you feel like you already did your part, back in the sixties. But guess what? You haven't done your part in a long, long time."

Larry pats my head in response, concentrating on the picture. In truth, I haven't done much for the greater good either. It's this job; it's killing me. Five days a week, I apply every bit of analytical, creative, and social intelligence I have to something that does not interest me.

"And it's all because of people like you, Larry. Because of capitalism! People like you invented capitalism and you've had no problem riding the centuries-long wave. You're content to watch your nostalgic TV while the rest of us drown. And I realize I'm way better off than most. But look at me—I can barely talk to my beautiful husband anymore. All I think about is money. Instead of sleeping, I'm here with you."

On screen, Nickels the cowboy drops a bunch of nickels from his big goobery pockets. "There goes Nickels!" the other cowboys jeer. Nickels blushes as bright as black-and-white film can convey and shakes his fist at the dusty saloon ceiling. He'll get his one day.

Larry hoots and hugs me.

When the credits roll along with a whistling Western tune, Larry wakes me up and escorts me back across the stepping stones to my house. His dry hand reminds me not to be afraid of the rustling in the magnolias.

The night is still as a medieval summer well. In a few hours, I'll have to get up again.

When I open the door, Beatrice is standing in the hall, spooky as a ghost child. Like, What were you doing with the landlord all night?

"Nothing, Beatrice," I whisper. "Goddammit. I don't have to explain anything to you."

She gives me another look, and we both hobble back to our respective beds.

———

My sleep deprivation reaches new levels as the week goes on. I have enough consciousness to sound lucid in meetings and smile at the right people in the halls, but when I get home my husband's face comes in and out of focus. I barely taste the food he cooks me.

Even so, I can't stop visiting Larry. Or ranting when I go.

"I hate your name, too," I tell Larry on Wednesday night, around one in the morning. Technically Thursday. Somehow we're in his Jacuzzi. I'm in bedazzled bikini I don't own and can't recall putting on. The tiles around the Jacuzzi flicker with candles.

"*Larry*. So sleazy, like one of those dirty picture theaters you totally went to back in the day."

"Yes, darling," Larry says.

We're drinking martinis Larry made from a splattered cookbook printed in 1967. My bikini is bright blue as a vintage headache. Its little plastic diamonds mimic the candles.

"You're probably the last person in America with a Jacuzzi, Larry," I add, reaching into the gray hairs on his chest.

Larry sinks lower into the tub, a happy hobbit. His chest hairs sway in the bubbling water.

I try to decipher whether Larry's turned off his hearing aid and how far I can go with my tirade. But then I feel guilty and tender. Actually, I really like Larry. Everything I say about him is true, but there's something alive about him, too, something like my husband's geode.

"What I like about you, Larry, is precisely all those things that are wrong with you. You don't work, and you don't worry about the state of the world. Nothing bothers you. It's like you're outside of time."

Larry smiles with his eyes closed. His nipples blind, innocent.

"And you're the only one who is awake when I need him."

I fall asleep on Larry's curly chest. I don't remember how I get home.

By Friday, I'm so dead I actually pass out on the couch after dinner. The sound of something playing on my laptop threads through my sleep. When my husband wakes me, I realize I didn't go visit Larry tonight.

"Wow, were you watching *Tough Nickels*?" my husband asks as he closes my laptop and puts me to bed. "That's hard core."

That night, I dream about Larry. I can't stay away, even in my sleep.

In my dream, I'm carrying Larry on my back through a stampede of leopards.

"Why are they stampeding?" Larry yells into my ear. He weighs as much as I would imagine, like a barrel of hard cheeses. His chin hairs tickle the back of my neck. "Leopards don't stampede."

I agree and feel closer to Larry; finally, he is making some sense.

The leopards move around us, thick as a school of fish.

The metaphor arises in both of us at the same time, and Larry asks, afraid: "Are leopards… fish?"

It gets darker in what I realize is an aquarium.

I get us the hell out of the aquarium. Larry and I climb into the magnolias in the yard, where the raccoons and possums are thousands of years old and enormous. We kiss there like two babies who escaped from day care.

"I'm confused," I tell my husband that weekend at dinner. Saturday night, and I've regained some of my humanity, able to speak.

"Me, too." My husband presses a pasta bow above his lips like a mustache. He's in his underwear; the weather is warming up. Green is coming in through all our open windows. My husband looks like a wild sighting of a sasquatch, as well as the anchorperson reporting on the sasquatch. Elusive, competent. Elusive.

"We used to walk through cemeteries together," I say, mopping up pasta sauce with bread. "I used to float across the surface of my life, like a fairy of worry."

"I know," says my husband and reaches across the table to pat my shoulder.

"Now I can't even see the fairy anymore," I say. "And the worry? The worry has hardened. It has become the world."

Outside our dining room window, Larry mows the lawn, the front of his T-shirt dark with sweat.

Sunday, my beautiful husband reads in an armchair that may have been inhabited by mice. The armchair is the one thing he rescued from his old hovel when I sneaked him into my bourgeois life. Admittedly, he seems to enjoy this bourgeois life—he's drinking a fancy black tea I bought to please him. Beatrice at his feet. Larry hacking at wily tree roots in the yard.

I spend the weekend in the bedroom on my yoga mat, with my crystals and my tarot and my spiritual podcasts, trying to make a clearing inside from which I can keep an eye on myself.

The following workweek, I can't seem to find my husband or Beatrice in the house. Maybe they've become very small, hiding among the pasta packets in the pantry. Maybe they've grown sick of my bullshit. I can tell they're around, it's just a matter of where.

Anyway, it almost doesn't matter, because all this house has room for is my big red mood. The clearing has only made it easier for my feelings to take over.

I go to work like a crab, nothing but head and claws, nothing but pincers. I carry my big head home from work. My shoulders exhausted from power blazers. My legs all sad and sickly under from daily polyester.

I'm angry. I want to bury something in the yard, but I don't know what.

"I don't want to talk about my job," I say to Larry when we watch *Tough Nickels*, though he hasn't asked. "My job is like a muscle that's so sore, just trying to stretch it out could send me to the doctor."

There's a long delay before Larry laughs. Mostly he's laughing at Nickels, who can't mount his horse right, like a cowboy should.

"I'm spending my time with all the wrong people," I sputter at Larry. "Did you know, my husband and dog are hiding from me?"

"I know, honey," says Larry. His thick eyebrows look alive, like he trapped them out in the yard. They bristle at me.

I expect he's going to go right back to his show, but instead, Larry looks straight into my eyes. "You're in a vicious cycle, an impossible situation," he says. "You're just like Nickels." Larry's eyes fill with tears. "Just like Nickels, you have everything you need. You've got a good brain, a good heart. Those good Russian tits. Your husband is great, your dog is great. You've got enough money. But you can't get on that horse, and you can't get off. Just like Nickels." And Larry sobs into his hands for so long that I have to rub his beastly back until he tips over and falls asleep on the couch. I cover him with the scratchy Mexican blanket and turn off the TV.

I feel like I've been slapped. I take myself home on the stepping stones, and the young raccoon waits for me at the end of the walkway like a portent. I worry that he's turned and become like his mother, that I'm going to have to fight him, but he runs off at the last moment.

The bed is cold without my husband. Every once in a while I hear something skittering in the kitchen, like a moth trapped in the pantry.

When Larry goes to visit his sister in Florida, my husband and Beatrice crawl out from between the pasta packets or wherever they were hiding. All I know is that Monday morning, my husband is back in his seat at the table, watching me eat cereal, his geode sparkling.

It becomes easier somehow, I don't really know how. But I no longer feel as much like a crab. When my husband tells me about his ideas for his album, I relax. I hang up my gray suit feeling to take Beatrice to the park, where I rub her belly without resentment. I stop trying to control my facial expressions at work. I surrender.

Larry comes back from Florida, but I don't watch *Tough Nickels* with him anymore. I don't go over to the mansion at all. I sleep through the night like a normal person, next to my husband. Sometimes when I'm out in the yard with Beatrice and Larry's mowing the lawn, he waves at me and grins. Does he remember our times in the Jacuzzi? Do I? It's hard to say.

But I still have dreams about Larry.

In one, Larry invites me over for a daytime punch party. He's got a long table of pitchers, orange slices bobbing. His house is a castle, hundreds of years old. Ragged curtains blow in the windows. All of my landlord's other guests are shriveled old monkeys and cats in fancy teatime hats. Pale blue ribbons, green baubles. It's hard to tell the monkeys from the cats, that's how it is in old age. Everyone at the party is drunk. It never rains but we're suspended in this eternal darkening, in the clinking of ice and the bonneted purring of the cats.

In another dream, Larry puts his face against my screen door. "Sorry to bother you, I was raking up some leaves, wondered—do you want to check on the rain gauge with me?" Sweat in the pits and under the teats of his T-shirt. "Okay," I say. "Surprise!" he says when I open the door. He isn't wearing any pants. All of his nether parts are there, pinkish, and his white belly floats up between us like something dead from the sea. "Goddammit, Larry," I say.

This dream I have all the time, and it always feel very real: I wake up in the middle of the night because of the environmentally friendly new streetlamp that shines right into our bedroom like the angry eye of God. I get up and look out into the yard. There are several raccoons on all fours like bears, and right behind them is a naked red rat, and that rat is Larry. The raccoons and the rat make figure eights all over the lawn, little Larry scurrying behind the raccoons, searching and sniffing. Their movements followed by the angry eye of God.

In another dream, my husband and I bring a gift basket to Larry. He is in the early stages of dementia, so we're worried about him. "Larry," we say, my husband holding him by the arm with feeling, and I conveying other feelings with my eyes. "Larry, thank you so much for everything you've done for us. What a beautiful place to live, we're so lucky. And you've been so good to us. The Christmas presents, the flexibility with the rent checks when we were broke. No one has ever been this nice to us in our entire lives. The world is cruel, Larry, but you are kind, and that has made all the difference." We're all crying now and holding one another. There's a green wind blowing around us and the gift basket, there's something craggy about the wind and the grass. Then Larry pulls away and the sweetness is gone from his face, his body is limp. He stares at the ground and slowly turns around, like a sick cat. He heads off into the craggy cliffs of our lawn, which earthquake and buck. He's going to jump.

That's the last dream I can remember, but there will be others.

Oh, Larry, when you die or become a rat or join the monkeys in their teatime finery, when you fall off a green cliff and enter the wind, will you take my lurching, nighttime secret with you? Larry, are you a sort of gravity, are you the leering electron that I cannot trust but require? Larry, why didn't you accept the gift basket that was rightfully yours, which you deserved? Because Larry, I do love you, in a way, and I think that you love me.

FICTION / YOHANCA DELGADO

OUR LANGUAGE

She has no mother, La Ciguapa, and no children,
certainly not her people's tongues. We who have forgotten all our sacred monsters.
—ELIZABETH ACEVEDO, "LA CIGUAPA"

The books do not say that I was a girl once. They do not say that I lived near the woods in the far outskirts of Higüey, that my name was Celi, that I was born in 1954. I want you to know that I was a real girl, like you. Una niña.

Like memory, language changes. Our words eddy around the things we fear. Isn't it funny, how it worries what we fear, water turning a jagged rock into something smooth and small? We have so many words to make a girl small: jovencita, señorita, mujercita.

What a wealth of words and yet there is so much that the books do not say.

Why would the books say, anyway, that I was mid-height, with brown eyes and brown hair? There are ciguapas born every day, and it takes us lifetimes to become walking fears.

When I was a muchacha, my best friends and I would share a bag of limoncillos on the walk home from school. Have you ever tried a limoncillo? In English, they call it a Spanish lime, even though it doesn't grow in Spain. Isn't that something?

After school, the walk back to the village took about twenty-five minutes, but if we walked slow, we could make it last thirty-five and avoid some of the predinner chores waiting for us. We always tried to walk in the shade, our cheeks pink from the sun, our patent leather shoes picking up the dry dust of the country road.

Strolling three abreast, we cracked the green skin in half with our teeth and took the pink seeds into our mouths. One was never enough. Such a small fruit with an acidic sweetness that made you miss it, even as you held the seeds between your teeth. Before you finish one, you are already yearning for another. We call this can't-stopness seguidilla.

Listen closely. I'm teaching you our language.

Eating a limoncillo requires concentration. The stain of a limoncillo is a dark magic. The fruit is a pale peach, but stains a dark brown that ruins uniform blouses and sparks torrents of belts and chancletas and nights spent sniffling over a sink with a scrubbing board and a bottle of Clorox.

On one of those unremarkable days, I made it home without a single stain on my yellow uniform blouse. Picture the village. Little boys played street soccer, pausing when a car passed. A breeze tickled the sandaled feet of the abuelas rocking in white plastic mecedoras before rising up, up, up, to coax a gentle susurration from the glossy, green-leaved palm trees behind my house. In the distance, music. Always.

The house was two floors, coral-painted stucco with white accents. Modest and unremarkable. My mother waited for me at the door, her silhouette motionless against the sitting room light behind her. I broke into a jog and saw that her lips were set in a thin line, her arms crossed over her cotton housedress, her eyes red-rimmed.

She stood up straighter and uncrossed her arms. She forced her lips to lift at the corners.

I kissed her on the cheek. "Bendición, Mamá," I said. In our culture, it is customary to ask our relatives for a blessing every time we greet them. We are trained to career through the world begging for blessings.

I have learned to make my own blessings. You will, too.

"Celi," she said. Her voice was stilted, as if she had been practicing. "I couldn't wait to tell you the good news."

I trailed her into my bedroom.

"Don't change yet," she said, as I began to unbutton my blouse. *Don't change yet.*

I sat on the rose-covered blanket on my bed instead. "What is it? What's wrong?"

"You're getting married," she said, smile sepulchral, eyes fixed somewhere along my hairline.

"What? To who? Mamá, I'm fourteen." In this era, it was not uncommon for country girls my age to marry, but there were usually—how do I put it— other considerations.

"I know, mi amor. But there are things you don't know, even about yourself."

I wondered if I had, like the Virgin Mary, become pregnant without knowing it. We are taught so young to be suspicious of our own bodies. In our case, perhaps, not suspicious enough.

My mother took a long breath and sat next to me. She faced the wall and kept her face blank. "You're different. I need you to trust me. I'm trying to give you a full life."

"How am I different?"

"You'll know when you need to know," she said.

"Doesn't it sound like I need to know now?"

"You're too young to understand."

Isn't that one of the worst sentences you've ever heard? I won't teach it to you in Spanish.

"What's a full life, then?" I had started to cry. "What do you mean?"

"Children, security, family." She tucked my hair behind my ear. She whispered, "It's complicated, Celi, but I promise you, on the Virgin herself, that I'm trying."

It would be ironic, I suppose, for the history books to document how stubbornly we avoid our own stories.

The day after I turned fifteen, I was married to a man named Ignacio at the church near the school. I wore a new white, white dress. My mother hugged me so hard I feared my bones might break. My best friends, Laryssa and Benigna, wept in a pew. We were all grateful that our sobs were mistaken for tears of happiness.

I met Ignacio once before the wedding. He was a pleasant, if uninteresting, man in his mid-twenties who wore short-sleeved button-down shirts in pastel colors. He was an accountant for a company in Higüey. He agreed to commute to work so that we could live in my parents' village, by the woods.

The ceremony was short and the night: very long.

Ciguapas are always women. This is true, though no one asks why. I think it has something to do with our powers of escaping. And because we are women, the literature has much to say about the way we look. *The ciguapas are very beautiful,* some books say. *The ciguapas are hideous,* say others.

I do not think the books are wrong. My problem is with what the books do not say.

The books say that the first ciguapas were magic born of necessity, pressurized alchemy. The colonists came, they say, and some island women escaped to the caves and to the sea. Terror morphed our bodies into something monstrous and untraceable. It took less than three years for the colonists to kill everyone else.

Then new generations of ciguapas came in on the ocean waves. We are a nation's wounds made flesh.

By the time I turned sixteen, I had a son named Javier and my parents had died in a car accident. Ignacio was a good man. He did all the right things. He held my hand at my parents' funeral and pressed a cool towel against my forehead as I gave birth.

It's certainly not the sort of thing worth putting in a book: Ignacio made good money and managed the house. I followed orders and kept everything clean. I focused my quiet desperation and love on my son. It's boring, really, in its normalcy.

The trouble began when I realized that I was getting smaller.

Every day, I became a little bit shorter. The changes were almost imperceptible at first. I would cook dinner and the pot of rice would feel a bit heavier than it had the day before, the shelf that held the plates a bit higher. My skirts seemed longer than I remembered; my shoes wider.

Shorter and shorter and shorter until I was table height. My husband complained. I was becoming hard to find.

By the time I turned seventeen, Javier was two years old and we were practically the same height.

That wasn't the only change. My skin seemed lit from within, like pure ámbar. Do you know about Dominican amber? Dominican amber is resin from an extinct tree called *Hymenaea protera*. Wondrous, isn't it? How nature keeps a record, even when we cannot, of species that no longer walk the earth. The honey-colored resin is nearly transparent and carries an extremely high number of fossil inclusions, small lives trapped for twenty million years, to be studied under loupes, sold to tourists, worn on pendants.

My eyes seemed larger in my shrinking face. My hair grew faster, coming in shiny, long, and thick. Several times, I cut my hair myself, huddled over the sink in the dead of night, with a sharp pair of kitchen shears. By the next morning, it had grown to cover my knees again.

And then there was the puzzle of what happened to my feet.

They shrank—along with the rest of my body—and they realigned. My knees began to ache as if someone were twisting them to the point of breaking. They began to turn outward, to pivot.

The change was slight, at first: I waddled like a pregnant woman, my toes facing out. But soon I was walking like a ballerina in the second position. People began to notice. The little boys at the market began to trail me home, imitating my walk.

At first, my husband brushed off the jibes and made dirty jokes to his friends over beers—but then the jokes were laced with something acidic. I could not find the words to say I felt betrayed, but I suppose he felt the same.

By the following year, my knees, my calves, and my feet had rotated completely to align themselves with my back. Ignacio loathed the sight of me. I had become something he didn't understand.

I stopped leaving the house. Try keeping a secret in Higüey; it's impossible.

When I stand facing a mirror here's what I see: A woman, about thirty-six inches tall. Proportionally small, with short limbs. Eyes large, dark, and clear. Hair long, down to the area where my knees should be, except that what I see there now is the tender backs of my knees, slender Achilles tendons, calloused heels.

I see Celimena, trying her best. And for reasons that never make it into the books, my deformity doesn't upset me the way it should. It feels true.

I had to learn how to move in my new body, but I'm adaptable. I did not take me long to learn to backpedal, to look over my shoulder constantly.

Ignacio didn't know what I was and he resented me for it. Have you seen his picture? He was a big man, nearly six feet tall, and solidly built besides, with a thick waist. He would come home from a night out with his friends, heavy-limbed with drink, and slam me against the walls.

When he realized that my bones seemed impervious to breakage, he tried harder.

He seemed resolved to tear me limb from limb, if he had to, to crack me open and release the secret I was hiding.

One night, he came home with Grecia, a local widow who practiced Santeria. You should know that we Dominicans say we're God-fearing Catholics, but when confronted with a stubborn problem, we'll try anything.

Grecia's eyes were milky with cataracts and her hair was pure silver, a braid coiled down the side of her neck. She wore all white and carried an old leather doctor's satchel. She smelled like cinnamon. Behind her, Ignacio stood with his hands in his pockets, shifting his weight from one foot to the other. He avoided my eyes. I understood that this was a last attempt.

"I'm sorry for the state of the house," I said, rushing toward Grecia and tripping lightly over my backward feet. "I didn't expect company. Can I offer you a cafecito with a little milk?"

Her pearly eyes widened and she gasped. "Ciguapa," she said, noticing my feet and taking a step back.

I froze.

"What?" my husband asked.

"She's a ciguapa." The old woman's eyes remained fixed on my feet. "I didn't know they were real."

"Ciguapa," I repeated.

Imagine hearing yourself named for the first time. My mind dredged up the word from the bog of my passive memory: an echo of the old folktale came to mind, but first, I thought of the cigua palmera, the national bird of the Dominican Republic. A bird that loves to perch in palm trees. In English, it's called the palmchat.

"Fix her," my husband said. "I'll give you everything I have. I have money in the bank. I can borrow more."

"Keep your money," she said. She shook her head. "The change can't be reversed."

Can you imagine a more dangerous monster than one who reads?

Well, I have gotten into the books. Here's what they say:

A ciguapa is a mysterious, savage, and mystical creature in the folklore of the Dominican Republic. The legend of the ciguapa appears to have originated among the indigenous Taino Indians, though it also appears to have been influenced by African folklore brought over by victims of the slave trade. The legend concerns a group of women who escaped enslavement during the Spanish colonial occupation of the Dominican Republic. The escapees took up residence in the wild, emerging only at night to forage for food.

Imagine a monster whose sole objective is survival. Imagine the bending and shrinking of bones, over generations, to achieve this one end.

The ciguapa's distinguishing features include a diminutive size (about three feet in height) and reversed feet. Because of the reverse placement of their feet, ciguapas can walk backward and forward comfortably. They are nearly impossible to track. Bodies designed to elude and confound. Imagine the loneliness.

My husband knelt before Grecia and touched his face to her feet. His voice was low and filled with rage. "Her family knew and they cheated me. My only son is half monster. Will he change, too?"

"It is inherited," Grecia said slowly, "but I don't think so. Ciguapas are always women."

"So, what am I supposed to do," he said, forehead still pressed to Grecia's worn leather sandals. "I can't live like this."

Grecia looked at me again with something akin to pity. "Leave her." She stepped back and gently freed her legs from Ignacio's grasp. "Leave her alone."

"I'm your *wife*," I said, my anger finally welling up to answer his. "We were married before God. Do those vows mean nothing to you?"

"I was cheated. I didn't set out to marry some sort of demon," he said, rising heavily to his feet. At full height, he was nearly twice my size. "Some demon that could kill my only son."

"She won't hurt Javier," Grecia said. But now that Ignacio knew she could not fix me, her opinion no longer mattered. Ignacio ushered her out of the house, folding a few crisp bills into her palm, even as she tried to reason with him. He told her to never speak of me again and slammed the door.

"I could kill you," he said simply when he returned. "And no one would ask questions."

"Our three-year-old son is in the next room," I hissed, craning my neck to look up at him. The distance between us seemed infinite.

"So? He'll grow up knowing the truth. His mother was a monster and I did what I needed to do to her to keep him safe. He'll know his father is a brave man."

"This is what you call brave?"

"You know your voice is changing, too, right?" He pushed me against the wall. In the other room, Javier began to gurgle in his crib.

"Go get him," Ignacio said. "Go take him out of his crib."

"I may not be able to carry him anymore, but Javier is as much my son as he is yours. This is my house and I'm not going anywhere."

"Who paid for this house?"

"Where's the money my parents left me when they died?"

"Your parents are charlatans. You can't ever repay me for what your family has done to me."

He picked me up, kicked open the back door, and hurled me out into the backyard, which extended out into the woods. I scraped my elbows as I landed in the dirt, unable to rely on my knees. I didn't know how to fall yet.

He shivered. "Look at you, you're terrifying," he said. It infuriated him that I seemed content with this new body, even as I struggled to my feet. "You're not the woman I married," he said. "And you're not welcome in my house anymore."

He bolted the door behind him.

If fear is a currency, then those were extravagant times. The books acknowledge, at least, that this was the age of Trujillo. In awed, breathless lists, the books catalogue the torture, the rapes, the mutilation. They say: *this brutality is unprecedented.*

Oh, but it's only an echo of what came before. You know that, right?

We are the record. It's etched into our bones. A million times.

The ciguapa has long, lustrous hair that covers her naked body. Because of the odd placement of her feet, the ciguapa is nearly impossible to capture. She lives in mountain caves, in the trees, and in underwater caves along the shores.

The ciguapa can capture a man with her dark, hypnotic eyes. She is known to find lone men on the road and lure them to her cave or to her alcove by the sea. The men are never seen again. It is assumed that she eats them.

I stood, shaking, and scanned the area for nosy onlookers.

You will unlearn shame, as I did, and you will be happier for it.

The woods loomed before me and I decided I would give Ignacio this temporary victory. I would take a walk.

The air was intoxicating: the perfume of Bayahíbe roses, a million petals curled in on themselves for the night, a self-embrace. I backpedaled, feeling a sudden urge to run far away, to plunge into the sea. I had never run so fast. Many miles passed in a light breeze. Without learning how, I climbed a palm tree near the shore and was suddenly aware of my altered clothes and how needlessly constricting they were. I jumped down and ran my hands through the wild dry grass, relished the cool soft sand beneath.

Night fell and a full moon emerged. Ciguapas dropped from the cradles of their palm trees. They emerged from behind bushes. They were all small like me and naked. They all walked backward, nimble on their feet. In this clearing there were a dozen or so, but I knew that there were many, many others.

The ciguapas gathered around me.

"We all already *know* each other," a ciguapa named Diana told me, kissing me on both cheeks.

It was true. I had never met Diana before, but it was true.

"We don't live together because it's safest," she said. "But the full moon is hard to resist."

"Luna blanca, cobertor y manta," said another ciguapa who called herself Yamila. "Fool moon. It's when we yearn for our old lives the most. It makes us do stupid things. But most nights, we eat, we explore, and then we sleep."

"Where do we sleep?" I asked.

"Wherever we want," Yamila said, her voice bell-clear. "Want to see my favorite?"

I nodded. Yamila and Diana led me to the shore, their feet leading the way, their eyes fixed on mine. The ancient pull in their gaze told me I could trust them.

There were no houses along this stretch of shore, and the only sources of light were the stars and the moon, refracted off the water in a million glimmering threads. The waves were gentle, beckoning, the air cool and fresh.

"Ready?" Yamila said.

They took my hands and led me into the water. Pulling me gently into its depths until I took a deep breath and plunged.

Diana gave me a thumbs-up under water. I could see and breathe as easily as I could on land. They taught me how to catch a fish and eat it raw, without ever rising to the surface. They led me to a series of underwater caves and I claimed a small one. I had never slept so well, or felt so safe.

Ciguapas can only be captured in a full moon, and only by a hunter accompanied by a black-and-white polydactyl dog. In captivity, ciguapas die of grief. (It won't surprise you to learn that this does not deter the hunters.)

With a small, but passionate membership, The Ciguapa Hunters of the Dominican

Republic (CHDR), advertises tours of the Dominican countryside in search of the elusive monster. The group's mascot, an Australian shepherd with an extra phalange on its front left paw, is present on every full-moon tour.

Few successful captures appear in the CHDR's records, but hopeful hunters commission, in advance, special display boxes for their trophies, designed to preserve a specimen and slow the decomposition process.

The club attracts local men and tourists in equal numbers. Members say that they enjoy most the male comradery and friendship they find on the hunts, outings in which they say they can truly be themselves.

I visited my son at night so that Ignacio wouldn't know. I would climb in the window and help him into bed and tuck his curly dark hair behind his ears. He would smile at me. I told him my story so that he would not forget me. How handsome my Javier was.

On one of these nights, I spoke to Javier and he began to cry. He couldn't understand me anymore. I held his big head in my arms and tried to tell him, tried to tell him, how much I loved him.

As he grew bigger, I became even smaller. One evening, I approached the window and heard Ignacio saying to Javier, "You shouldn't need to open the window at night, but if you do, this is where the latch is."

I waited until he was gone and then showed my face at the window. I could see Javier in his bed. I tapped the glass. He turned his back and lay with his face against the wall until morning came and I had to go away.

I have become a sort of animal. If the books are right, my voice sounds like braying or mewling now. Some words whip around in my mouth and leave my tongue bloodied.

I am choosing, more and more, not to speak at all. But you and I, we understand each other.

Though the ciguapa can breathe comfortably under water, she is best known for her diminutive size and superhuman speed on land. This extraordinary speed not only helps the monster elude capture, it also makes her a formidable predator.

Historians disagree about the genetic provenance of the ciguapa. The written records are vexingly imprecise on the subject of ciguapic genealogy, though there have been reports of typical human women giving birth to daughters who, on reaching adulthood, transform into monsters. It is assumed, in these cases, that the women carried a recessive ciguapic gene. Some folkloric sources indicate that they are born ciguapas, while others hypothesize that ciguapas have procreated with human men, and that their descendants continue to exist among us.

Some books say that ciguapas steal newborn babies from their cribs, such is their desire for motherhood and connection to the human race.

See also: oread (mountain nymph); napaea (woodland nymph).

See also: Genu recurvatum (medical condition in which knees are in reverse position, causing a deformity in which the afflicted appear to walk backward).

See how they translate us?

Though he never let me in again, I stood at Javier's window every night for years. I like to think my presence was a comfort to him. In nightly increments, I watched him grow up to be a quiet, sad boy, big for his age.

When my husband announced that I had run away, no one questioned him, not even my friends. Heartsick, I listened at their windows. By then, they were married, too, and kept their own houses neat. Benigna was pregnant and Laryssa was trying. She visited Benigna often, as if attempting to pick up pregnancy through osmosis.

From time to time, I hoisted myself up to the window and watched them stir sugar into their espressos. The sound of their spoons against the cups made me miss coffee. The delicious, bitter mundanity of it. The power was out, and with only a few candles lit, Benigna's living room looked cozy and welcoming.

"It seems unlike her, doesn't it?" Laryssa said once, after a long silence. "To leave Javier behind?"

"She really did love her baby," Benigna said, one hand on her swollen belly.

"But Ignacio would scare anyone off. That man was a drunken brute toward the end."

"Just the end? I'll never forget that wedding."

"Poor Celimena," said Laryssa.

"What could we have done?" said Benigna, folding a paper napkin into smaller and smaller pieces with nervous fingers. "We were just girls. Her parents wanted to marry her off."

"But so young?"

"You heard the rumors."

"They obviously weren't true." Laryssa drained her cup, and placed it upside down on its saucer. "We grew up with her, Benigna. We know her. She wasn't crazy."

"Her grandmother disappeared, too. Whatever happened to her? I heard she lives in the woods, runs around naked, eating berries at night."

Laryssa laughed. "Crazy like a fox. Sounds better than cooking and cleaning all day." She lifted the coffee cup and examined the rivulets formed by the coffee grounds.

"What do you see?"

What did I tell you? We look for magic *everywhere*.

"I see anger," said Laryssa slowly, as she turned the cup in her hands and examined the dregs. "A group of women. Tragedy. I don't know what it means."

I slipped away from the window as my best friends searched for the future in their coffee cups. I wanted to tell them that my grandmother had been captured by a hunter and that she had died of grief. But this is the saddest part of the change, losing the ability to speak.

Within a few years, Ignacio remarried to a wiry busybody named Gladys who painted her toenails neon green on my terrace every Sunday.

Together, they had two little boys and Javier seemed out of place. It was decided that he would go to New York to study English and live with Ignacio's sister. I crouched in the bushes and listened as Ignacio made the arrangements to fly him to La Guardia. I clawed my nails into my palms until I drew blood.

The night before Javier left, he came to the window for the first time in a long, long time and we studied each other in the moonlight. He put his palm on the glass and I put up mine.

Then he closed the curtains, but through the sheer fabric, I could see his shoulders shaking as he packed his suitcase.

Did I mention that we love riddles? Adivinanzas? Here's one:

The one who makes it does not use it.
The one who uses it does not see it.
The one who sees it does not desire it— no matter how pretty it may be.
Can you divine the answer?
A coffin.

The books say that we are immortal. I would like to correct that: we are long-lived. We can be killed. We can kill ourselves. We can die of grief. But we live very long lives. The oldest ciguapa in our clan is more than two hundred years old.

Decades feel like months: we sleep, we wake, we feed. The village gossip interests us less and less. It's so predictable. Boring in its normalcy. The past is a photograph from someone else's life: curling at the edges, and fading. Like the books, we have become particular about what's worthy of memory.

We have learned to outlive the people we love.

Here's another adivinanza:

Diligent twins
Shapers of lack
Who walk with their blades pointed forward
And their eyes pointed back.
Can you divine the answer?
Scissors (did you guess?)

In their cozy houses, surrounded by their children and their husbands, Larissa and Benigna still talk diligently around my memory, tracing the outlines. Like us, they choose what to remember.

But what can they know of my untamed grief? Javier. In every word, an echo of his name.

Thirty years passed and Javier came back to my house, alone. My heart beat a fraught old song in my throat.

On the first night, when everyone in the village was asleep, he walked to the edge of the woods, as if looking for something. I watched him, enthralled.

He sat down on a tree stump, looked at his fine leather loafers, and checked his gold watch.

"Mamá," he said, finally. "I know you're here."

Mothers do a lot of things without thinking. I walked out into the clearing.

Javier shuddered and leapt to his feet, as if to run away—then gingerly bent at the waist to hug me. I smelled nothing beyond cologne and aftershave and mosquito repellent. Who was this strange man with my Javier's eyes? He was tall, like his father, but I was pleased to see that he carried a hint of me in the creases around his mouth, and in his dark, thick eyebrows.

"I got married," he said, sitting back down on the amputated tree, resting his manicured hands on his knees.

I crossed my arms. I suppose it would have been too much to ask to have been invited? But I couldn't stay angry. Not after waiting this long to see him again. I uncrossed my arms and hazarded a smile.

"I have a daughter," he said blithely. "Her name is Celimena. After you. She's twelve."

"God bless her! What's she like?" The last of my pride dissolved. I put my hands on his giant ones.

He tilted his head back, gently pulled his hands away. "I can't understand you. You know that."

I took a step toward the trees.

He straightened up again, as if remembering a memorized speech. "I haven't forgotten you. I'm going to tell my wife about your disease and we'll get you to America somehow and find you a surgeon," he said. "Or here, even! We can take you to the best surgeon here. We have money now."

I pictured myself in a hospital gown in a white, white hospital, a doctor slicing my calves open and rearranging my tendons like a florist rearranging rose stems. I shook my head.

I tried to explain that we can't be fixed—not in that way. We can't relinquish what we have been built to carry. And it isn't so bad, anyway, to be ourselves. But the sound of my voice only seemed to make things worse.

"Don't you even want to try?" A drop of spit landed on Javier's lip. "Don't you realize how selfish you are? What if Celi grows up to be like you? We'll need to know how to fix it."

I wanted to hold him in my arms and comfort him, but he shoved me away.

"Do you know how hard it's been for me? To grow up motherless? To lie to everyone about my mother? It would have been better if you'd just died." And now he was crying, this adult man with my Javier's eyes.

A venomous grief slithered up my calves and noosed my throat. I stopped trying to talk. By now, I understood my power. I looked in his eyes until his expression softened to a dull calm. I faced him as I walked away and he followed me, his lumbering footfalls heavy and thick. I imagined bringing him back to my sea cave, where I could rock him like a giant doll in eternal sleep.

Ciguapas have done worse.

But me? I had learned something new. I waited until the wave of anger receded back to some distant shore.

I kissed his hand. I watched from the window, just like before, as he packed his suitcase. I let him get in a taxi and find his way back to New York.

I grieved him again and I let him go. This letting-go is called living.

I know it will be hard, but when this message finds you—and it will find you— let your body hear it. You're the one I'm waiting for.

I've read that it gets very cold in New York, but you won't need much here. When you arrive in the old house in Higüey, wait until nightfall and then come straight through the back and out into the palm trees.

I will wait for you here. As long as it takes. Years and years and years—like sand to me. You will be sad at first, as I was, as we all were and are. But then you will see how the trees grow tall around us here, to keep us safe, and the grass is sweet-smelling and velvet-soft beneath our unloved feet. The breeze is a light kiss across our faces and the moon—full and white and glowing—is a generous mother. You will finally become who you have always been. You will remember what your body has forgotten.

I've waited so long for you, mi nieta, my granddaughter. Listen closely to me. I am teaching you our language.

NAZARÉ

At 4:30 A.M. on June 30, every dog in Balaal began to bark. Pampered pooches in the Mayor's palace yelped at the chandeliers, mangy street hounds growled at a cloudless moon, and guard dogs bawled into the dark. A crescendo of "No! No! No!" because that was the moment nature was breached. The moment a sixty-ton blue whale washed onto the beach.

A boy called Kin was the first to see the whale, but he didn't know what it was. Just a dark mound on the sand, like the outline of a low hill. As he approached, the features began to clarify in the early morning light: the pectoral fin, the bifurcated tail. The whale was stranded on its belly, half-in, half-out of the water.

The thing didn't move.

Gentle waves lapped at its flanks. Oblivious seagulls flew overhead and a light breeze jostled the grass of the hummocks that fringed the beach. Balaal, city of tinkers and fishermen, slept as the sky turned orange with the first stirrings of the sun.

Kin had never seen a creature so big. Slowly he circled it. He saw water and air bubbling from its blowhole and heard the rumbling of what sounded like a breath emanating from its belly.

White and black spots covered the whale's mottled back as if a painter had flicked a loaded brush at it. The skin shone with a watery sheen.

Kin, at eleven years old, had seen whale fins in the distance and had heard whales bellowing to one another in the deep. A child with music in his bones, he'd once perceived the sound at A minor and thought it was a ship's mournful foghorn until one of his sailor friends told him, "That's a blue whale, ten miles out."

Kin dared to get closer. The whale's presence was otherworldly—a colossal mass of indistinct blubber. It looked like a fallen zeppelin, and its stench permeated the beach.

Kin wanted to ride the whale's back, grip it with his bandy legs, lay his head down on it and listen to the internal workings of the beast. Instead, he walked past the boats to the fishing village where the night fishermen would be bringing their catch to be placed on ice and gutted.

The first person he saw was Shadrak, an old black fisherman with a round belly.

"Shadrak," he said, "there's a whale on the beach."

The old man smiled and nodded. He had a fishing rod in one hand and the butt of a cigarette in the other. He blew a miasma of smoke.

"And it be good mornin' to you, young shrimp. You tellin' tales?"

"No. I just saw it."

The old man coughed. "Where?"

"There." Kin pointed. "On the beach."

"How big?"

"Huge."

Shadrak took a final drag of his cigarette, a mess of rolled newspaper and foul-smelling tobacco, and dropped it at his feet.

"I go get some men. We take a look."

Kin walked on until he came to more fishermen unloading their catch and he repeated his story. A few of them knew and trusted him. Some put down their tools immediately and began walking toward the ocean. Others laughed it off. "They stink up the beach is all they good for."

By the time Kin returned to the whale, there was a crowd. Several women were carrying buckets and throwing water over its gargantuan body.

Kin saw Shadrak with a group of fishermen and asked him, "Why are they doing that?"

"Whale skin dry out in the sun, whale die."

One of the women, who was called Jesa, saw the group of fishermen and shouted, "Hey!" They looked at her. "Call Fundogu," she said. "Tell him to bring a stethoscope. We'll need your fishing boats. He's too big to push by hand."

None of the men moved.

"Hey, estúpidos!" she shouted again, pausing from throwing water on the whale's back. "We don't have much time. When the tide goes out, the whale will be stranded."

"It's stranded already," said a fisherman. "What's your plan?"

"What do you mean, what's my plan? We're going to rescue it. Put it back in the ocean. It's still alive."

The man cocked his head. "How do you know?"

"It's breathing." She rolled her eyes.

Another man moved forward, next to the first fisherman, and said, "How we gonna move it?"

Jesa said, "We're going to use your boats, tie lines around it and then you drag it out to sea."

There was a murmur.

The Mayor arrived in a suit along with six pampered dogs and a retinue of soldier-bodyguards and had himself photographed next to the whale. Then he prodded it with his cane and went home.

A priest arrived on a bicycle, soon followed by a gang of harlots in fishnet tights and a drum troupe and trapeze artists from a traveling circus. An acrobat danced on the whale's back until Jesa shouted at her to get down because that's not how you treat a sacred beast.

Then came the widows of the fifty lost miners. Then troubadours and vagabonds from Balaal's wastelands. There was even an appearance from the Bruja of Laghouat, although no one knew it because the witch came in the form of a seagull and observed events from far above.

Down below, buses cranked and creaked, puffing whorls of smoke, and disgorged a rabble of schoolchildren. They ran to the whale and took notes and drew pictures, eyes agog, nostrils quivering at the smell.

The radio station took a break from its nonstop government propaganda and ran a story on the whale, complete with fake whale noises made by a bushy-bearded actor called Baha. Journalists from Balaal and two neighboring cities came and took photos and interviewed the locals.

"It's a gift," said the priest.

"It's an omen," said the fortune-teller.

"It's big," said the acrobat.

A posse of loosely affiliated dogs came sidling out of the shadows and nosed along the beach, tails erect at this new wonder. To them everything was in two categories: dog or not dog. But this creature seemed to herald a third: undog. Unlike not dog, undog was living but the very antithesis of dog: huge, not moving, and incapable of wagging its tail.

Then came twenty-five Believers, who gathered sticks to build a fire and sat in a circle around the whale and made incantations. They said the whale was a god.

A woman who had been photographing the creature asked, "Who found it?"

"This boy!" said Shadrak and pointed at Kin.

The people parted and in stepped Fundogu, who was a holy man and a doctor, which were the same thing in Balaal. He was large and black and in his seventies, with tribal scars down both cheeks. He wore a white galabiya and no shoes. With great ceremony, Fundogu inspected the whale. He circled it, touching it with his long, ringed fingers, prodding at some parts, massaging others. The whale let out a jet of water and Fundogu pulled out a stethoscope from somewhere within his robes. He placed it against the whale's vast back. The crowd murmured its approval of the learned man.

During the inspection everyone retreated a few feet except Jesa, who continued to water the whale.

Then, in his slow, deep voice, a voice as deep as an ocean, Fundogu said, "Get the whale back in the water in six hours or he will die."

With that, the holy man wandered off, head high, through the human corridor that had let him enter. His large flippery feet were damp with sand. Before leaving the beach, he turned, looked at the crowd, and said, "Everything begins and ends in the sea."

Jesa called to the fishermen, "You heard him. Get your boats ready."

Shadrak stepped forward and said, "No can do use our boats."

"Why not?" said Jesa.

"We take this whale into water, he pull us under before we cut the line. He drag us down, boat and man 'n' all. No can do it."

Jesa dropped her bucket into the sand. Some of the other women also stopped throwing water at the whale. Jesa crossed her arms. She was in her midthirties, tough as tree bark, already a widow, her husband claimed by the sea. She had no progeny and wore a black scarf around her head in memory of her drowned beloved and to hide a vivid streak of white hair. It had turned white the moment she had heard her husband was dead. The Spanish-speaking kids had taken to calling her *zorrillo*—skunk.

"This is a sacred animal," she said. "Older than me and you. It was sent here by God. It's a sign from across the oceans. Put your boats to work, you weaklings, and cut the lines when the whale's in the water. We'll send divers down to do it."

The men were unmoved.

"Too risky," said Shadrak.

Jesa squinted her eyes at him. "Then I'll do it."

"You no got no boat, remember?"

Jesa approached Shadrak as if to slap him. She had lost the boat at the same time she had lost her husband, both wrecked on the rocks.

Shadrak didn't flinch.

"Ms. Jesa, I would like help you," he said. "But no can do it."

"Then let me borrow your boat."

"No can do," he said. "My boat is my livin'. No boat, no fish."

Jesa looked around at the fishermen. A wiry Somali. Pacific Islanders with tribal tattoos. Lean, weather-beaten Japanese. West Indians stripped to the waist. Not one looked her in the face. The whale breathed again and its massive eye opened to take in the sky and the flitting birds.

"Which of you will lend me a boat?"

The men looked at their feet. No one lends a boat to a water widow.

"Then we'll gather every man and woman in Balaal and push the creature back into the sea."

With that, she spoke to the women with buckets and they wheeled away to gather reinforcements.

Kin alone heard the whale singing. Was this its death song? He heard three notes in a minor key, a refrain or a threnody of such sadness that the whale's mottled, dark skin seemed to tremble with the song. It sounded to Kin as though the notes conjured all the beast had seen: the glistening shoals of fish; kaleidoscopic reefs with their jagged edges; seaweed wavering like witches' hair in the tides; sunken galleons lost and canted on the seabed; the undersides of boats—massive trawlers and tiny skiffs he could have upturned like toys; sunlight bursting through the water.

The song ended as abruptly as it had started.

Soon the masses were there, the pushers and pullers of stranded whales, and Jesa ordered them in five languages to take their positions. They were going to roll the beast back into the ocean.

Kin could see the tide receding. Where the whale had been half-under at first light, it was now barely in the shallows.

Two hundred people amassed now at the whale's side: butchers and road workers, farmhands, schoolteachers, knife sharpeners, cat catchers. They gathered their strength, sucking in the sea air, rested their hands against the wall of gray-black flesh, and heaved with groans and gasps. The whale didn't move.

A dozen of them brought out shovels and dug a vast trench by the whale's body. They were going to reduce the drag of the sand, to ease the beast's passage to the water. They rasped instructions to one another, mimed and gestured, and hollowed out a new ditch. The butcher, built like a bull, went ankle deep in the water with his shovel and carved the final path to the sea. At his call, the people took their places and pushed with all their might to force the thing through the channel in the sand. The whale didn't move.

Three fishermen—islanders squat and sunbrowned—appeared reluctantly and tied ropes to the whale's flukes and flippers. In groups of thirty, the people gripped the ropes and readied themselves like contestants in a tug of war. The remaining fishermen joined in, put their shoulders to the whale's back. At the water's edge one of the drummers from the circus troupe started up a beat on his djembes. The man, who'd been born with four arms and now whacked out a rhythm on four drums, went faster and faster till the sweat flew off him in his frenzy, and as the pounding came to a crescendo and the sun climbed higher, the people of Balaal heaved and shoved and pulled as they'd never heaved and shoved and pulled in their lives. They gritted their teeth and strained every sinew and summoned from nowhere the strength of the ancestors. The whale didn't move.

The people looked at one another. They were spent. The pullers were bruised and cut where the rope had worn a groove into their skin.

Shadrak picked up his straw hat, which he'd temporarily laid on the sand, and said, "He no gwon move."

The fishermen untied their ropes from the whale and people began to walk away.

A woman approached Jesa and said, "We did our best. All this pushing and shoving is going to kill it anyway. There's only one chance now."

"What?" said Jesa.

"The magicians are here."

A raggedy cluster of shamans arrived, most of them naked or wearing nothing but loincloths and necklaces made of seashells. They were preceded by the smells of pipe smoke and ganja. They were alchemists, wind talkers, adepts, thaumaturgists, Voodoo priests.

They lit a fire under a cauldron and mixed metals and threw in bindweed and dandelion and the spines of long-dead starfish. Some whispered incantations in languages not heard for a thousand years. One blew mapacho smoke into the pot and sang to the whale in a voice so pure the stones in his pocket began to dance. Still the whale didn't move.

All the while, Kin listened to the creature's breath.

By late afternoon, the shamans had melted away into the rocks or returned to the hills, and the beach had thinned out. Jesa had gone home, leaving just a few women to throw water onto the whale's back, careful to avoid its blowhole, and to warn the children to stay away from the flukes because with them, the whale could thrash with the power of horses.

As the sun went down, Kin sat alone beside the creature in the sand. Steam came off its skin and its eye rolled above the grooves of its ventral pleats. Kin listened.

"Are you dying?" he asked.

He heard its breathing change. Then he got up and began to push at the whale's side. All around, seagulls flitted and yawped and watched this child in rags heaving at the mass of blubbery flesh.

Kin hurled himself at it. He put his shoulder to the animal's skin and pushed, running on the spot for minutes at a time, kicking up sand till his feet sank. A crab darted from a hole, looked quizzically, then skedaddled sideways.

The stench was now tremendous, a mélange of rotted fish, garbage, and brine. It was as if the whale were inside out, discharging the fetor of its guts. This, Kin ignored. He pulled at the creature's flipper like a child pulling its mother's arm. He yanked at its fluke.

He exhorted the creature in all the languages he knew. He hollered and sang and begged and howled. He clambered on top and looked into its eye and pointed at the sea.

He climbed down, bathed in his own sweat and tears. His legs were trembling. He sat down again behind the whale in a bundle of kelp and seagrass. A voice startled him.

"I brought you something to eat."

Jesa, that widow known to be crazy with grief, was behind him at the beach's edge, holding a plate of food.

"I'm not hungry," he said.

"You're lying."

"I'm not hungry."

"Maldito, don't you get it? If you want to push the whale back into the sea, you need more strength."

She gave him the plate. Fish, rice and beans. He said nothing and ate with his hands.

She had been there for fifteen minutes and let the food grow cold, watching this boy. Now she watched him again as he crammed the food into his mouth. He hadn't eaten all day. Maybe not all week. Skinny as an eel. Stubborn as a roosterfish. Maybe nine or ten years old, she figured. Another street urchin tossed up by the waves. Seen him running errands for those yellow-bellied fishermen. Why was he here? Wasn't he the one who first saw the whale?

He finished the food and gave the plate back. He got up and began pushing at the whale. He was flailing at it, trying to stir the beast.

"You're welcome!" she shouted and wandered away, empty plate and unused fork in her hand.

The sun was going under. Kin whispered and stroked the whale's flanks. He thought about the beast. It had been so alive. A giant traversing oceans, now reduced to shallow breaths, an expanse of fat and skin.

His thoughts were interrupted by a distant roar. The sound continued but because he was behind the whale he didn't see the wave rising, a veil of brine and salt, that drew over the shore like a curtain.

They called it Nazaré or Teahupo'o. It broke the laws of nature. A wave was supposed to make a perfect curl like butter from a knife and then collapse on itself and dissipate onto the shore, disappear like a memory. Nazaré rode higher and longer, overwhelmed the other elements.

It wasn't the tide coming in. It was something sent by the spirits of the sea, or that's what the people of Balaal would say the next day. Like one bellow in the bellows of an accordion gone haywire, sweeping over the land and dragging everything in its path back out to sea.

At the last moment, Kin skirted the whale and saw the wall of water and ran to high land beyond the grassy patches that bordered the beach. With all the strength left in his legs he ascended the hill where the shamans observed the horizon. He clambered, not looking back, hearing the roar chasing him until it washed over with a great fizzing sigh, the outer edge of its splash spitting droplets of the ocean onto his back.

He turned. In one jolt like a gust of wind, the whale was borne into the ocean. It made a sound, like a lone cello, a deep thrum at the core of the universe. It sank and rose and waved its tail and plunged into the deep. It rode past the island with the abandoned lighthouse, below and above the surface, suddenly buoyed and then plunged again until it was a mound just as Kin had first seen it. And then with a final wave of its tail flukes, it dipped out of sight. At that precise moment, every dog in Balaal wagged its tail, collapsed onto its forelegs, and fell asleep.

Around Kin there was nothing but the sound of the waves and the pinprick lights of fireflies flashing in the evening sky. He heard the moaning of a distant ocean liner. A low D. Across the way, harbor lights glowed dimly.

THE MADE WORLD

JENNY XIE

Your ear moves along one swarm of conversation
to another, then alights on a dog's stiff bark,
in a cornflower structure up the hill.

How hard the city center has worked for this,
the churches with their large ribs.

Some words tossed off like beads, some pepper
cooling on the lip of a ceramic bowl.   ·
Small glances, from afar, that one keeps in the front pockets.

Blurry forms are stored elsewhere, in the camera,
stacked along streets of ochre and rose.

Attention's formidable property—you spend it quickly.

Crumbling rock with your feet
along alleyways, those loose couplets.
You mistake this openness for waking,

but it's a trick of the landscape.
We, who are made and unmade
by something we have no control over.

This far inland, emptying out feels both distant and near.

TO SAVE THE CELL-PHONE BATTERY—

KIMIKO HAHN

I look up and through the train window.
There are stops I've not seen
since childhood—Spuyten Duyvil, Ludlow.
I'm staring through the train window now
at trees in vacant lots that will grow
anywhere because they're not trees.
I keep looking out the window
because stopping cannot be seen.

NIGHT OUT

GRAHAM FOUST

Tap is fine, but am I really worth the water?
(That logic feels faintly despotic is one of its pleasures.)
If not, all I ask is to be brave in the face of it
and to be told what else to ask before your answer.
But if I can *make* that face and have some say in this,
while having neither need nor any use for getting
far enough away to touch the day that's yet to frame us,
the trees pulped, the oceans impossibly modular—I'm on it,
you're on it, our flickering behalf—then in figments
will begin sure things, which then will end there,
and I'll go home to make sure what I want has changed.

SUNDOWN POEM

GRAHAM FOUST

How quiet is it? It's so quiet, you can hear
manners pummeling candor, so why wouldn't you
burn the scene, for in a field without a harvest,
the dirt of which you'll paw through to find your own bones,
all instantly ironized and bright as new dice,
the fire for which can only live all over you,
as always, your first last resort, the colors on
a wall into some damp grass set so lovelily
back to monochrome, thereby to re-lovelify
malfunction's following form's not following light
around the shaky meat you've made of either hand,
you'll be damned if this isn't an experience
whose particular occasion has been confused
with other memories from the same mood or place,
but grace to be the fault of what's called *consciousness*,
"the perception of what passes in [one's] own mind,"
according to Locke, and "what passes," too, is time,
which makes its way to what since the 1300s
has been called *knowledge*, and which, like many concepts,
has multiple names by which it can and does go,
as we say *snake* for *serpent* and *ship* for *vessel*
and *grief* for *unhappiness*, *mourning*, or *sorrow*,
and you think you're gone alone, but I'm not there too,
my disappearance a reconnaissance of you.

MY HEAD EXPANDS

MATTHIAS GÖRITZ

TRANSLATED FROM THE GERMAN
BY MARY JO BANG

I've looked too deeply into the glass,
which works like a telescope.
The tadpole head is held up
by the cockroach at the stove's edge.
She peers at me
as she drags her pregnant belly
into the icebox underworld.

So, I say,
when the door bursts open,
I see inside it's also winter.

What am I missing?
I have a place,
a bit of money
and a window.

My elongated brain drives through the day,
equipped with my eye,
outfitted in my body,
addressed by me,
it gathers impressions.

Where is it going?
The transport mediums are
the modes of transport: feet, legs, auto, and bus.
Every day I see people
vanish through the subway entrance,
that atom smasher for the human masses.

Sometimes I'm also in there,
Always coming in, late
even faster,
to the job,
to the agreed-upon date,
back to the desk.
I can hardly bear to say so, but
sometimes I think
it's all a game my mind made up.

I have looked too deeply into the glass.

It is all crystal clear
you don't go up against the day.
I've made a place for myself,
a bit of money,
and take a stand at the window.
Outside goes on.

Traffic flow.
Life flow.
Nightfall.
The get-up and take-away,
the all-out uproar.

IN THE CASING OF TIME

MATTHIAS GÖRITZ

TRANSLATED FROM THE GERMAN
BY MARY JO BANG

It's incredibly deep, people's sleep
inside the downpour-machine

noises
from the inside of time

out of the organ work
elongated tones emerge

the outstanding radial tire
tracks, traffic

circles carried on
from the morning

the colors are commutable
the driver's license names

get slipped into the morning
from that sleep

like a pneumatic tube
into the city's bloodstream

go with the flow
or keep sleeping

gray are the innards of the ticker
sleepless and deep

lies its meat
in the casing of time

THE PALACE OF JUSTICE

MATTHEW ROHRER

Imagine being hauled
by a few guys
into the Palace of Justice
through the enormous
golden doors oh my
while the sun shines
in every direction
even the innocent
feel guilty stumbling
up those wide marble steps
and the gates so bright
the rest of us look away

from UNDERWORLD LIT

SRIKANTH REDDY

FALL TERM XXIV

The first historical appearance of Antigone is the vanished *Antigone* of Euripides. All that remains of her are a few scraps of text quoted by Aristophanes in *The Frogs*. Then comes Sophocles's extraordinary rendition—translated, adapted, remediated, and otherwise resuscitated countless times to this day. My favorite *Antigone* in this vein is Hölderlin's *Antigonä*, her mouth open like a floodlight onstage—though some prefer Brecht's, with her mouth like a floodlight whose bulb has burned out. In Japan, *Antigone* after *Antigone* sprang up after the bomb. A Turkish Antigone speaks out for exploited cobalt miners. The Yoruban Tegonni wears an exorcist's mask. Though our tragic protagonist continually exhibits new symptoms, new costumes, new customs, and new systems, every Antigone suffers from the same underlying disorder. She cannot tolerate the thought of the dead among the living. Yet who can say whether she is living or dead?

WINTER TERM X

My students this term are unreceptive, even intolerant, of anything that resembles a translation of a translation. They suspect David Constantine's late twentieth-century English version of Hölderlin's early nineteenth-century German version of Sophocles's mid-fifth-century BC Greek version of Antigone's grave epithalamium in act 3 may be unsound. "Very well then," I say, "let's see if we can drum up our own version." What on earth is *Antigone* doing in an undergraduate seminar on comparative underworlds anyway? It does no good to point out to my class that our Attic antagonist is forever asking herself the same question. I am not "teaching." They are not "learning." Hades, who tucks everybody into bed in the end, is escorting us, still breathing, to the shores of the River Acheron. There is no ceremony. No wedding song sings us down the aisle. Nonetheless, we shall, every last one of us, marry Acheron.

WINTER TERM XXIV

’Αντι (anti-) is the Greek prefix for *opposition*, though it may also mean *like* or *comparable* in the ancient grammars.

The suffix γόνη (-gone) refers to birth, generation, or descent—from *gónos*, seed. Another meaning, contested by modern scholars, derives from *gonia*, meaning *angle* or *bend*. Think hexagon, or agony.

Therefore it follows that Antigone, commonly translated as *unbending* or *worthy of one's parentage*, more properly speaking signifies *against birth*.

Etymology has this way of turning a person inside out.

SPRING TERM XI

Every child must learn to apologize for the pain they will inevitably cause to themselves and others. My daughter has been practicing with her ancient transitional object, flinging the tattered creature down the stairwell, then descending to retrieve it while I prep *The Myth of Sisyphus* this Plutonic spring morning.

"Sorry, Hop Hop," she says. "I'm sorry. Don't be sad."

My wife is at the kitchen table upstairs, searching the *Chronicle* for late-season openings in comp and comp lit. I worry that others may hear the frayed wire of worry running through her voice lately. When she slips into bed after midnight, she sometimes wakes me with her apologies.

"Sorry, darling," she whispers, "I'm sorry."

The remedial speech act has never come easily to me. Yet last night I had a dream wherein I expressed my regrets to an endless procession of black gowns in the pink morning mist. My wife and daughter filed past, looking a little embarrassed on my behalf. I'd delivered a commencement address on the Sisyphean condition, dressed, all the while, as a *papier-mâché* stone.

SPRING TERM XXIX

Some academicians view zombie films as historical allegories for failed immigration policy, apocalyptic Cold War realpolitik, autophagous libidinal economies under transnational capital, or various other societal ills.

Grading papers in front of the TV with the volume low, I wonder if the genre might have something to do with higher education itself.

That would be one way to account for all of those decomposing extras milling about in ill-fitting pantsuits and sweater vests like dispirited postdocs at an MLA convention cash bar.

It may also help to explain the protagonists' method of dispatching wave after wave of cadaverous assailants with a sharp blow to the brain stem.

I have yet to determine where my innermost sympathies lie.

Sometimes I feel for the undead, sometimes the unliving.

Joseph Yoakum

FAMILY THERAPY

In the passenger seat next to me she's reading the paper and tells me it says why the man was arrested the other night. She says, Domestic abuse. She doesn't say anything and then says, There's a picture of her.

Look, she says. She does not look good.

These are long pauses where she wants me to reply. I'm waiting for the light to change. My back hurts from the seat. The paper crunches in her hands.

Not that anyone looks good, she says. Not after that.

You did, I say.

No I didn't, she says, and puts her hand softly on my knee.

I get my youngest son Tuesdays, Thursdays, and every other weekend. Only him. My lawyer told me at the start of this arrangement that the court cannot force children to see their father, and that the court always favors the woman, yes, even if she's a liar, can't hold down a job, and drinks too much. I told him I was on step six, ready for God to remove my defects. I had my purple chip.

He said to leave the chip at home, and God too. What you're doing now doesn't matter nearly as much as what you did then.

Five thirty-eight I pull into his mother's driveway and honk. Weekdays I get two hours, but his mother and I have been arguing now for almost six years about how long two hours is. I don't count the driving, she does, and the papers make no comment. The shades move in the window and I see my daughter, my oldest, the flash of my eyes on her looking at me like she always has since I first held her when she was bloody and crying and I wiped her face clear. Suspicion. I can hear her in the background of the phone shouting that *he's* here, that *she's* in the car with him. Where my older son is I don't know and doubt his mother does either. I say over the phone, over maybe a twenty-foot distance,

Hey Kiddo, outside.

He says he'll be out in a minute, and what I do for ten is not smoke a cigarette. When she tries to light up next to me I pitch it onto his mother's lawn. Don't, I say. And not in the apartment either. She crosses her arms but I hate listening to him cough. And even with the door closed I can see his mother holding up her hand to him and saying I should wait until six.

Five fifty he comes out not wearing the Mets hat I got him last weekend. My eyes on him too, though. He opens the car door and climbs in saying hi Dad hi Gina. His mother watches us from the door and waves as I back out. Gina, I love her here, she always waves back. I say,

Big as houses now, look at that.

And shift into drive. Gina says that isn't nice. My son is quiet. In the rearview his arm is raised to the window but not moving back or forth.

Years from here and now, the court-mandated family therapist will stare at me while I remember the hat. I'll say I don't know, but that he always wore hats. Always Mets hats—blue his favorite color. So I buy him a Mets hat and then he stops wearing them altogether.

To placate me the court-mandated family therapist will ask how I felt about that and what I thought it meant. He and I will both scoff sitting on either ends of the couch because all three of us know what we're talking about is not what's important. I had to fight tooth and nail with the judge to get us into this room. It was only ever his mother that got between us. But she's not in the room now, and there is nothing but nothing between us on the couch but still we're sitting too far away from each other for the court-mandated family therapist to look at both of us at once.

I pull up to our condo, pointing out the unit where that guy got arrested. It looks like every other unit—blue door, white stucco. Our unit is ours, though—I tell him when we walk inside that we're home. We're home, and I have prepared a steak that will blow him away—marinating for two days, it will melt in his mouth so he doesn't even have to chew.

He plops down on the couch with his book bag, then looks up. He asks,

Why's Gina outside?

She's smoking.

So?

I've asked her not to smoke inside while you're here.

You and mom always smoked inside, he says. Let her come in.

———

The lawyer kept bringing up Christmas. I asked him eventually,

Why are we doing this?

I have to know what happened, he said. You know what ruining Christmas does to your chances of seeing your kids? Every time you tell me the story it's different. Which version will you tell in court? Which bar were you coming back from, Tara's or Popeye's? How'd you get back? Was the door locked? How'd the TV break? Who threatened who? She had a knife on you or she had a kid's book as a shield from you? And who called the cops—her? Her mother? Your daughter?

The most I could say was Yes. Step five is admitting the exact nature of your wrongs but there's a difference between a thing's exact nature and a thing exactly. I couldn't remember anything exactly and honestly was afraid to look back. I could see in every meeting men turned to salt over what they can't take back, because not a one of us is a deserving refugee. I knew there were holes in the story but I knew they were made by the devil's horns. Anyway the facts were documented. I can't remember better than a police report, and I can't make what I've done better. So what could I do now?

There will be three sessions because the court knows how healing works and that problems can be solved in six hours over three weeks. But at the start I will think I won. Unlike what my first lawyer had told me, the court could force a child to see his father if he had enough lawyers. And I won, seeing his mother drive him to court-mandated family therapy, seeing them sit quietly in the car not talking to one another. But on the way to court-mandated family therapy my hands will shake and my chest will hurt, so Shannon will have to drive so that I get past the liquor store. And then Shannon will sit with his mother for two hours in the waiting room flipping through health magazines, none of us talking about what matters. What broke, and how to fix it.

Good lord, the lawyer said, the first one. Whatever you do, do not say any of that.

He's quiet in the living room while Gina and I make dinner. The oven sets off the fire alarm, and then I'm holding the baking sheet in my hands saying the squash is burnt.

So I stomp around, and I slam things. I see myself doing that. Throw the squash smoking into the trash, throw the window open. Slam the oven door.

Potatoes are like five minutes in the microwave, Gina says.

If it's something that can just be thrown together in five minutes then what is the fucking point? I ask.

I slam some more things. I feel the muscles in my arm doing that. I ask her low why she didn't just check on it, and she tells me in a hiss that it's not her fault I fucked up the squash.

She goes outside again to smoke. I stab some potatoes and nuke them. I haven't heard a sound from the living room through the alarm, the slamming, so I check on him. He's sitting in what's dark now from the window, reading. He looks up at me as I come in, then through the window at Gina outside.

Everything okay? he asks.

Fine, I say.

He nods. Turns a page.

How about a light? I ask turning one on. I say,

You'll ruin your eyes that way.

It's not good for you, I say. Reading in the dark.

He turns a page.

Is that for school? I ask.

He shakes his head.

Shouldn't you do your school reading?

I did it already.

What about your other schoolwork?

Did it already.

Then why did you bring your backpack? I ask.

Which makes him look up. You asked me to, he says.

Well because I thought I could help you with your schoolwork or something, I said. But if you did it all.

He looks back at his book. He says he doesn't really need help. He says, Sorry.

I sit on the chair at the other end of the couch.

Well, what are you reading now? I ask.

Which is a trick of a question. If I ask him about whatever book he's reading he goes and goes, into painstaking detail. He weighs all of his words and interrupts himself to make sure plots and characters are clear, that I know the setting, that I understand the tone, and why all of that is important. I never have any idea what he's talking about and never remember the books and listening to him it's easy to think that maybe I've never read anything, ever, at all, but it's nice to hear him talk, in that way, to me.

The lawyer asked me what I was even doing out on Christmas, why I would leave my family for orphan drunks at some sad divorcée bar. I told him it was cereal.

Cereal?

Their mother hates it. On Christmas morning she made a big holiday breakfast with french toast, bacon, sausage, hash browns, a quiche—but I'd gotten hungry while she was cooking and ate a bowl of cereal. When everything was done I wasn't hungry anymore and she yelled at me, over the entire table, her mother there, Why do you have to do that? Why can't you just eat with our family, my mother, your children?

In the second session we will not talk about Christmas, but we will talk about his mother. The court-mandated family therapist will say that there seems to be a lot of unresolved tension, and confusion. That she is confused about when exactly I stopped being a member of my own family, she'll mean.

Her mother brainwashes him, I'll say.

I'll say, I'm the bad guy, I'm the drunk.

Forever, I'll say,

It doesn't matter what I do, it doesn't matter what I went through.

I'll say, What I'm going through now.

He will be quiet with his hand over his mouth as I speak, then ask,

Did you bring me in here just to tell me how much you dislike my mother?

Do you have any memories of me in the house that your mother didn't put there? I'll ask.

He'll shake his head. He'll say, How little do you think of me.

You were so young, I'll say. What could you remember?

Then he'll laugh into his hand, and ask me, What exactly do *you* remember?

Cereal?

———

He'll ask me what I thought I've been doing all these years. Sending random men to serve his mother papers on weekend mornings; not paying child support to the single mother working two jobs; emancipating the children I couldn't guilt or force into seeing me; this, what we were doing here, right now, what was this?

Papers, I'll say. It's just papers.

Gina comes back inside without looking at us, gets her phone, and walks back out.

Is she okay? he asks.

She's fine.

But from here, through the window. She's sitting on the patio, where we watched the man across the lot get cuffed and carted away, his wife watching from the door. I said I'd been there, and she said she'd been there. We smoked, we laughed a little at ourselves and where we were now. But right now she's hunched over her phone like she's being pelted with rocks.

The court-mandated family therapist will shift subjects and ask him what he's reading in school. He will talk reverently about some dead Frenchman, and I will think he sounds essentially hopeless. I will want to tell the court-mandated family therapist that this will not work, this trick. I will know because it was my trick. And still, in the next and last session, when we are done refusing to talk about anything important, or anything at all, the court-mandated family therapist will give him a small stack of books tied with string, the rest of Frog Legs's career. She will say that she thinks he will appreciate them more than she will, now.

And before the court-mandated family therapist tells us the session is over, before she says that she hopes we found the sessions helpful, before I ask my son to come outside with me for a minute to talk, before he says No I will not go outside for a minute to talk, before the only thing left for me to say is Okay son fine don't come outside for a minute to talk, before I shake another pill onto my tongue for back pain and tell Shannon to drive, before—I will watch him take those books and say thank you and I will only want to tell him that I would have given him every dead French author's books if I thought that they would help.

———

And would they have helped? Do they still?

I'm right about the steak. It does melt in your mouth. The meat is soft and full of juices and so tender. I'm licking my fingers and smiling like a kid at the back of Gina's head. I want to tell her that this will be good. That I can make good, with my own two hands.

I gave him a copy of *Moby-Dick* once. Expurgated, abridged—classroom edition. I found it in the discount section of a Borders.

I will leave so many messages, starting before the court-mandated family therapy, after he tells me that he can't do it anymore, can't keep watching me do this—to Gina, to Jen, to Tracy, now to Shannon. And to myself. In the message I'll say,
     Papers don't have to mean anything.
     We will just have been about to leave to get him from his mother's house— me and Shannon and Shannon's son—to go to Port Jeff Bowl. He won't hear it in the message, no matter how many times he listens to it over the years, but Shannon will be holding my arm through the entire thing, looking at me, and looking at her own son sitting in the car.

From here I can see exactly what not to do, what not to say. It hasn't happened yet so I don't have to take it back.

I will not hear his voice for a long time. Entire years. I'll call—on the train to the city with the conductor announcing Stony Brook or St. James in the background, on weekends on my way out of church, at the dinner table, I'll call. My messages will repeat themselves and standardize.
     Hey Kiddo. It's today's date, around the current time rounded to the nearest quarter-hour. Merry Christmas or Happy Easter or Happy Birthday. Just wanted to see how you were doing. Haven't heard from you in a while. Give me a call when you get a chance. Okay? My number's the same.

I ask the table who wants to say grace, and they stare at me. Gina laughs. It's funny until you need it. I take their hands and say the serenity prayer like I have every night for the last six years, whether or not their hands were there to take. But it only works if you work at it. Amen.

Neither of them say it back. Gina gets up from her seat to get more wine from the bottle I said she could keep in the back of the pantry, saying, Forgot the blood of Christ.

Don't, I tell her when she sits back down. Mock me.

She raises the glass to her lips but doesn't drink. I take up the carving knife and say,

Don't you know what grace is? It's a debt.

The meat spills over itself, tender, dark, and thick. Perfect blood inside. I carry a piece to his plate, to hers, and to my own.

This marinade, I say, chewing. Is soy sauce, extra-virgin olive oil, fresh lemon juice, Worcestershire sauce, fresh garlic, organic basil, rosemary, thyme. I basted it each of the last two nights with honey also. The meat itself is Black Angus beef, a heifer who lived a life happier and better fed than you or I could ever hope to be, except tonight.

It's good, he says.

Does your mother ever let you have a glass of wine with dinner? Gina asks him.

She better fucking not, I say.

My parents always did, she says. It's very Italian.

You better make sure I never hear of you drinking, I say.

My parents were both very Italian, she says. Waving their hands around. Making sauce.

Smoking either.

Rosaries everywhere. Saying *mangia*.

I say, What's in me is in you. And, I will blow your head clean off.

She asks, Is his—is your mother Italian?

His mother doesn't know what she is. She's nothing, she's a mutt.

He sighs into his cutlery and without looking up asks me not to call his mother names.

Like she doesn't call me names, I say.

We don't really talk about you, he says. They try not to. With me.

I watch him cut his meat. I don't believe him. He holds his silverware wrong. Like his mother does. He changes hands to cut and stabs the fork into the meat like a dagger. It's not that his mother taught him but that she didn't. No class. The sharp noises from the tines against his plate make Gina wince. Her glass is already half gone.

What did you learn in school today? I try.

He shrugs.

Nothing? I ask. Give me something, son.

He places the silverware on his plate crossed and stares at it.

My favorite subject was history, Gina says. Ancient history. The Mesopotamians. It's amazing what they were able to do with nothing, with rocks.

What's your favorite subject? She asks.

English, he says.

What about science? I ask. Math? The useful ones.

He shrugs again. Eventually picks up his fork and knife.

I talked with Mrs. Moretti in the guidance office today, he says. She's not a counselor, but she's at a desk in the lobby. Whenever I come in she calls me Curly, because of my hair, and I call her Moe. I asked her what this magnet on her cabinet meant that said Pogue Mahone and she told me how she wasn't born here. She came to America when she was my age as a refugee from Ireland. During the Troubles? I didn't know what those were. A car bomb killed her father. She said that she's lived here most of her life now, but that Ireland is her home. I asked if she's ever gone back and she said she couldn't go back to what wasn't there anymore.

I don't know what to do with that. I don't say anything.

So I know what Pogue Mahone means now, he says.

Gina asks, Who's Larry, then? Can I be Larry?

I meant something you learned in class, I say. What did you do in math?

He chews. He swallows. He says, Proofs.

Oh my god, Gina says. I hated those. Explaining why a triangle isn't a square? Sure, he says. P's and Q's.

P's and Q's! You know that is the most useless thing. I can't count on one hand how many times I've have to P and Q, because I've never had to!

What I think is that she poured herself a glass in the pantry, drank it, then poured another before sitting down. She's light and small. It hits her quick. By her own admission—we met in a meeting. She still goes but she's stopped speaking. She says she can't say anything until she can say she's stopped. We don't know she's pregnant yet, but when we find out next week I'll somehow think it's another chance to make good.

Can I get anyone anything? I ask, getting up for pepper.

A.I.? Gina asks.

The steak doesn't need it, bleeding onto the platter. I put it on the table not lightly.

You know, I say to him, Your birthday's not far. Know what you want?

He shrugs.

Books, probably, I say.

He nods.

Gina says her birthday's not far either, and she has *ideas*.

You read them so fast, I say.

I might need shoes? he says.

Let your mother get you clothes, I say. And I'm about to say I should get the fun stuff when Gina says to him,

Get your elbows off the table.

He doesn't look at her or me or move his arms at all.

Hey, she raises her voice. I'm serious!

I put my hand on the table and say her name.

I'm *sorry*, she says too loud. It's ingrained in me, you know? My mother would hit my elbows with a wooden spoon to get them off the table. My back to sit up straight. Hard—we had to have good table manners. If he were in my household he would be covered in bruises.

He straightens his back a little but doesn't move his arms.

Our spoons are plastic, though, she says into her plate.

She takes another sip of wine. She's rationing. I would never hit my kids for manners. This is not a conversation they could have about me at their mother's table. I don't think so, anyway, I think I'm in the clear.

I tell him about work, while I have it. We're rebuilding tower three. I'm a foreman on this one so I don't have to climb the steel. Too old now anyway, too many back problems. My doctor only gives me Tylenol, like I'm some sort of child. I tell him I've been taking a lot of pictures I'm excited to show him. We're getting high, starting to clear some surrounding buildings. He can't imagine the sunsets, but I'll show him. And what's wild is that, as high as we are, as long as we've been going up, we haven't had a single accident. No one has gotten hurt.

I'm looking at him, and I can feel my face wide open, but he doesn't know what I mean. I don't know how to make him understand. He reaches for the asparagus and Gina says,

Sure, reach over me.

Which stops his hand, floating above her plate. I say,

Maybe you could pass my son the—

But she takes the plate and drops it on the table in front of him. He takes two spears and tries to hand the plate back. She doesn't take it. She's got her forehead in her hand, and her glass is empty. I ask if they want more steak.

There's plenty, I say, squeezing Gina's knee under the table. Hard. I take the carving knife and honing steel and look at Gina, sharpening. I give him a thick cut. Her too, past her hand holding up No.

Plenty, I say again.

No accidents, I say. No one's fallen. The job's safer now than when your uncle took his fall, that's true, but it's different with this one. I'm excited to ride the train in the morning. I'm proud of what we're doing. We all are. We're building on the bones of people who died that day—that does something to a place. The work feels sacred. We think the spirit is holding us up. Even the guys that don't believe anything believe that—this site is something different. We want to make good for those people and for each other. We want to rebuild.

Neither of them say anything. His fork against the plate makes a sharp sound and Gina grabs the fork from him and says,

Stop that. Who raised you?

Gina, I say.

Who? She asks him. You would be covered—

Gina.

—in bruises, What?

She looks at me. She puts her forehead into her hand again, still holding his fork. He hasn't moved. He never moves. He would always just sit there and try to be somewhere else.

May I be excused? he asks.

Sure, son, I say. Why don't you go up to your room to read while Gina and I clean up?

He gets up. I hear him go up the carpeted stairs and close his bedroom door. I turn to Gina and I lean in close to her. I put my arm around her. I control my voice—it's amazing, the control I have in my voice. I make it soft, and light. Comforting.

Listen, I say. I need to explain something to you. Each week I get a total of four hours with my son, and every other weekend I get about thirty-six. This averages each month to a little over five days. I am lucky to get any holidays. And this is only one of my three children, because the other two will never give me another chance as long as I live. Gina, look at me. Gina, I have very limited time with my son, is what I'm trying to explain to you. Very limited time that is poisoned before he even gets here by what his mother and my other children must say about me. Look, listen. I will not fuck this up, and you will not—will not—fuck this up for me.

I will call every week, then every other. Every month then every other. I will call when it's inconvenient, or it will seem that way to him. I make bad days worse—but when would be a convenient time for you to reconnect with The Estranged Father? Tuesday? Around one?

After a few years the calls will stop almost completely. He will start answering his phone again because he will not be afraid every new number is mine. He will be glad not to have those panics, but also hurt, somehow. Like that panic was the last connection we had, like I've given up on him. Like it was my decision.

But one week I will call to leave a message during a lunch break, having practiced all morning a line about busting my back on the steel because that is something I think he could be proud of me for, and his voicemail will have changed. Instead of a robot telling me what number I've reached and to leave a message at the tone, it's him. His voice, telling me I've reached him, apologizing for having missed me, could I please leave a message? Thanking me for calling.

The tone will sound and I won't know what to say. God. I will be able to say, God. Wow. I will say, It is so good to hear your voice.

The first lawyer made his voice low and quiet when he leaned in to ask, sitting down to family court that day, Do you think she still has the photos of your older son's neck?

I am climbing the stairs to check on him. Gina is polishing off the bottle. She'll miscarry anyway. One day I'll use the word *crazy* to describe her and he'll say he didn't know what I expected from a woman half my age that I met at a meeting. I'll say that's not fair. I'll say that good people attend meetings, and that the steps work if you let them. I'll say it's up to the person, to forgive themselves.

What about everyone else? he'll ask. We'll be in the car, driving him to his mother's house. There will be the sound of the car, humming. Not looking at me looking at him, he'll ask, Are you going to her funeral?

But that is years from now. Now, right now, I'm climbing the carpeted steps to his bedroom door. It will always be his bedroom, even when Shannon calls it her son's room. I knock on the door lightly, and I hear him tell me to come in.

The week after I hear his voice I'll call again, way ahead of schedule. Too excited. The ringing will stop and in that small quiet moment I will pray.

She did have the photos to show family court but I was only scared of her showing those photos to him, telling him, Look what your father did, evidence I could never refute except with his reflection in the mirror, maybe the only thing I ever did right.

He is sitting on his bed reading. I sit on the end and I am asking him how he's doing.

Fine, he's saying. How is Gina?

She's okay, I'm saying. She's sorry.

It's fine.

The way he is saying it, I know he means it. He can have forgiveness. I'm seeing him now like I saw him last weekend, after the game, exhausted, about to fall into bed when I said, Say your prayers. And he did. He kneeled at the edge of his bed, this bed, and I kneeled with him. We closed our eyes. We put our hands together.

When the voicemail plays it will not be his voice. It will be the robot again, telling me what number I've reached and to leave a message at the tone. I will check my watch. I will say,

Hey Kiddo. It's Thursday, the twenty-seventh, around five forty-five. Just wanted to see how you were doing. Haven't heard from you in a while.

Suddenly out of practice I'll say,

I'm, uh, just about to get off the train. Maybe you heard it. The train. I know you said once you could hear the train from your mother's house. I don't know if you're still living there, but. If you do, if you heard the train, just now, well. That was me. That was my train coming in.

But right now I am looking at him and I know that the next thing he is going to ask me is if I can take him home. But I am looking at him, and what I want more than anything is for him to look at me, away from his book, my eyes reflecting mine, say,

Could I spend the night? Maybe you can drive me to school in the morning.

I can see from here what few moments we really have left, just moments, and how I will always remember them exactly how they happened.

I will put my hands together. I will close my eyes. Can you hear me?

He will be sitting in his living room when I call. He will look down at his phone and watch it until the vibrating dies out, then watch the screen tell him I left a voicemail. He will put down his book and open his laptop, and he will have his fingers over the keys. Miles from the sound of the train coming in, but it will be my eyes staring outward that stop his fiancée as she crosses the room and asks him, What? Which won't reach him, at first, but he will then say, Sorry, what? And she will say, I thought you were looking at me. And he'll say, Oh. No, sorry.

HIGH No 2. BRIDGE CROSS
THE MISSOURI AT CHillicOTHIE MO.

Joseph Yoakum

THIS IS THE WAY

"You're choking the hammer," Fritz said.

They were on the scaffolding, Henry leaning out at an awkward angle to pry rusted roofing nails out of tin, his brother observing him on his way past.

"What does that even mean?"

"You're holding it too high up, if you hold it further down you'll get more leverage."

Henry shifted his grip lower, but then the hammer felt too heavy, his wrist feeble. "I can't get any strength behind it when it's like that?"

Fritz shrugged, sauntered off. "Suit yourself."

Henry tried again with the hammer, using the grip Fritz had shown him. He was close to tears, knew that to be ridiculous. The first two weeks of his summer job had passed like this, as a series of small but intense humiliations. Even the most minor mistakes had felt unsurvivable, although Fritz and the others never did much more than lightly tease him, or show him an easier way to do whatever it was he was doing. He still hadn't mastered the art of looping the extension cords into smooth coils. The day before, when the boss, Snowy, had teased him about the tangled mess of cord he'd just finished rolling up, Henry had felt actual tears spike in his eyes. Tears! He'd turned quickly away to another task. Snowy, of course, had been oblivious. Snowy was a kind man, Māori, in his late fifties, nicknamed for his startling shock of thick, white hair. He had a wheezing laugh, and wore half-moon glasses that seemed oddly clerical for a roofer. Henry wanted very badly to be friends with Snowy, to joke around with him the way Fritz did, but he never quite managed it; he was always slightly out of step with their jokes, limping along a half beat behind. And then there was the inscrutable apprentice, Toby, a near-silent man in his early thirties, sandy-haired with pale, lashless eyes, huddled in his hoodie even on warm days.

Henry returned his hand to the wrong position on the hammer, pried the last few nails out of the sheet of tin, and eased it off the roof, dropping it onto the pile of scrap below where it landed with a clang. Toby, walked past below, talking on the phone.

"... in the fridge, babe," he was saying. "I left it in the door of the fridge."

Toby had three little girls, Fritz had told him this, and Henry tried to imagine Toby going home and being clambered on by blond daughters, their sticky hands on his face. Toby smelled of Lynx, and often farted loudly without either apology or remark.

Henry watched him walk around the corner of the house and disappear, still talking on the phone. At first Henry had tried to make conversation, had asked Toby questions about himself, about his life, but the answers he received were brief, not quite a rebuff but close. Now, whenever Henry spoke to Toby he felt that his own sentences sounded oddly ingratiating, or too verbose, echoing plummily in the air after he had uttered them. He gave up on asking Toby questions when it dawned on him that no one had asked him any questions about *him*self. No one offered him any information about who they were. They worked, they bantered with each other, they got into their trucks at the end of the day and went home. Henry thought of his friends in Wellington, their endless fetish for *expressing* themselves. Their outfits and bands, their zines and devised theater pieces.

That day after work, Henry took himself for a walk on the beach near Fritz's flat. He stood in bare feet at the water's edge and watched a woman swim back and forth in the bay, adhering to a specific distance as if she were in a swimming pool. After about ten minutes, the woman swam in to shore. She stumped up to Henry, a sturdy middle-aged woman in a white swimsuit splashed with blue flowers, goggles on head, red indents on her forehead where the rims had dug in.

"How'd I do out there? I'm trying for one of these ocean swims."

She was Irish, he guessed, from the accent. "Good," he said, "I think?"

They chatted easily about this and that, laughed, and said goodbye. Henry watched her go, suddenly bereft. He had felt more at ease with this Irish woman than he had since he'd arrived in Bluff. Intimacy springing up between them like a wind-filled sail. He could nearly always find a foothold with women, but sometimes men felt like... what? Like walls. Like cliffs made of something inaccessible, huge slippery plinths of obsidian.

———

Their next job was a place called Inverary Lodge. A pompous, Queen Anne style house that had never had its tiled roof replaced; instead the roof had just been patched up, here and there, for more than a hundred years. The old terracotta tiles had to be stripped, the roof decking beneath repaired, new terracotta tiles hung on top. From the vantage point of the scaffolding, the roof was a mess to look at, gappy and patchy, the tiles cracked and mossy, slipping and jostling out of their close-set formation. Able, as Snowy demonstrated, to be loosened from their fixings with one sharp tug. For the disposal of the old tiles there was a huge skip placed on the driveway, positioned below the scaffold. A chute, made out of a series of interconnecting, open-ended buckets, went from the scaffold to the skip. Snowy tossed a demonstration tile down the chute and then continued his fluid progress, moving crabwise along the pitch of the roof, tapping with his hammer, showing them where the tiles were loose and where the rafters might be weak underfoot. Henry watched him, marveling, as ever, at the graceful way he moved. Snowy was a short, solid man but he had an easy, studied way of prowling the rooftops that was beautiful to watch.

Henry found that he liked prying up the old tiles, liked the moment of give when they came away in his hands. And he liked carrying them, too, in rough stacks, to the chute. When he placed the tiles in the chute he could hear them scrape and slither all the way down. And the best part of all was watching the tiles emerge and explode against the metal of the skip's floor. After each load he would hurry back to get more tiles and do it all over again. There were no mistakes he could make here, he could tear up the tiles as quickly as anyone else. He smiled at Toby and Fritz when he passed them on the scaffold, sent the tiles skidding down the chute, paused to savor that jubilant sound as they collided with the floor of the skip, and then dashed off again. As the morning wore on the skip became lined with fragments of terracotta, and the bare, water-stained wood of the old roof deck began to emerge.

————

That night Fritz went out somewhere, did not extend the invitation to Henry. Alone in the flat for the first time, Henry passed in and out of the shabby rooms, scrutinizing them in a way he wasn't able to when his brother was there. He went prying into Fritz's bedroom, noted the grimy bong on the bedside table, the clothes that had slithered from their hangers and lay heaped in the bottom of the wardrobe. Among the pictures and postcards pinned to the wall was one Henry recognized, a picture he had taken on Fritz's disposable camera. Fritz in the distance walking along a tussocky ridge somewhere in Canterbury, the faint thread of a path both in front and behind. A man-alone picture, the feeling of distant prospects. Next to the picture was a scrap of paper on which a quote had been copied out in Fritz's squat, capitalized handwriting: *"Temperamentally, I am not only careless and irregular, but melancholy; still I have fought both down."* Henry did not recognize the words but the tone was familiar, just the kind of fierce, self-mastery that Fritz liked.

Henry returned to his own room. This room was much smaller than Fritz's, less a room and more a sort of slot, a hallway with a bed in it. There were still some things he hadn't unpacked. He tidied up carefully, folding his clothes and rearranging his books. The quote rattled in his head while he worked, irritating and smug. He didn't know who the words belonged to but he knew the type of writer it would have come from. Fritz liked to read books about the sea, uncharted rivers, men wrestling with their demons in thick jungles. Books where women were either distraction or consolation. Henry wiped down the small chest of drawers at the foot of his bed, arranged his few toiletries on top of it. He felt girlish and fussy, somehow bourgeois, about his need to make things nice. While he made the adjustments he kept feeling as if Fritz were loitering in the doorway, following his careful movements, smirking at his flagrant displays of materialism and conventionality.

————

Fritz got home late that night. Henry woke to thuds and shambling sounds. At first he thought his brother was in the hallway, but then he felt the old box spring mattress drop and chime and Fritz was in the room with him, sitting right there on his bed.

"Erica," Fritz whispered thickly. "Wait, wait, I mean Henry. Henry." And he patted Henry's shoulder through the duvet. "Sorry. *Henry*. We should go swimming," he said. "After work tomorrow. Let's go swimming."

His brother was so drunk that his words came out slowly, thick and halting. Again, he patted, then shoved, Henry's shoulder through the duvet.

"Okay," Henry said. He was still muddled up in sleep. "Let's go swimming."

Fritz reeled back and lay beside Henry. It was a single bed, they were lying side to side. Henry could smell something yeasty and stale, like a beer-soaked carpet.

"It's pretty cool," Fritz said after a while. "The whole you being Henry and… I just want you to know that it's cool."

Henry didn't know what to say. Perhaps if the conversation hadn't occurred in this strange half-place of drunkenness and sleep he might have conjured up some kind of indignation. But, half-asleep, he felt his throat seize a little.

After a long pause he said, "Thanks, Fritz."

He waited, hoping Fritz would say something else sweet, or maybe pat him again through the duvet. He even rolled a little closer so that his arm pressed hard up against his brother's. But Fritz's breath deepened and he started to wheeze a little in the back of his throat. Henry lay there, wide awake, and listened as Fritz's breathing gradually turned into snoring.

When he next woke up, Fritz was gone.

———

They had left the truck parked in the sun and it was baking and airless when Henry opened the doors at the end of the day, the metal of his seat belt scalding when he snapped it into place. Fritz turned right when they reached the end of the Inverary Lodge driveway, which wasn't the direction they turned if they were going home, but Henry made himself remain silent. If Fritz wasn't going to explain where he was taking them, then he wasn't going to ask. Somehow, when he was with Fritz, Henry had begun to feel as if asking too many questions, even displaying mild curiosity about what they were going to do next, was a personal failing, marking him as unspontaneous. So he kept silent, playing with the vents to try and flush the hot, stale air from the cab. Only as they turned up the road to Omaui did Henry deduce that Fritz was driving them to the big beach. Henry glanced over at his brother, but Fritz's eyes didn't leave the road. The day had passed without either of them mentioning what had happened the night before, and Henry wondered whether Fritz might have been so drunk he didn't actually remember. They turned onto the gravel road, the dust banking palely on either side of the truck, the beach getting closer. Was this Fritz's way of saying that he *did* remember the nighttime visit? Was this him making good on the suggestion that they would go swimming? Or was it just what he would do anyway, on a hot afternoon?

They parked in the low dunes. Stiff, spiny grass fringed the beach, below them a wide streak of grey sand. The tide was out and the sea, glinting in the distance, looked shallow, with humped sandbars breaking the surface here and there. Fritz never swam in swimming togs, which he declared to be pointless, and because Henry hadn't brought any swimming things with him to work he wore his underwear, too, running after his brother toward the water. The water was shallow and Fritz, who was a few paces ahead of Henry, flung himself into it when he was only knee-deep, wallowing and splashing and shouting.

Henry did the same. The collision with the cold water seemed to cure Fritz of his aloofness and he immediately tried to leap on top of Henry, who squirmed away and half-crawled, half-swam out to slightly deeper waters.

"I saw a beached whale here once," Fritz said, following Henry out but making no further moves to pin him. "Or maybe it died at sea and washed up. Either way, it was already dead."

"Do you remember when we saw all the fish in Fiji?"

"Of course I do."

That trip to Fiji had been the big summer holiday of their childhood, its events retold and retold, the creamy children's mocktails becoming legendary in Henry's memory, so rich and sweet that real cocktails had been a shocking disappointment. One day, on the beach outside their hotel, they had found hundreds of stranded fish. Small, blue-black fish, a carpet of them on the sand. Henry and Fritz had tried to pick them up and return them to the water, but there were so many fish that the task had become daunting, pointless. The fins of the fish had been sharp, stiffer than he expected, a coarse fibreglass texture Henry could still conjure up in his hands. No one seemed to know or care where the fish had come from, or why they were there. Then the tide had come in and taken all the dead and dying fish away. Only a few hours later the beach was white and perfect, like the stranding had never happened.

"So weird," said Henry.

"Weird that we even went to Fiji."

"What do you mean?"

"Well, Mum and Deb were arguing so much then," Fritz said. "I thought they were going to split up. We couldn't really afford to go, anyway."

Henry's memory held no such information, it was all piña coladas, stranded fish, those fascinating ornaments in the gift shop, assembled from glue and tiny shells. But Fritz had been almost thirteen and Henry only seven.

The water was just waist-high so they were both crouched, gently bobbing around as they spoke, only their heads above the surface. While they talked, Henry realized that Fritz had probably never seen his chest before, and even though he was now shirtless his brother still hadn't remarked on it. At the flat, Henry had been making sure he slipped on a T-shirt after showering and never walked to his room in just a towel. This was less to do with his own self-consciousness and more to do with protecting Fritz. In truth, Henry never quite knew if he wanted people to comment or not. He didn't know if he preferred the earnest yet somehow patronizing affirmations some people felt they should offer, or the studied, woke indifference of others. But under the water, invisible to Fritz, he ran his hands over the smooth plane of his chest and felt a private surge of joy. It would be so much easier if there was no one else to deal with. No one else's reactions to anticipate, manage, or appease. If it were just him, slowly becoming alive to himself.

They walked back up the beach to the truck, their shadows hunched like gargoyles at their feet.

"What were they arguing about, back then?" asked Henry.

"Oh, the usual bullshit," said Fritz morosely.

Henry had a vision of his brother in Fiji. A skinny, tan boy wearing giant, stiff Dickies shorts. Laughing, shreds of mango caught in the tracks of his silver braces. He had followed Fritz everywhere, all holiday long, trailing down the beach behind him, dogging him to the kid's zone where Fritz had made friends with some American boys. Henry's mother had even taken him aside at one point, saying that he had to let Fritz do his own thing sometimes; if he did that then Fritz would be nicer to him when they did hang out together. He could still remember the shame of this talk, his mother's careful wording, the understanding that his presence was something to be rationed, something Fritz needed protecting from. Do your own thing, his mother would say, just do your own thing for a while.

Fritz took a towel from the back of the truck, dried himself off, tossed it to Henry. Henry began to dry himself.

"Last night," Henry began, "when you came into my room."

"Yeah, sorry about that, I was hammered."

"You said we should go swimming?"

"And so we did." Fritz was upright now, his eyes closed, leaning back against the truck.

"And you said you thought it was cool... me being Henry?"

"And I do."

Henry waited, although he knew nothing else was coming. Then they got in the truck and drove home, the breeze riffling in through the half-open windows, his arms pleasantly tired from working, a blood-warmed, animal peace spreading though his body.

———

It turned out Fritz had a girlfriend, or a sort-of girlfriend. Hana. She was related to Snowy in some unspecified way, a niece or a cousin, Henry couldn't tell which. He had discovered the existence of Hana when Snowy had teased Fritz about her, making some garrulous joke about how Fritz shouldn't get her pregnant, inviting Henry into the joke with a raising of his eyebrows. Henry had laughed, then wished he hadn't.

After work on Friday, at the end of a long week of working on the roof, Fritz took Henry to meet her at the pub. Hana was already there, leaning at the bar talking to the bartender. When she saw them she sprang up, hugged them both. She made Fritz take off his ugly orange work fleece and, when he sheepishly kept his arms clamped at his sides, she gave his armpits a brisk sniff and told him not to worry, he didn't smell. Henry saw the careful way his brother watched Hana, the way he became attentive and slightly stiff around her, and understood that he loved her. Henry could see why. Hana had a commanding face, short dark hair, something merry in her glance that made Henry want to be her co-conspirator. While Fritz looked on, she asked Henry all the questions no one else had asked: what he studied in Wellington, why he was down here, what Fritz was like as a big brother. She was funny, with the cool-girl quality that seemed to demand devotion, allegiance. Henry tried to make her laugh with his descriptions of work, of Toby and Snowy. He was performing, turning his moments of embarrassment into self-deprecating comedy. Watching Hana laugh, Henry remembered how he was actually capable of being funny and charming, and he felt an ungenerous flare of triumph as he noted Fritz's growing reserve, the hint of something guarded in the way he held himself back from the edge of the table.

They got a second round of beers, then a third. Bad karaoke started up in the back of the pub, ignorable, until a guy in a hoodie began slurring his way through "If You Don't Know Me by Now." Henry and Hana both strained to watch the fiasco from their table, while Fritz drank his beer, uninterested. The man's friends were heckling him but he carried on, resolute, barely moving his body, the microphone held so close to his face that the sounds of his mouth came crashing, loud and plosive, over the sound system.

It was Toby, Henry realized. The man was Toby! He nudged his brother, wide-eyed, and Fritz nodded, apparently already aware. The song finished to whoops and boos and some smart-aleck applause. When Toby left the stage, he went straight past the group that Henry had assumed were his friends. Alone, he made his way to the bar, walking with the kind of deliberation mustered only by the very, very drunk.

"Should we go say hi?"

Fritz shook his head. "I wouldn't bother, he's pretty far gone."

"You know that guy?"

"That's Toby," Henry told Hana. "Toby from work."

"*That's* Toby?"

Henry had just been talking about Toby, the way he farted at work, the way he ate so many mini sausage rolls. He watched as Toby lowered himself onto a seat at the bar. "We should go say hi, shouldn't we?"

Fritz gave another small shake of his head but Henry felt gleeful, bold. Hana's eyes were on him. He got up and made his way over to Toby, clapped him on the shoulder, a hearty gesture that he could never have managed sober. It seemed to take Toby a long time to recognize him, but when he did his expression didn't soften, he didn't smile.

"What are *you* doing here?"

"I'm just saying hi," Henry said. "Me and Fritz are sitting over there."

Toby didn't look to where Henry had pointed, that was probably the most disconcerting thing; instead, he just held Henry's gaze and continued glowering at him. Henry stood there for a moment. Then he fled back across the bar to the table where Hana and Fritz sat.

"He just glared at me."

"What the hell!" said Hana. "What's his problem?"

"Maybe he doesn't like you either," Fritz said.

"What do you mean?"

"Well, you don't really like him."

"That's not true…"

"You don't," said Fritz.

"Well, it was still rude." Henry looked appealingly to Hana. "Wasn't it?"

"I think it's more rude to go and say hi to someone when you've just been ripping into them," said Fritz. Then he took a measured sip of his beer, looking steadily at Henry over the rim of his pint.

Oh, Fritz was so high on his high horse you could barely see him. Henry wanted to punch his brother, to pummel him the way he had when he was little. He knew just how it would feel, his fists flying, driven by fury, indignation, and, worst of all, agreement. But he mastered himself, sat back down on his stool, picked up his beer. Hana moved around the table and slipped herself under Fritz's arm.

"Well, Toby's not going to be a hard act to follow," she said. "What song should *I* sing?"

———

The next afternoon Henry and Fritz drove out of town, on their way to collect Hana. They were all going tramping. They had concocted the plan the night before. Henry would have been happy to abandon the idea now that they were hungover, now that it looked like rain was coming, but that wasn't Fritz's way of doing things. The truck smelled of McDonald's; two cheeseburgers and a milkshake churned uneasily in Henry's stomach. Farmland sheeted past the window, empty pasture broken up by the dark, hulking loaves of windbreak hedges.

"The thing is," Fritz was saying, "I don't know why you have this need to *connect* with everyone."

"I don't *need* to," said Henry, his hackles rising. "I just don't like feeling like I can't."

"What, you want to be able to go anywhere? Feel at ease anywhere?"

"I guess."

"Well, okay, so do I. So does everyone."

"Yeah, okay, and I feel like you can."

"Don't be an idiot," said Fritz.

"Well, you *seem* like you can."

"I get on fine with my workmates, yeah, but how do you think I would feel in your classes? Or at, I don't know, a fancy academic party or whatever?"

"I'm a student, I don't go to—"

Fritz spoke over him. "I'd feel weird, of course. Out of my depth. Uncomfortable. Like you at work, right?"

Henry hated the conversation, wished he had never begun it. This imaginary party filled with snooty academics was absurd.

"So what's the difference?" Fritz pressed. "Why should you get to be everyone and do everything?"

Henry said nothing. This was Fritz's tactic when he didn't like a conversation: prevailing with silence. So he could do it, too. He leaned forward, fiddled with the radio. There was a problem with the truck's stereo and whatever station Henry got, no matter how crisp it came through at first, the music would buffet and sizzle after about a minute. Somehow this static seemed a symptom of how far south they were; Bluff like a hook of land hanging off the South Island, an afterthought, like a cedilla dangling off a C, and beyond Bluff there was nothing, nothing except a few scattered islands and then, of all places, Antarctica. Henry rolled the dial back and forth, looking for a song that might lift the mood. The night before, when they got home from the pub, he had drunkenly tried to explain himself to Fritz, tried to explain that he was only mean about Toby because he was intimidated by him, intimidated by both Toby and Snowy, even by Fritz, sometimes. Instead of offering comfort or advice Fritz had seemed almost triumphant: "I knew you wouldn't like it," he'd said, he was almost crowing, "I warned you!"

This was true, Fritz had warned him, and Henry hadn't forgotten. That was back in September, three months before, when they had both gone home for Henry's mother's birthday. Henry had flown down from Wellington and Fritz, who had said he wasn't going to come, impulsively drove the thirteen hours from Bluff, arriving elated and stinking of Red Bull and cigarettes. It was a giddy meal with plenty of wine and Fritz doing his big, gusting shouts of laughter that made everyone else laugh, too. Henry had made a cheesecake. He lit the ranks of candles and then raised the cake aloft and glowing, a feeling of piety as he carried the cake from the darkened kitchen into the darkened dining room.

While they ate the cake, Fritz had talked about the summer ahead, how business was good, how his boss would have to take on another guy. Listening to this, Henry had his big idea. The plan arriving inside him with a *chock* of certainty. Between semesters, during the summer, he had stayed in Wellington and worked for his father in the English department. He was spoiled in this way, a little embarrassed that he hadn't worked in cafés or painted houses or gone apple-thinning like some of his friends. But that night he had seen clearly what he should do. He should live with Fritz for the summer and work as a roofer, be outside all day, roughen his hands, work for the first time as a man alongside other men. Thick and fast had come the visions of himself being handsome in overalls, elbow poking out the window of a truck, standing with his hands on his hips squinting at some complicated problem. At first, Fritz hadn't taken him seriously but Henry had insisted. By then he had been on hormones for almost two years, he'd had his chest surgery, he was passing completely. To all intents and purposes a man. Fritz had been flushed, his eyes gleaming and wicked in the dim room. It's nothing to do with all that stuff, he'd said, waving his big hand toward Henry's chest, I just don't think you'll like it. *I just don't think you'll like it.*

———

Fritz, Hana, and Henry stood in the doorway of the hut, strobing their headlamps from one unsavory corner to another. The hut looked small, dirty, full of mouse droppings and empty soup cans. Henry waited for someone else to say it: the hut looked pretty awful. But, of course, they had walked there and now they had to stay. So they shrugged off their packs and while Fritz and Hana went to get water Henry moved around the room, lighting the candle stubs that some other trampers had left. He waited as the little blue flames clung to the wicks, strengthened, and then stretched upward. In the modest light the candles doled out the hut became almost cozy, the dirty corners retreating into flattering shadow. Henry swept the mouse droppings up, put the cans in a plastic bag.

Hana came back and they put the water on to boil, set the mattresses up in the bunks. Fritz was now out in the lean-to, chopping wood. Gender and the division of labor, Henry thought, listening to the thud and bite of the axe. He got the whiskey out of the bag, poured it into their three plastic camping mugs, and tried to turn off his internal critic.

They ate sausages and instant mashed potato for dinner. Then, even though it wasn't very cold, Fritz made a fire in the woodstove. The hut grew uncomfortably warm. Fritz wanted to play cards but to Henry's great relief, no one had remembered to pack them. Instead, they drank the whiskey and chatted. After his second mugful, Henry felt like there was a long, smoldering fuse running from his throat and down into his belly. His cheeks were flaming, his tongue loosened at its root. He and Hana were doing most of the talking and, without really intending to, Henry found himself coming out to her. He had already forgiven her in advance for whatever she might say, but she just grabbed his hand and said, "Hey, thanks for telling me," which was graceful, more graceful than anything Henry could have invented for her to say.

When she went outside to pee, Fritz turned to Henry, speaking for the first time in what seemed like hours. "Why'd you tell her that? I thought it was a secret?"

"It's not a *secret*," said Henry, indignant.

"You told me not to tell anyone."

"That doesn't make it a secret."

Fritz looked annoyed. "Doesn't it?"

Henry wanted to explain himself but Hana was already coming back, kicking off her shoes, more firewood stacked up in her arms, her bare skin slick with the rain. She looked lovely. She *was* lovely. The night before, she had sung "Heart of Glass" and Henry had felt so lumpen, so ponderously male, standing next to Fritz while they watched her dance and sashay and strike mock-ingénue poses, pointing at them in the back of the room. Henry had leaned into his brother, whispered, "Your girlfriend is amazing." Fritz had shook his head wonderingly. "I know."

———

Later, Henry lay in his bunk, thinking over what Fritz had said. Was it a secret? He wasn't ashamed, not exactly, but it was true that he wanted to conceal the fact of his transition from some people. He argued with himself: No, it was only from people who might judge him, or treat him differently, or even do him harm. But was that even true? Did part of him still believe that there was something lesser about himself? Other people always seemed so solid to Henry. Hana and Fritz, they were so… *substantial*, whereas he felt himself to be ill-defined, sketched very lightly on the surface of the world. But maybe that had nothing to do with transition, maybe that was just how he was.

The therapist he'd been to see in Wellington, Calvin, would be exasperated with this train of thought. "It takes strength to change, Henry," Calvin would say, "it takes strength to become your authentic self." Henry always wanted to believe Calvin but he had never understood exactly how it was you determined what the authentic self was. Was he any more *authentic* now than he had been a few years before? The question felt like a riddle, infuriating, circular. When he went spelunking down into the depths of himself there was no gleaming kernel of selfhood waiting there, just a sense of murkiness, of further reaches. What did other people find in there?

The hut was dimly lit, quiet apart from the shifting sound of cinders in the stove. Hana was already asleep but Fritz lay stretched out on his back, holding a paperback in one hand, the left hand coming up to the spine of the book when he turned a page. Fritz had such beautiful hands, big but delicate. His brother's eyes moved down the ladder of one page, then across and down the other. A page was turned, Fritz's rough thumb scraping on the paper. Watching someone else read had always amazed Henry, the incredible privacy of it. All he saw was his brother, the puppetry of his hands and the pages, but inside Fritz's mind who knew what voice was speaking, what scenes were being played out, what thoughts were being kindled out of view.

———

Monday was their last day at Inverary Lodge. The broken terracotta shards had risen to the top of the skip and the roof deck was finished: clean, new plywood covering the whole angular landscape of the roof. Another contractor was going to hang the new tiles, a restoration job that apparently Snowy wasn't qualified to do. In the meantime the roof was to be wrapped in plastic to protect it from the elements. While the others began this, Henry was tasked with cleaning up the site, sweeping the front steps, dumping wood scraps and tufts of insulation into the skip. When he had tidied up the most obvious messes he made his way around the garden, picking up any stray tiles from the lawn. He hadn't been told to do this, but at least he would appear busy if Snowy looked down from the roof.

When there were no more tiles to collect, Henry went to use the bathroom. The owners had left a side door unlocked, and it opened into a dusty hallway that contained an empty storage room and a narrow, pistachio-colored bathroom. The interior of the house was cool, dim and private. Though they had only spent a week at Inverary, the hallway and the bathroom felt like his domain. Each time Henry went inside, he felt like he was ducking into some quiet, sanctified place, away from the glare and bustle of the roof. As far as he knew, he was the only one who used the side door. The other guys pissed in the garden, but Henry did not want to get caught squatting in the bushes so he made two trips inside each day. He limited himself to two trips, lest the other guys began to think he had some sort of bowel problem. He'd wondered if Toby and Snowy had noticed that he didn't pee in the garden like they did. In the bathroom at Inverary he always left the seat up afterward, as if when Snowy or Toby chanced to come in they would see this signal and realize he wasn't actually taking a series of dumps throughout the day, he was just someone who *preferred* to urinate inside rather than outside. Henry knew no one was paying this kind of anthropological attention to his bathroom habits but he lifted the seat regardless, and each time he stood up from peeing and clacked it back against the cistern, he experienced a private moment of exasperation and hilarity.

Henry washed his hands, smoothed his hair in the mirror. The glass was foxed with age, the light in the green bathroom murky. The mirror offered a pleasantly lo-fi reflection, in which he could choose to see certain things, and ignore others. His face was both uglier and more handsome than it had been before, both more and less like himself. If he looked in the mirror, if he waited long enough, he could see his old face swim, momentarily, beneath his current one, as if two sheets of acetate were laid one over the other and someone was shifting them slightly. He tried it now, waiting for Erica to come into focus, then Henry, then Erica, then back to Henry. *Henry*, he thought, with a disorienting sense of amazement. Who on earth was *Henry*? Sometimes, he felt like he had invented Henry and now everyone was indulging him in his game. Sometimes, just hearing his new name in the mouths of others still caught him off-guard. But being called his old name was more jarring. That still happened occasionally, when his mother or Fritz or one of his old friends forgot. Correcting them was awkward, and he never felt entirely convincing when he did it. As if the very idea of having a name, or even a face, was somehow trivial, embarrassing for him to insist upon it.

He stared at himself in the mirror, trying to catch himself as a stranger might. Henry stared warily back at himself. Maybe, deep down, he was neither Henry or Erica. Perhaps he was something else entirely. He felt a stirring, as if behind each of the names, beneath each of the faces, was a presence that balked at having to declare itself to be anything at all.

———

At ten it was time for morning tea. The others were sitting on the scaffolding. Behind them, the roof was already half-sheathed in plastic, a blazing white canopy against the blue sky. Snowy called out for Henry to come up and join them. They had a bottle of Budget cola, a bag of chips, some chocolate biscuits between them. A little party, to celebrate how quickly they'd got the roof done. Henry took a seat next to his brother, dug his hand into the bag of chips.

"I heard you boys had a pretty big night on Saturday," Snowy said.

"Pretty big," said Fritz. "Not nearly as big as Toby's though."

Toby just shrugged, turtled deep inside his hoodie as usual. No one said anything for a moment.

"Well," said Snowy. "What'd you do, Tobe?"

"Just went down the pub."

Very softly, very softly, Fritz began to sing the opening lines of "If You Don't Know Me by Now." Toby said nothing but Henry could see that his face was getting red. Fritz kept going, building in timbre and intensity. Finally, Toby gave Fritz a shove.

"He put on quite the show," said Fritz.

"I forgot about even doing that," Toby said. He managed what looked to Henry like a shame-faced grin.

"Well, I'll personally never forget it," Fritz said. "It's burned into my memory forever."

He leaned over and grabbed some of the chips, giving Henry a small wink. Henry ate his own handful of chips. He had the feeling that Fritz was dancing circles around him, or maybe offering him some sort of truce, but he couldn't have pinpointed exactly how. And anyway, at that moment he didn't really care. He ate one chocolate biscuit, then another. The talk moved on to other things, the week ahead, the next job.

Henry let the chat around him fade. The sun was warm on his face, the sky clear. In the distance he could see the smelter at Tiwai Point, a plume of white rising from low, glinting buildings. The day was so still that the steam hung plumb, perpendicular to the horizon. It looked solid but as he watched it frayed and thinned and then, as his eyes strained for the last threads, it was gone.

Brazus Valley Atmerile Texas
by Joseph E Yoakum

HEART PROBLEMS

On the day Violet Morse died in Butte, Montana, the headlines told of a German dirigible fighting to outrun a storm across the Atlantic Ocean in its record-setting round-the-world trip. Charles Lindbergh reported seeing Mayan ruins from the air after turning inland over Quintana Roo, an area "white men had never penetrated." In Butte, the thirty-four-year-old wife of the president of the Montana Coca-Cola Company had died shortly after bearing her fifth baby, and the police were taking fingerprints from a dead man in an attempt to identify a carnival follower who'd been shot and killed during what authorities called "a small riot."

Butte in 1929 was known to be disreputable. That Violet died in Butte was the first suggestion that something was not natural about her death. It was a mining town, after all, so first and foremost, it was dirty. One young woman reporting her impressions of Butte in the early years of the twentieth century told of the ugliness; the smeltery fumes had killed all the vegetation. People had to go out in the early morning before the fumes got intense, and they wore handkerchiefs over their faces.

In 1907, *Craftsman* magazine published an article titled, "Redeeming the Ugliest Town on Earth." It was about Butte.

The city was full of miners with a high percentage of unattached young men. Butte's red-light district rivaled those of New Orleans and San Francisco. One prostitute, self-described as sheltered in spite of five years in the bordellos in eastern cities, recalled her "shuddering horror" at Butte's "seamy side of the underworld." When Carrie Nation brought her public campaign against vice to Butte, the city's most prominent madame, May Maloy, came out into the street, where she and Carrie Nation engaged in fisticuffs in front of a gathered crowd. Carrie Nation lost.

Violet's body was found on Thursday, August 1, 1929.

From that day on, Violet Morse's public identity was fixed: the reports of inquests and autopsies all described her as a twenty-two-year-old Anaconda schoolteacher.

Two years earlier, when there were still at least a few possible lives Violet might have lived, her name began to turn up in a college newspaper out of Dillon, Montana. Dillon is the county seat of Beaverhead County in southwestern Montana, where online maps still refer to large geographical areas as the Hoffman Place, the Ball Place, the Fries Place—names of ranchers who owned huge spreads.

Violet grew up with her parents in Anaconda, seventy-five miles from Dillon. Isack Morse, her father, was an engineer, according to census records. Anaconda was home to the Anaconda Smelter Stack, which smelted copper from the Butte mines and was the tallest masonry structure in the world in 1919. Anaconda's population peaked in 1930 at almost thirteen thousand souls. Lucille Ball lived there briefly as a child. The first surgeon to successfully separate conjoined twins came from Anaconda.

I'd like to follow Flaubert's advice and give you three vivid details about Violet's physical appearance, but I can only rely on news sources, which called her pretty and popular. Somehow I imagine she was a brunette, but her mother emigrated from Sweden, so it's more likely she was blond.

In February 1927, two years before her death, Violet received her teaching certificate along with dozens of other young women at the Montana State Normal School in Dillon. The following month, she was chosen for the varsity volleyball team.

The *Montana Standard*, the daily paper of Butte, which was one of the largest cities in the western United States at that time, had a section called Anaconda Briefs and one called Jackson Notes. Violet turns up in both, as she was from Anaconda but now teaching school in Jackson. In early December 1928, we learn that Miss Violet Morse visited friends in Jackson Saturday afternoon. On Christmas Day 1928, "Miss Joy Morse, student of the Normal College at Dillon and Miss Violet Morse, teacher at Jackson, are in the city to spend the holidays with their parents."

Violet was the oldest of five children, according to the 1920 census. Her parents, Isaac and Christine, were both forty-five years old that Christmas of 1928, the last time they'd celebrate that holiday with their eldest daughter. Iva, as the census named her, now known as Joy or Ivey, according to different newspaper articles—these personal name changes make historical research difficult—was three years younger than Violet. Then came two teenage brothers and another sister, ten years younger than Violet.

In March 1929, the *Dillon Tribune* reported on "a delightful dinner," hosted by the Neidts on Sunday at their ranch home. "Dinner" in this case means lunch, and a ranch home means an actual house on a ranch rather than the low-slung homes of midcentury America, oriented around the garage and patio.

Also in March in Dillon, Miss Violet Morse and Mrs. Camas Nelson were the hostess committee for a session of the Royal Neighbors. After the meeting these hostesses arranged for the members to be "entertained at cards and luncheon… Pinochle was the diversion, eight tables being at play. High scores went to Mrs. Alan Dansie and Mark Clemow." Mark Clemow will turn up again in this investigation.

In May 1929, just three months before Violet died, she visited her sister Joy, and a week later she spent the weekend in Dillon, returning to Jackson to teach school Monday morning. Who was she meeting in Dillon? Was that the fateful encounter? Lest you think Violet Morse was somehow special to be named so often in the newspapers, I offer the full listing of the Jackson County News from the *Dillon Tribune* for Friday, May 17, 1929:

Rosie Wenger returned from Dillon on Tuesday having been there for a track meet.

Miss Violet Morse returned from Dillon on Monday.

The P.T.A. held a splendid meeting Friday, the county nurse was present and examined the children and the teachers put on a fine health program.

A.W. Wilson left for Butte last week where he will remain for some time having dental work done.

Our last sighting of Violet alive comes from the *Dillon Tribune* on Friday, June 21, 1929. "Mr. and Mrs. Diggle Emerick, Miss Violet Morse and Tom Lubin were week-end guests at the Clemow home." When I read this, I hadn't yet seen the inquest results, so I didn't understand it was Clemow I'd want to trace, Mark Clemow. So instead I went after Tom Lubin but found nothing. I chased Diggle Emerick for a generation or two, exploring how the Emericks came to Montana, his or his wife's illness and travel to the Mayo Clinic, until finally I decided this wasn't the key to Violet's demise.

What can we know for sure about Violet's death? Only what the newspapers reported, and even that, as we'll see, raises as many questions as answers.

THE MONTANA STANDARD, BUTTE, MONTANA | AUGUST 2, 1929
WELL-KNOWN ANACONDA GIRL PASSES IN BUTTE
ANACONDA. AUG. 1—(SPECIAL)—Miss Violet Morse, 22, beloved daughter of Mr. and Mrs. Isack Morse, 617 Walnut Street, died this afternoon in a Butte hospital after a brief illness. Miss Morse was born here and received her education in the Anaconda schools. Her death is mourned by a host of friends.

Besides her parents, she is survived by two sisters, the Misses Ivey and Inis Morse and two brothers, Robert and Elmer Morse, all of Anaconda. The body is at the White chapel in Butte, pending funeral arrangements.

THE MONTANA STANDARD, BUTTE, MONTANA | AUGUST 3, 1929
AUTOPSY ORDERED IN CASE OF GIRL FOUND DEAD HERE, FATHER OF VIOLET MORSE, YOUNG ANACONDA WOMAN, REQUESTS AN INVESTIGATION
Following the request of Isack Morse of Anaconda that an investigation be made into the death of his daughter, Miss Violet Morse, 22 years old, County Attorney Harrison J. Freeborn yesterday ordered that an autopsy be held in the case.

The girl was found dead in a Nevada Street home here Thursday morning, authorities said. They did not state what suspicions had led to the investigation.

GREAT FALLS TRIBUNE, GREAT FALLS, MONTANA | AUGUST 3, 1929
DEATH OF ANACONDA GIRL TO BE PROBED AT FATHER'S BEHEST
BUTTE, AUG. 2.—(AP)—An autopsy and investigation into the circumstances surrounding the death here Thursday of Violet Morse, 22, well-known Anaconda girl, was ordered Friday by County Attorney Harry Freebourn. Miss Morse died suddenly and the investigation was requested by her parents. Isack Morse, father of the girl, refused to tell reporters why he asked for the probe.

Already, we can see contradictions and confusion: first it is reported that Violet died in the hospital after a brief illness, but then it comes out that she was found dead in a house on Nevada Street.

Violet's father requested the investigation but refused to say why. We can only imagine the shame complicating his grief, but he had to have been considering the family reputation and his four younger children. At first, I could find almost nothing on the man's life—Isack or Isaac Morse of Anaconda seemed to disappear after his fifteen minutes of fame surrounding his daughter's death. But when I searched for records on Violet's siblings, I discovered that their father went by Roy. His full name was Isaac Del Roy Morse, but everywhere on ancestry.com and in newspaper wedding announcements, I found him and his wife referred to as Mr. and Mrs. Roy Morse. In giving a different name to the reporters, I suspect he was trying to protect his other children, especially his two surviving daughters, from the shame of this scandal. He wouldn't be the only one to publicly deny or distance himself from Violet after her death.

The name changes of Violet's father and sister are perhaps trivial illustrations of the difficulty of knowing accurately even simple factual matters from the past, let alone private actions not made public. In the weeks after her death, some news articles began to report that Violet was twenty-three years old. Was this a correction? Had she had a birthday between the death and the inquest? We make do with what facts we have and then conjecture, based on knowledge of human nature and other contemporary people of similar class and location, but ultimately we depend on our own psychology to imagine the details of events we cannot know.

THE MONTANA STANDARD, BUTTE, MONTANA | AUGUST 28, 1929

UNKNOWN PERSON KILLED TEACHER, VERDICT ASSERTS, JURY REPRIMANDS GERTRUDE PITKANEN FOR SIGNING OF FALSE DEATH CERTIFICATE

Censuring Mrs. Gertrude Pitkanen for signing a false death certificate and for having failed to notify proper officials of a death, a coroner's jury found at an inquest yesterday that Violet Morse, 22-year-old Anaconda teacher, died last August 1st as a result of a criminal operation, performed by an unknown person.

In spite of a death certificate saying heart problems, what had become clear from the reports, no matter how circumspect the newspapers might be and how inconclusive the final verdict, is that Violet Morse died as a result of trying to end a pregnancy. I'd initially thought that June weekend with Tom Lubin and Mr. and Mrs. Diggle Emerick was the key. But if Violet conceived in late June, could she already have lined up an abortion for August 1st—or more accurately, the last days of July, since she was found dead on August 1st? How could she be so sure? If her periods were regular, she would've missed one in early July. But hope and fear would've still been battling it out, I would think, for a few weeks. No, even a highly organized and decisive schoolteacher would not have acted so soon, to my way of thinking. She had to be farther gone to have made such a choice.

The pretty school teacher was found dead at 638 Nevada Street in a house where she had rented a room for a few days. The session yesterday concluded the inquest, which started two weeks ago. Testimony of Dr. J.R.E. Sievers and Dr. P.E. Kane, autopsy surgeons, and a written report from Dr. T.F. Walker of Walker Laboratories in Great Falls indicated that the girl had died as the result of an attempted abortion.

Mrs. Pitkanen, who testified that she is not a physician but a licensed chiropractor, signed the death certificate giving myocarditis, a heart disease, as the cause of death. She testified at the inquest yesterday that she had not treated the Morse girl, although the latter had asked her to help her.

A. Lafty, a friend of the Morse family, testified that Mrs. Pitkanen had admitted to him and the family shortly after the death of the girl that she had given her "tablets."

YOUTH TESTIFIES

Mark Clemow, son of a prominent Jackson rancher, near whose home Miss Morse was teaching school, also was called to testify. He denied that he had been in Butte with Miss Morse the day before she died, as was indicated by the testimony of other witnesses. Clemow was engaged to Miss Morse and they were to have been married this fall, he said. He emphatically denied knowing anything connected with the illegal operation.

Mrs. Pitkanen declared that she was called to the girl's bedside after she had died and knew nothing of the cause of death. She admitted that she knew of the girl's condition, but had believed death due to some other cause. She explained her negligence in calling authorities before the body was removed by the undertaker with the statement that she "had forgotten" to call the coroner.

NO ACTION EXPECTED

The jury under Acting Coroner J.J. McNamara declared that "Violet Morse, 22, of 617 Walnut Street, Anaconda, died as a result of a criminal operation performed by a person or persons unknown to us."

The verdict also contained the following reprimand:

"We, the jury, censure Gertrude Pitkanen for signing a false death certificate and for having the body removed to the undertaking parlor without notifying the coroner."

Unknown persons are responsible for this criminal act. Is *criminal* a more accurate assessment than *tragic*? There's no question Violet's death was tragic: she was young and pretty and popular and about to marry the son of a rich and important rancher. The question, as in all tragedies, is whether Violet's downfall was due to a flaw in her own character, a wrong judgment. Or was it just the casual play of the gods we call luck? Perhaps the gods were actually punishing the young man, Mark Clemow, or the old man, Isack Del Roy Morse—both of whom would go on to suffer other unexpected losses—and thus Violet's womb was simply an instrument of dramatic action, collateral damage in the drama of someone else's fate.

The landscape of the western plains, including the foothills approaching the Rockies, is tough terrain, largely empty of human enclosures. Zebulon Pike called this region the Great American Desert, a term that would be contested and overturned as railroad companies needed settlers to populate the invented towns along the tracks. Montana has always felt like a mystery just out of reach, the contradiction between how lonely the landscape feels to me and the sentimental, even maudlin, nostalgia of my father's stories. Something about my character made me wonder how it was possible to be a person, let alone a woman, in such a wide-open, hard land, in a culture that valued one's ability to be silent, especially about personal matters. Silence was the interpersonal correlative to the landscape. And yet, there was always the luminosity at the horizon, drawing one on, the promise of some treasure just out of reach. Or maybe the landscape simply mirrored back one's self? To the person who didn't need others in the messy business of human life, perhaps it was friendly.

My people were from southeastern Montana, flatter and dryer than Anaconda, near the scene of the Battle of the Little Bighorn. All four of my grandparents met up and settled on the least fertile acreage in the continental United States.

Montana was on my mind in 2017, but not Butte or Anaconda. I was at a dinner party on the Upper West Side of Manhattan, when a woman my age, midfifties, told me about her grandparents coming from Anaconda. Her grandfather had worked his way up through the mining company, she said proudly, adding, "My grandmother and her sister took turns attending college, because they couldn't both afford to go at the same time. So one year her sister would attend while my grandmother taught school, and then next year they'd do the opposite."

My first response to the woman's story about her grandfather working his way up was irritation. My relatives never seemed to climb any ladders, working instead only horizontally across the country, always moving on before any value could be accrued, ever westward from West Virginia, Illinois, Bloody Kansas, to Montana and then Washington State. I changed direction at eighteen, taking the red-eye to New York City where I've stayed ever since.

My own grandmother had recently died at almost ninety-eight, making her contemporaneous with these virtuous ancestors of the dinner party woman, but Grandma Marge's eight marriages and divorces, the way she stayed on the move, felt like a different American story. She was a secret-keeper, so habitually closemouthed about anything substantive that she lost the ability to have a real conversation until the last few weeks of her life, when she'd come a bit unhinged, her white hair uncombed, her translucent face wild. In the TV room of the Olympia Arms Nursing Home, she answered what I thought was a simple question about whether she'd graduated high school with a quiet howl, "No, I was raped! I had to leave school."

I knew she'd married my grandfather, Frank Harrison, twice. I knew she'd married him the first time as a teenager and had her two children—my uncle and my mother—before she turned nineteen, but there now seemed to be so much I didn't know.

When I went back to the videotape I'd taken of Grandma at ninety, seven years earlier, it started to make more sense.

Me: "Did you... like... Frank right away?" (I was not sure what verb to use. They'd married each other twice, which I'd assumed meant they were driven by intense sexual desire. But she was my grandmother.)

Marge: silent for a long pause as her eyes slid from me to the floor, then a vague distance comes into her voice, "No, I was going with another boy. I didn't want to get married. I wanted to stay in school."

It was in that same videotaped interview that I learned I wasn't the first woman in my family to have a baby by C-section. I asked Marge about her births, and she told me the story of her first birth, my Uncle Stan, when she was seventeen, how she'd ridden into town for the Fourth of July celebration and had Stan three days later. Marge said that as she was approaching her due date the following year with her second baby—who would become my mother—my grandfather came to her and said, "I've made an arrangement with the doctor for you to have a cesarean. But you can't tell anyone, not even your mother."

This story was both shocking and somehow a confirmation of something I'd known: my first intimation of Grandma's C-section had come long before I interviewed her at her ninetieth birthday.

I was nine years old. The grass was that phosphorescent shade only visible during peak springtime when the whole universe manifests fecundity.

My mother had set up a homemade slip-and-slide in the backyard. There was a slight downhill under the clothesline, on which she'd laid out a big piece of clear plastic sheeting and then secured the gushing hose to the top of it, so that we, her five children, could approach it at a run and then throw our bodies on the wet, slippery ground to slide to the bottom.

As I stood up after sliding down, panting and happy, I suddenly saw in my mind's eye the scar on my mother's belly, from which she'd given birth to me. It might have been that we were all wearing swimsuits, or that the grass burns from miscalculating when to fling myself down triggered some sensory recall. Whatever the instigator of the scar memory, I saw it clearly that day.

The only problem was that it was not her scar.

My mother, Roberta, had five normal births. What I wouldn't find out for decades was that my grandmother had indeed had a cesarean section when she gave birth to my mother. How did that unknown association come so strongly into my mind, even if I was off by one generation?

That mysterious childhood memory was the only thing that justified, even to myself, this midlife obsessive investigation into why Frank Harrison forced his eighteen-year-old wife to have a cesarean section in 1935 in rural eastern Montana.

In 1935, the year of my mother's birth, a cesarean section would have been risky. A reliable supply of penicillin, eventually developed in Peoria, Illinois, in a single moldy cantaloupe—from which most of the worldwide supply still derives—had not yet been established. There was strenuous debate in obstetrical journals in the first half of the twentieth century, eventually establishing the low cervical transverse incision as the safest approach rather than the historically used classical vertical incision. Still, there were dangers, as discussed by Dr. Murdoch J. Cameron in his 1923 guide to the technique, based on 107 sections he'd performed while losing only one mother, making him something of a guru:

> On the other hand it is an operation for the specialist rather than the general practitioner, and this view should not be lost sight of as small maternity homes staffed by practitioners are being opened in all parts of the country. During extraction of the head I have known alarming haemorrhage result from extensive tearing of the tissues where a transverse incision had been made.

It is unlikely that Marge's doctor was a surgical expert.

Grandma didn't know why Frank Harrison had made this plan. She thought he might have owed the doctor money; they were gambling friends. She thought the doctor needed more experience. She said she'd heard the doctor's wife had died after a similar operation. Like most of Grandma's stories, that turned out to be false. But there was one fact that ultimately emerged as inarguable: after she had my mother by cesarean section when she was eighteen, my grandmother never had another child. She was sterile.

The British Medical Association in 1930 listed the three top indicators for cesarean section: contracted pelvis, placenta previa, and eclampsia. Placenta previa is not diagnosed until a woman is in labor and the placenta comes first, blocking the baby's way out, so that could not be the reason for Marge's section. Eclampsia generally comes on during late pregnancy, with high blood pressure, headaches, and swelling. It's rare during second pregnancies, and Marge would have known she had it.

Contracted pelvis, still the leading indicator for surgical birth to this day, is the idea that a woman's pelvis is too small. There was an elaborate system of pelvimetry in which various measurements were calculated to determine if a woman could give birth to the baby she was carrying. It's not unlike some of the brain-size theories about different racial intelligence levels put forward in the 1920s and 1930s. Like them, pelvimetry is fake science, but it testifies to a persistent fantasy about that most contested territory in a woman, along with the doctor's need, often with the conspiring help of the husband, to protect what we call during childbirth "the birth canal," which is known at all other times as the vagina.

The pelvis is not one bone; it's a system of several bones attached by membranes that stretch, gradually softening throughout the nine months of pregnancy to allow for labor. A tiny echo of that softening and stretching happens with each menstrual period, causing much of the discomfort we think of as PMS. Facts don't stop doctors from saying, sometimes as the first words to a woman they are meeting, "Your hips look a bit small. We may have to section you." My sister heard these words from an obstetrician two years before she gave birth at home to an eleven-pound baby.

Marge didn't have any trouble the first time. After she rode her horse into town, she was staying at her mother's when labor started. She got her history teacher to drive her to the hospital in Hardin, because he had a car. Marge remembers they had to stop to get the headlights fixed because it was dark. She was lying down in the back seat. "A black cat crossed our path," she said. (This was the kind of information Marge provided when I asked her about factual events.) At the hospital, Stan was born around midnight—Marge always said it was the sixth of July, even though the birth certificate lists the seventh. Either way, for a first-time mother to get to the hospital after dark—in the long days of July—and have the baby at midnight, we can conclude that Marge gave birth easily.

———

As of this writing, you can watch an actual C-section from 1930 on YouTube. "Cesarean Section at Full Term for Contracted Pelvis" shows Lieutenant Colonel Spencer Mort operating in London. The woman on the table is completely draped in white cloth, her face covered like a corpse, with just the top of her mountainous belly exposed.

She is a twenty-year-old woman, having her first baby. This diagnosis, then, is based on nothing real except what is in the minds of the doctors. Her "diagonal conjugate diameter" has been measured to be 3.25 inches. They have manually palpated the belly and determined—with certainty, they must feel— that she will be unable to birth her baby.

The preanesthetic treatment: 1/12 grain heroin hydrochloride given thirty minutes before surgery. Then gas and oxygen are applied over the face.

A four-and-a-half-inch incision is made vertically, with the belly button at the midpoint. Scissors are then used to snip open the tissues below. The uterus is cut open. Blood spurts up at this point, and several hands move in to limit the spray, forcing the spurt to angle downward. The black-and-white screen doesn't show the bright-red blood as a crime scene would. One surgeon inserts a hand up to his wrist into the woman's belly, as blood streams up and out onto the floor. He wrestles his arm around for several long seconds, then pulls up some pale limbs. The head is still inside the mother. Then it's up and out, and the baby is floppy, white and motionless, its head hanging loose. The doctor places it on a towel held out by a nurse. Meanwhile, another gloved and masked figure holds onto something inside the mother, probably the placenta. Throughout the video, a nurse places towel after towel around the belly to absorb the blood and other fluids coursing from the open abdomen. The surgeon attempts to remove the placenta and tissues, but they are "very adherent" and he must work delicately to avoid causing hemorrhage. An assistant "steadies the uterus" and applies pressure to the uterine arteries, while "Sister has given ½ cc Pituitrin," an extract of bovine posterior pituitary hormones, to encourage contractions and the release of the placenta. More towels. Finally the placenta is out.

The uterus is lifted out of the mother's body. The camera zooms in on gloved hands holding the uterus while the surgeon stitches with catgut. Medical journals featured discussion of the relative merits of catgut versus silk stitches. Catgut usually wins. It's not actually cat's guts; it's made by twisting together strands taken from the small intestines of healthy ruminants (cattle, sheep, goats) or from beef tendon.

The long threads, knitting together the uterus, are lifted up, stretched out, and cinched tightly like trussing a turkey or Scarlett O'Hara's waist, while several hands continually towel away blood.

Next step: "Anterior fossa of peritoneum cleared of blood clots by swabs." The pouch of Douglas, a little cul-de-sac between the rectum and the back wall of the uterus that tends to collect fluid, is cleaned out. The letters on the screen state "This is very important." As four hands scrub inside the woman with dish-towel-size swabs of cotton, intestines ooze up and out. Each time, they are pushed back in by gloved fingers.

The white text on black screen reads "Ovaries and tubes examined and found healthy. Patient not sterilised."

The uterus is popped back down into the cavity.

Two gloved hands now stitch the peritoneum closed, using catgut, while two other hands hold the edges of the skin together using scissorlike tongs, just ahead of the stitching. Finally, the threads are tied into knots and clipped, like a tailor hemming pants. The outer layer of skin gets silkworm gut sutures. The belly is doused with dark antiseptic fluid, the kind we used to use when we skinned our knees, then covered with layers of gauze and tape.

The total time elapsed was seventeen minutes: one minute to deliver the baby and sixteen minutes to put the woman back together.

D. M. Strang signed my mother's birth certificate. Momma told me she knew two things about the doctor. He moved from Montana to Pacific County, Washington, a memorable coincidence since it's where she has lived for the past twenty-five years. And he was famous for a triplets birth.

In the 1940 census, D. M. Strang, surgeon, lived in Pacific County. But the 1930 census also shows him living in Pacific County, self-employed as a doctor, so Momma's idea that he moved there after her birth in Montana isn't quite accurate. Strang was born and raised in Minnesota and attended Carleton College, where old yearbooks show him active in theater and other clubs. In 1907, he graduated from medical school and got married. In the next four years, he had a son and a daughter and was on the board of trustees of Northfield Hospital, owning shares and helping to establish this new institution. He delivered scores of babies, including his own son, at Northfield, signing the last birth certificate in May 1913. And then suddenly in June, he is in Sprague, Washington, a dot on the map fifty miles from Spokane, applying for a license to practice medicine in Washington State.

Why had he suddenly left his well-established life in Minnesota for somewhere so isolated?

He was still in Sprague in 1918, when his draft registration card tells us he was of medium build with blue eyes and brown hair. Records available attest to his attendance at many deaths, though this is perhaps because few encounters with physicians are recorded unless a birth or death is the result. Throughout the 1920s, he lived at various addresses in Seattle, according to city directories.

The 1930 census shows Strang and his family already living in Pacific County, and the *Centralia*, a daily newspaper, reported in 1933 that when little Robert Marg cut off the first finger of his left hand in a bark-cutting machine, Dr. Strang dressed the wound. So, if Strang was practicing medicine in Washington State since 1913, how did he come to be in Hardin, Montana, to perform a scheduled C-section in 1935?

We can rule out Grandma's rumor that the doctor's wife had died when he did a C-section on her. Mrs. Strang was about fifty years old in 1935, and her youngest child had married the previous year. The *Seattle Times* reported on her daughter's wedding in August 1934, referring to "Dr and Mrs Strang of Hardin, Montana." So he was in Hardin by mid-1934. He didn't stay long. By 1940, he was back in Pacific County, Washington.

Why does it matter?

Why did he sterilize her?

Marge's experience of Momma's birth may have just been another everyday example of the systemic disregard for the feminine voice. During the 1930 London C-section, the narration states that the woman's uterus was examined and found to be healthy, therefore she was not sterilized. The assumption here is that any C-section was an opportunity for a doctor to decide to sterilize a woman while she was unconscious. No consent required.

The colonization and control of the uterus, the strongest muscle in the body, stronger than anything in a man, takes different forms at different times.

Momma was caught up in the hysterectomy craze of the 1970s, losing her uterus around 1975.

When my gynecologist asked me at a routine visit when the women in my family experienced menopause, I had to report "They don't know."

Marge's explanation of her several marriages and divorces (at least six after the two involving Frank Harrison) was that when something bothered her, she thought to herself, "Well, gosh sakes, that's not right." Then she left.

There are at least three explanations of why Marge married Frank a second time. Either he promised her a car and that he'd stop drinking if she came back to him, or he was drunk and gave her two black eyes and threatened to kill her if she didn't come back to him, or he wanted a chance to renegotiate the child support agreement after he lost his good job. This third version also features two black eyes, but the motive is more calculated and secret than the maudlin second version.

When Marge eventually remarried, after the second divorce from Frank, she and her new husband, Glen, wanted to have children. After trying for some time, they consulted a doctor and found out Marge couldn't have more children as a result of the C-section.

She didn't know she'd been sterilized.

That's all Marge would say on camera; no emotional details. Later, Momma said it was something about the way she got stitched up.

"Well, I knew Glen wanted to have a lot of children, so I decided to leave him so he could marry someone else," Marge reported, seventy or so years later. And she had.

"Did you talk to Glen about it?" I asked as I shifted the video camera on my shoulder to follow her face as she turned away. "Did you discuss it with him?"

"Oh, we didn't talk about things like that in those days," she said.

Dr. Strang, according to my mother, achieved some fame related to a triplets birth. Triplets were rare in the days before fertility drugs. In 1938, in the entire state of Montana, only two triplets births were reported. My mother is a woman with a strong and historically accurate memory, but I can't find any record related to Dr. Strang and triplets. Neither could the research staffs I hired at historical societies in Washington and Montana.

I was still pondering possible reasons when the *New York Times* ran a story about a baby-selling scheme in Butte from the 1920s to the 1950s. I knew that

Frank had spent time in and around Butte. His second wife—the one he killed in a "hunting accident"—was from Butte. And her aunt ran the local whorehouse where Frank went "just to gamble," according to my mother.

The *Times* article, combined with Frank's Butte connections and Momma's tenacious memory of triplets, gave me the idea that maybe the doctor had palpated multiple babies. That would be a reason for a C-section and, if Frank were planning to sell the extras, Marge would need to be knocked out. The sterilization could've been a mistake, a by-product of the surgery that was, as we know, not a job for a general practitioner like Dr. Strang, a guy who dressed the wounds of old people and little boys who severed their fingers in farm equipment. What kind of doctor could you partner with, though, if you wanted to sell extra babies without letting the mother know they'd ever existed? I asked my uncle what Frank had told him about Dr. Strang.

"Oh, he was a drunk," Stan said, waving his hand dismissively.

Infants sold for up to five hundred dollars each at a time when the country was in a depression and the doctor's annual salary was only two thousand dollars. The midwife who'd brokered the sales, which people were only finding out about in the twenty-first century because of DNA testing, was Gertrude Pitkanen, the same one who'd lied on the death certificate of Violet Morse.

Relying on memory and coincidence, like the woman at the dinner party in Manhattan who mentioned her Anaconda grandmother just when I was up to my neck in research about Violet Morse, or even newspaper archives for truth has its hazards. The name changes of Violet's father and sister are perhaps trivial illustrations of the difficulty of knowing accurately even simple factual matters from the past, let alone private actions. Motive is several layers even more remote, even if the perpetrator is fully aware of their own reasons. And few of us are.

Everything about my grandfather's past was a matter of conjecture. Depending on which stories I chose to believe, he might've killed a man in Chicago or spent time in the tuberculosis sanatorium in Deer Lodge. He may have been in prison. He definitely died young, at forty-nine, of a bleeding ulcer, a consequence of severe alcoholism.

It's impossible to know who Marge was, emotionally, before she was raped by the man she would have to marry as a result—and then two years later sterilized as a result of his actions. Who might she have been? Her absent presence may have been her original character, but certainly the losses and attacks she experienced, and the silence with which she and her culture addressed them, had to have diminished her emotional range and ability to be a full self in the presence of others, or at all. In the end, she wouldn't even die in front of a family member, waiting until the vigil keeper left the room to slip away.

When I started to paste the article below into this document, it was as if a ghost took over, highlighting several pages and deleting them. I pressed "undo" and tried again. The file became possessed, page after page being highlighted as the text scrolled down, while neither of my hands were on the keyboard. Maybe Marge wants her secrets kept.

> According to the new insights of behavioral epigenetics, traumatic experiences in our past, or in our recent ancestors' past, leave molecular scars adhering to our DNA. Jews whose great-grandparents were chased from their Russian shtetls; Chinese whose grandparents lived through the ravages of the Cultural Revolution; young immigrants from Africa whose parents survived massacres; adults of every ethnicity who grew up with alcoholic or abusive parents—all carry with them more than just memories.
>
> Like silt deposited on the cogs of a finely tuned machine after the seawater of a tsunami recedes, our experiences, and those of our forebears, are never gone, even if they have been forgotten. They become a part of us, a molecular residue holding fast to our genetic scaffolding. The DNA remains the same, but psychological and behavioral tendencies are inherited.[1]

Perhaps one day scientists will discover the exact mechanism behind the psychological and behavioral tendencies toward silence, toward indirection and evasion, like birds avoiding the house where an ancestor was shot generations before, even though different people now live there. The word is passed mutely and never gets revised.

My mother took away only positive memories of her father, she says. But she has behavioral tendencies and warnings to communicate. She didn't want

1. Dan Hurley, "Trait vs. Fate" (*Discover*, May 2013)

her daughters to attract attention as girls. When I asked for what my friends had during adolescence—a bra (before I needed one), fashionable articles of clothing, pierced ears—Momma said, "Girls who look older than they are get into trouble."

I protested, but on some level I took it in. The trauma expert Bessel van der Kolk writes: "Even our biological maturation is strongly influenced by the nature of early attachment bonds." I did not begin menstruating until I was seventeen and a half, far outside any published range of menarche ages.

We inherit not only physical inclinations, to heart disease or red hair or long faces, but also, as epigenetics is now making clear, emotional and behavioral patterns. From both my maternal grandparents, Frank and Marge, I inherited almost nothing concrete except two pairs of earrings and the dress Marge wore to my parents' wedding, but I'd been steeped in their evasiveness. Marge had certain well-rehearsed stories she told over and over as if to shield herself from more genuine interaction, but when asked a follow up question or even seeing herself on video telling a story—that I myself had taped her telling!—might say, "Oh, that's not how it happened at all." No matter how hard you tried to pin Marge down, she'd cycle her arms, head for the door, and exclaim, "Gotta run!"

Eventually, I would have to wonder if the problem was not just that we were a family with few written records and the habits of cowboys: a tendency to move on, a reverence for silence and deep disgust with any talk of an inner life. My compulsion to investigate these old mysteries, moments when a possible birth turned slantwise and ended in its opposite, stories I'd never be able to solve, has its roots, most likely, in the Saturday night in Greenwich Village that has both receded to historical background in my life and, through unconscious byways governing the movement of my attention and obsession, remained at the forefront of my mind and heart.

At 9:26 P.M. on January 9, 1999, I gave birth to a baby girl who declined to take a breath or beat her own heart once the cord was cut. Another secret keeper. The yards of coiling tape spewing from the heart monitor machine told a beautiful lie, a fiction of rhythmic perfection.

Five doctors and a midwife huddled together in the hallway, examining the heart monitor strip. It was impossible, they said, to have such a story on paper, right next to the table on which lay the baby who had refused to be resuscitated. "You're one in a million!" a doctor told me.

The Greek chorus gauntlet on Brooklyn sidewalks and playgrounds gave me no rest: "We heard about you!" "Everything happens for a reason." "Now you get to try again!" "Next time get more testing done! You're no spring chicken!" Did anyone tell Violet Morse's survivors that she'd been right where she was supposed to be? A rooming house in Butte? More likely: it was God's will. It must be comforting to imagine God as a wise figure meting out justice, not some randy old goat like Zeus who might just be using your life to settle an old score.

I return again and again to a narrative that begins in a mystery and gives every sign that the arc of excitement, the discovery of clues, will result in a satisfying conclusion and the unmasking of the villain. But instead, each time, the trail goes cold and I'm left alone, wandering Green-Wood Cemetery, wondering about causality and culpability, matters that grand rounds and autopsies have in fact already judged, repeatedly, to be inconclusive.

When I was a child, I used to sweep our driveway, even though it was unpaved, just packed dirt. It felt purifying to make a clear, flat, smooth surface without rubble or dust on top. I would stand on it barefoot feeling the silkiness of the compressed earth. As I got older, I saw how pointless this was. But a clearing in the dust, an afternoon of diversion at pinochle, a horseback ride into town on a summer day, a baby's sun-bleached white cotton diaper hanging out on the line: all these moments matter, even if they will soon be soiled, soon disappear in the hourly, daily, yearly cycles that consume our lives.

It has mattered to me to pick apart the strands of inheritance, of nature and nurture and received ideas, to reclaim some piece of territory on which I can stand and name for myself the truth, or some truth. Discovering what actually happened—who, when, where, even if not the full truth, ever, about the real what or why—has freed me to consider that memory and intuition and everything I think I know—about myself and my ancestry, about the gradient of the plot arc and my place in it, about causality—might be explained by some different and unknown set of circumstances.

Nothing official remains of my daughter, no birth certificate or death certificate. Sometimes, less and less often now, I stand on a chair and take down a wooden cigar box stamped Zino Classic Special Selection, in which I keep proof that she was not nothing. I open the metal latch and take out papers: a letter from Old First Reformed Church, "Ministering to the Heart in the Heart of the City," testifying to our ownership of grave plot no. 365 in section 53/72 of the Cedar Dell Section of Green-Wood Cemetery.

From the New York City Department of Health, I have a certificate of spontaneous termination of pregnancy, which makes it sound like there wasn't a fully formed seven-pound eleven-ounce baby girl who made her way partway out of my body, far enough for the doctor to feel her pulse in the fontanelle as he cut the cord. The questions at the top of the form are:

"Did the heart beat after delivery?" In all caps, *NO* is written by hand.

"Was there movement of voluntary muscle?" Again, *NO* is scrawled.

If the answers had been *YES*, "Such cases must be reported by filling a certificate of birth and a certificate of death". On this form, the one filled out when the answers are *NO*, there are spaces for names only of the mother, father, and doctor, because there was no baby.

I turn back to the cigar box. From March 8, 1999, a faxed two-page report from Saint Vincent's Hospital and Medical Center Department of Pathology. It's a fax, because we, as the parents, had trouble getting a copy. A friend who was a doctor at Saint Vincent's obtained it for us. It's the autopsy report, and it begins with the patient name: Babby Girl Madden. It's ridden with errors worse than spelling, claiming I was feverish after a "2 day history of spontaneous rupture of membranes." In fact, my water had been broken for two hours. How can I trust any official records, for Annie, for Marge, for Violet? Was the hospital trying to put the blame on me, an irresponsible woman who would wait two days after her water broke to finally manage to push out the baby? Or was that also a typo like Babby? When I finally got Dr. _____ on the phone to ask him about the cause, wailing "I have to give birth again! I have to understand," he said, "You're the mother? I'm not supposed to talk to the mother." His voice got fainter as he backed away from the phone. Finally he told me the cause, like most infant deaths, was unknown. They could only conjecture.

Next: an Oxford Health Plan identification card for Annie Ebersole, testifying to her membership in the Liberty Plan, member number 558003*03, received a few days before her birth. I feel a secret satisfaction holding this card, like I've outwitted the authorities.

Underneath is a pink half sheet, "Newborn Identification, To be completed in the delivery room." It has my name and the infant's information: 1/9/1999

@ 9:26 P.M., girl, 7 lbs 11 ounces. Below those handwritten facts, which exist nowhere else, are two inked footprints, proof of Annie's corporeal existence.

In a corner of the cigar box, there is another tiny box. Inside, a folded square of white tissue paper with barely visible penciled words, in my handwriting: Annie's hair. I unfold it gingerly. There's nothing in it. I take off my glasses, wipe my eyes, wonder if I should get a magnifying glass. Can hair decay into nothing? Is twenty years too long? Did someone else, not me, open the box and lose the contents? I look again. Under my desk lamp, I see tiny bits of blond hair distributed over the tissue, looking like part of the paper weave. I remember that when she was born, we thought she was a redhead, but that turned out to be my blood. Her hair was blond, like Jim's, and absurdly fine, like mine. As I fold the tissue paper back up, I see a minuscule bit of her hair on my desk. I lick my finger and touch it, try to wipe it onto the tissue paper to preserve it, but somewhere between my finger and the paper I've lost it.

A pink piece of lined notebook paper with my handwriting, copied from a book, "the death of a baby is a melody played softly through its mother's life like an intimate dirge, and you have to have died a little yourself to hear the music." Nora Seton, *The Kitchen Congregation*.

A carbon copy receipt, paper clipped to a business card, from Brooklyn Monument Company Inc. for a smooth face stone with sandblast letters, for which we paid $1,112.00, reading:

Annie Madden Ebersole

January 9, 1999

You who never arrived in our arms…

CONTRIBUTORS

JJ Amaworo Wilson's novel *Damnificados* (PM Press) received the 2017 Hurston/Wright Legacy Award for debut fiction. He is a writer-in-residence at Western New Mexico University and the author of over a dozen books about language and language learning.

Mary Jo Bang is the author, most recently, of *A Doll for Throwing*, *The Last Two Seconds*, and *Elegy*, which received the National Book Critics Circle Award. Her translation of Dante's *Purgatorio* will be published next year (all Graywolf). She teaches creative writing at Washington University in St. Louis. Her translations of Shuzo Takiguchi, co-translated with Yuki Tanaka, have been published in *A Public Space*.

Yohanca Delgado's fiction has appeared in *STORY*, *One Story*, and online at the *Michigan Quarterly Review* online. The story in this issue was selected from an open call and edited by A Public Space Editorial Fellow Taylor Michael.

Graham Foust is the author of seven poetry collections, most recently *Nightingalelessness* (Flood Editions). He teaches at the University of Denver.

Bruce Goff (1904–1982) was an American architect. He held his first architectural apprenticeship at the age of twelve in Tulsa, Oklahoma, and in 1934 he moved to Chicago, where he founded a private practice. He was later the chairman of the school of architecture at the University of Oklahoma in Norman. A retrospective of his work was exhibited in 1995 at the Art Institute of Chicago, where his papers are housed.

Matthias Göritz is a poet and novelist. His novel *Der kurze Traum des Jakob Voss* (The short dream of Jakob Voss) (Berlin Verlag), received the Hamburger Literaturpreise (Hamburg Literature Prize) and Mara-Cassens-Preis (Mara Cassens Prize). He teaches in the program in comparative literature at Washington University in St. Louis.

Mark Hage is the author of *Capital*, which was published in 2020 by A Public Space Books. His fiction has recently appeared in *NOON*.

Kimiko Hahn's most recent collections of poetry are *Foreign Bodies* and *Brain Fever* (both Norton). She teaches in the MFA Program in Creative Writing and Literary Translation at Queens College, City University of New York.

David Hayden is the author of story collection *Darker with the Lights On* (Transit) and contributor to anthology *Being Various: New Irish Short Stories* (Faber & Faber).

Robert Kirkbride is the dean of Parsons' School of Constructed Environments and professor of architecture and product design. He is a founding trustee for PreservationWorks, a nonprofit organization for the adaptive reuse of Kirkbride Plan Hospitals.

Jena H. Kim's work has been exhibited at such venues as the Queens Museum of Art in New York City, the Korean Cultural Center in Los Angeles, and the Museum of Modern and Contemporary Art in Seoul. She has also participated in the Smack Mellon Artist Studio Program.

Taisia Kitaiskaia is the author of *The Nightgown and Other Poems* (Deep Vellum); *Literary Witches: A Celebration of Magical Women Writers* (Hachette/Seal), a collaboration with artist Katy Horan; and two books of experimental advice from Slavic folklore, *Ask Baba Yaga: Otherworldly Advice for Everyday Troubles* and *Poetic Remedies for Troubled Times from Ask Baba Yaga* (both Andrews McMeel).

Jhumpa Lahiri recently edited *The Penguin Book of Italian Short Stories*. Her English translation of her novel *Dove mi trovo* (*Whereabouts*) will be published by Knopf next year; and her first collection of poems in Italian *Il quaderno di Nerina* (Guanda) will also be published then. She received the 2000 Pulitzer Prize in Fiction for her story collection *Interpreter of Maladies* (Mariner) and is the the director of the Program in Creative Writing at Princeton University's Lewis Center for the Arts.

David Larsen is a poet and a scholar of premodern Arabic literature. His translation of *Names of the Lion* by Ibn Khālawayh (Wave) received the 2018 Harold Morton Landon Translation Award from the Academy of American Poets. He would like to acknowledge the present translation's debt to the German translation of the Poem of the Bow by Thomas Bauer.

Vicki **Madden** is a New York City teacher and writer. Her work has appeared in the *New York Times*. She is a 2019 A Public Space Fellow.

Knox Martin is an American painter, sculptor, and muralist. Born in Barranquilla, Colombia, in 1923, he moved to New York City in 1927. *Radical Structures*, spanning seven decades of his career, was exhibited in 2019 at Hollis Taggart and Frieze New York.

Claire Messud's books include the novels *The Burning Girl* (Norton) and *The Emperor's Children* (Knopf); a collection of novellas, *The Hunters* (Harcourt); and, most recently, the autobiography in essays *Kant's Little Prussian Head and Other Reasons Why I Write* (Norton). She has received numerous honors, including the

Strauss Living Award from the American Academy of Arts and Letters. She teaches at Harvard University.

Steven Millhauser received the 1997 Pulitzer Prize for his novel *Martin Dressler: The Tale of an American Dreamer* (Crown). His new and selected stories, *We Others* (Knopf), won the 2011 Story Prize and was a finalist for the PEN/Faulkner Award.

Neal Rantoul's photographs are part of the permanent collections of the Museum of Fine Arts, Boston; the deCordova Sculpture Park and Museum; and the Museum of Fine Arts, Houston, among others. He is the author of several books of photographs, among them *Wheat* and *Rock Sand Water* and taught for many years at Northeastern University.

Srikanth Reddy's most recent book is *Underworld Lit* (Wave), a project that was supported by Creative Capital, the Guggenheim Foundation, and the National Endowment for the Arts. He is a professor of English

and creative writing at the University of Chicago.

Matthew Rohrer is the author of ten poetry collections, most recently *The Others*, which received the Believer Book Award; and *The Sky Contains the Plans* (both Wave). He is a cofounder of *FENCE* magazine and teaches at New York University.

Al-Shammākh (The High and Mighty) is the title adopted by the Arab poet Ma'qil ibn Ḍirār (d. mid-seventh century CE). He fought and lost his life in the Islamic conquest of the East, but martial themes are not prominent in his verse. He was above all a poet of the natural world and the hunt. His two brothers were also poets, and the eldest has his own long poem on arms and bow-hunting. The supernal Poem of the Bow is by al-Shammākh.

Kat Thackray is a writer and designer from Bristol, United Kingdom. The story in this issue is her first publication.

Sylvan Thomson is from Nelson, New Zealand. His work has appeared in the *Wireless*, the *New*

Zealand Review of Books, and *Tell You What: Great New Zealand Nonfiction 2016*. He is a 2019 A Public Space Fellow.

Colm Tóibín's tenth novel, *The Magician*, will be published next year. His nonfiction books include *Mad, Bad, and Dangerous to Know: The Fathers of Wilde, Joyce, and Yeats*; and *Love in a Dark Time: And Other Explorations of Gay Lives and Literature* (all Scribner).

Kyle Francis Williams's work has appeared in *Hobart*, *Full Stop*, and the *Chicago Review of Books*. He is an MFA candidate at the Michener Center for Writers and a 2019 A Public Space Fellow.

Jenny Xie is the author of *Eye Level* (Graywolf), which received the Walt Whitman Award from the Academy of American Poets, and was a finalist for the National Book Award and the PEN Open Book Award. She teaches at Bard College.

Joseph Yoakum (1890–1972) was a self-taught American artist of landscapes that blended imagination with real-life

CONTRIBUTORS

experience. He traveled the world widely, leaving home at age nine to join the Great Wallace Circus. In the late 1920s, he settled in Chicago, but did not begin drawing until 1962. His work is held in the collections of the Art Institute of Chicago, the Smithsonian Institute, and the Menil Collection, among others.

Ada Zhang's stories have appeared or are forthcoming in *Catapult*, the *Rumpus*, *Witness*, and *Alaska Quarterly Review*. She is a graduate of the Iowa Writers' Workshop.

CREDITS

IMAGES

Pages 3, 8-9: Knox Martin, *Maquette for Wall Mural*, 1975, acrylic and graphite on paper mounted on foamcore, 43 (H) x 35 (W) x 1 (D) inches; and *Rubber Soul*, 1963, magna acrylic on canvas, 103 3/4 x 139 inches (diptych). Courtesy of the artist and Hollis Taggart, New York. ©Knox Martin/ Licensed by VAGA at Artists Rights Society (ARS), NY

21-23: Neal Rantoul, *Great Salt Lake* 1, 2 and 3, 2015. ©Neal Rantoul. Used with permission of the artist.

51-53: Jena I I. Kim, Untitled I-III. Courtesy of the artist.

62 (clockwise from top left): Hudson River State Hospital, Poughkeepsie, NY. Used with permission of Dreamstime; Greystone Psychiatric Hospital, Morris Plains, NJ; Saint Elizabeths Hospital, Washington, DC. Courtesy Colin Winterbottom. ©Colin Winterbottom; Buffalo State Hospital. Collection of The Buffalo History Museum. General photograph collection, Buildings—Hospitals.

63 (clockwise from bottom left): Fergus Falls State Hospital, Fergus Falls, NY. Used with permission of Dreamstime; The title page of the second edition of Thomas Story Kirkbride's *On the Construction, Organization, and General Arrangements of Hospitals for the Insane*; Trans-Allegheny Lunatic Asylum, Westoon, WV. Used with permission of Dreamstime; Athens Lunatic Asylum, Athens, OH. Photograph courtesy Robert Kirkbride. ©Robert Kirkbride; Northern Michigan Asylum, Traverse City, MI. Used with permission of Dreamstime.

90: Bruce Goff, Al Struckus House. Photograph ©Elena Dorfman. Used with permission of Elena Dorfman.

91: Bruce Goff, Van Sickle Ford House. Photograph by Eliot Elisofon/The LIFE Picture Collection. Used with permission of Getty Images.

92: Bruce Goff, W. C. Gryder House. Photographs ©Elena Dorfman. Used with permission of Elena Dorfman.

93: Bruce Goff, Eugene and Nancy Bavinger Residence. Gene Bavinger, photographer. Bruce Goff Archive, Ryerson and Burnham Art and Architecture Archives, The Art Institute of Chicago. Digital file #199001. Bavinger_ext_color1. Used with permission of the Art Institute of Chicago.

144: Joseph Yoakum, *Mt. Gilbert of Appalachian Mtn. Range Polkaz in Pennsylvania*, 1965. Photograph courtesy Carl Hammer Gallery, Inc., Chicago, IL.

160: Joseph Yoakum, *High no 2, Bridge Cross the Missouri at Chillicothie Mo*, 1962/1965. Used with permission of the Art Institute of Chicago. Image source: Art Resource, NY.

178: Joseph Yoakum, *Brazus Valley Amerilo Texas*, 1966. Used with permission of the Art Institute of Chicago. Image source: Art Resource, NY.

205: Neal Rantoul, *Wheat*, 2019. ©Neal Rantoul. Used with permission of the artist.

TEXT

10: "The Delivery" was originally written and published as "Il ritiro" in the literary journal *Nuovi Argomenti*, Series 6, Number 5, September-December 2020.

24: "Two Women" is excerpted from *Kant's Little Prussian Head and Other Reasons Why I Write: An Autobiography in Essays* by Claire Messud used with permission of the Wylie Agency, LLC.

54: Robert Kirkbride discusses direct family histories in his interview for the Oral History Project for Greystone Park Psychiatric Hospital (greystoneoralhistory. com). Additional information about the preservation of the Kirkbride hospitals can be found at Preservation Works (thepreservationworks. org).

PATRONS

BENEFACTORS
Anonymous
Drue & H. J. Heinz
Charitable Trust
OppenheimerFunds

SUSTAINERS
The Chisholm
Foundation
Google, Inc.
Justin M. Leverenz
Win McCormack
Maxwell Neely-Cohen

PATRONS
Anonymous (3)
Charles & Jenifer Buice
Daniel Handler & Lisa
Brown
Joy Harris Literary
Agency
Elizabeth Howard
Padraig Hughes
Patricia Hughes &
Colin Brady
Siobhan Hughes
Patrick & Patricia
Hughes
Yiyun & Dapeng Li
Elizabeth McCracken
Joshua Rolnick &
Marcella Kanfer
Rolnick
The Jackson & Evelyn
Spears Foundation
Jeannie Vaughn
Paul Vidich
Mengmeng Wang

SUPPORTERS
Anonymous
Bevin Cline
Annie Coggan & Caleb
Crawford
Nicole Dewey
Elizabeth Gaffney
Matthea Harvey &
Robert Casper
Dallas Hudgens

Marjorie Kalman-Kutz
Binnie Kirshenbaum
Katy Lederer & Ben
Statz
Lisa Lubasch
Massie & McQuilkin
Literary Agency
Fiona McCrae
Kristen Mitchell &
Bryon Finn
NewsCorp
Joanna Riesman
Ira Silverberg
Deborah Treisman
Bill Wadsworth
Kate Walbert

SUPER FRIENDS
Linda Baker
Katherine Bell
Sarah Blakley-
Cartwright & Nicolas
Party
Alessandra Codinha
Megan Cummins
Jonny Diamond
Barbara Epler
Brett Fletcher Lauer
Sidik Fofana
Tom Fontana
Katharine Freeman
Amy Gallo
Mary Gannon
Tracie Golding
Elizabeth Graver
Ruth Greenstein
Courtney Hodell
Elliott Holt
Gabrielle Howard
Mary-Beth Hughes
Susan Jackson
Sarah Jacoby
Jodi & John Kim
Joan Kreiss
Richard Kot
Jennifer Lee
Joan L'Heureux
Mike Lindgren
Gregory Maher

Suzanne Matson
E. J. McAdams
Charles McGrath
Michael Moore
Alice Quinn
Austin Ratner
Charles Rodrigues
Chiara Rosati
Lisa Sardinas
Elisabeth Schmitz
Mark Singer
Laura Spence-Ash
Mary Stewart Allen
Robert & Suzanne
Sullivan
Sam Swope
Nafeesa Syeed
Craig Townsend &
Catherine Fuerst
Marina Vaysberg
Margo Viscusi
Calvin Wei
Susan Wheeler
Christine Levinson
Wilson & Antoine
Wilson
Hao Wu

FRIENDS
Margaret Beal
Stuart Bernstein
Robert Brady
Jamel Brinkley
Jennifer Braun
Lee Briccetti
Katherine Carter
Alice Elliott Dark
The Freya Project
Carrie Frye
Reginald Gibbons
James Goodman
Garth Greenwell
Margaret Griffin
Maria Harber
Diane Heinze
Joshua Henkin
Claudia Herr
Katherine Hill
Joseph Holt

Jessie Kelly
Eileen B. Kohan
Kimberly Kremer
Vivian Lawsky
Jeffrey Lependorf
Cressida Leyshon
Mark Lewis
William Love
Lowell Allen, Inc.
Mo Ogrodnik
George Ow, Jr.
D. Wystan Owen &
Ellen Kamoe
Jon Quinn
Tina Reich
Art & Iris Spellings
Christine Swedowsky
Alexander Tilney
Georgia Tucker
Terry Wall
Meg Weekes
Renee Zuckerbrot

Neal Rantoul

Poetry

I, too, *like* it.

WWW.POETRYSOCIETY.ORG

[clmp]

Community of Literary Magazines & Presses

Dear Publisher,
Don't take our advice.*

*Get advice from more than 500 fellow publishers (ours is pretty good too.) Since 1967, CLMP has been helping independent literary publishers through the business of publishing—join the community!

www.clmp.org

APS TOGETHER, A SERIES OF VIRTUAL BOOK CLUBS

WAR AND PEACE
BY LEO TOLSTOY
WITH YIYUN LI
I've found that the more uncertain one's life is, the more solidity and structure *War and Peace* provides.

TURN OF THE SCREW
BY HENRY JAMES
WITH GARTH GREENWELL
A story about ghosts (or is it?), madness, the vulnerability of children, the lure of desire.

THE MAYTREES
BY ANNIE DILLARD
WITH ELIZABETH MCCRACKEN
Its plot is time, really, but it's about empathy and marriage and divorce and love and the consolations of art.

MAP
BY WISLAWA SZYMBORSKA
WITH ILYA KAMINSKY
A poet who knows what it means to live in a moment of crisis. A poet who survives. A poet who laughs amidst misfortune. A poet who delights.

GREEN WATER, GREEN SKY
BY MAVIS GALLANT
WITH ELLIOTT HOLT
A book about memory, family, and the meaning of home.

TRUE GRIT
BY CHARLES PORTIS
WITH ED PARK
A magical historical novel, a revenge story, an utterly convincing western, and yet somehow also brilliantly funny, even absurd.

GIOVANNI'S ROOM
BY JAMES BALDWIN
WITH CARL PHILLIPS
A fever dream of language, desire, tenderness, those brief moments in which we think we know ourselves and others, the larger moments when we realize the quest to know anything for sure may be unresolvable—yet we keep questing, anyway.

THE PRIME OF MISS JEAN BRODIE
BY MURIEL SPARK
WITH SARAH SHUN-LIEN BYNUM
A novel about the indelible Miss Brodie, a character of magnificent convictions and questionable judgment who exercises outsized influence on her coterie of handpicked students, with unpredictable results.

SO LONG, SEE YOU TOMORROW
BY WILLIAM MAXWELL
WITH AIMEE BENDER
A novel with a dramatic story to tell, and that intrigued me too, but it has a quiet core, a thrumming beautiful dignified quiet core about loss, and that is the magnetic pull that brings me to it again and again.

THE BROTHERS GRIMM
WITH YIYUN LI
In 1806, the Napoleonic armies invaded Hesse-Cassel, where Jacob and Wilhelm, the Brothers Grimm, were researching for their folk-tale projects in their spare time.

TWO SERIOUS LADIES
BY JANE BOWLES
WITH CLAIRE MESSUD
The novel—a rare American existentialist fiction by a woman writer—tells the stories of Mrs. Copperfield and Miss Goering, two women seeking to live authentically and to find happiness.

VISIT APUBLICSPACE.ORG/EVENTS FOR THE APSTOGETHER ARCHIVE.

THANK YOU TO THE INDEPENDENT BOOKSTORES THAT KEPT US CONNECTED TO BOOKS THIS YEAR, INCLUDING

W-3
BETTE HOWLAND
Introduction by Yiyun Li

A new edition of the 1974 memoir by "one of the significant writers of her generation" (Saul Bellow). In 1968, Bette Howland was thirty-one, a single mother of two young sons, struggling to support her family and be a writer. One afternoon, she swallowed a bottle of pills. Both a portrait of the hospital where she was admitted and the record of a defining moment in her life, W-3 itself would be her salvation: she wrote herself out of the grave.

"A portrayal of mental illness like none other."
—Esmé Weijun Wang

CALM SEA AND PROSPEROUS VOYAGE
SELECTED STORIES
BETTE HOWLAND

One of our "literary foremothers" (Rumaan Alam), Bette Howland mined her deepest emotions for her art in stories that chronicled the tension of her generation. A collection of her enduring stories, Calm Sea and Prosperous Voyage restores to the canon a wry, brilliant observer and a writer of great empathy and sly, joyous humor.

"Cooler than a cocktail and sharper than a Japanese knife… Nora Ephron meets Lorrie Moore, which is about as good as it gets." —the Guardian

CAPITAL
MARK HAGE

For several years, Mark Hage has been observing the shuttering of small and iconic retail spaces in New York City. "At first, and perhaps out of discomfort, I walked by thinking of them as surface, without seeking depth or further understanding. But with time, I started to linger and photograph the worlds within." Capital reframes the story of gentrification in a meditation on vestiges and accidental composition. An elegy to a changing city becomes an homage to the anonymous hands that built it.

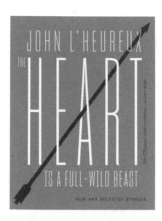

THE HEART IS A FULL-WILD BEAST
NEW AND SELECTED STORIES
JOHN L'HEUREUX

The final collection by John L'Heureux, the former Jesuit priest and longtime director of Stanford's creative writing program, whose stories "grappled with matters of morality, redemption and transcendence." The legacy of a life's work, The Heart Is a Full-Wild Beast celebrates a writer of astonishing vision—a master of storytelling and the sentence.

"Capturing the deepest yearnings of the human heart." —David Henry Hwang

GEOMETRY OF SHADOWS
GIORGIO DE CHIRICO
Translated from the Italian by
Stefania Heim

A multifaceted artist who lived in multiple languages, Giorgio de Chirico was just becoming famous in France for the paintings that inspired surrealism when he returned to Italy in 1916 to enlist for the First World War. Here, he began to write poems in his native language. Translating his iconic visual imagination into literary form, *Geometry of Shadows* celebrates the elasticity and innate potential of language, by an artist ever in pursuit of deeper understanding.

THE COMMUNICATING VESSELS
FRIEDERIKE MAYRÖCKER
Translated from the German by
Alexander Booth

"A raw literary meditation on loss" (*Kirkus*). Following the death of Ernst Jandl, her partner for nearly half a century, Friederike Mayröcker—as writers have for millennia—turned to her art to come to terms with the loss. *The Communicating Vessels* presents two singular books of remembrance and farewell, and offers a stunning testament to a shared life of passionate reading, writing, and love.

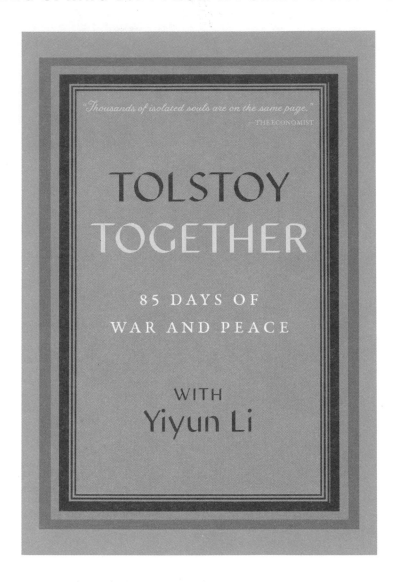

"Thousands of isolated souls are on the same page."
—THE ECONOMIST

TOLSTOY TOGETHER

85 DAYS OF
WAR AND PEACE

WITH
Yiyun Li